CARTER DICKSON
IS
JOHN DICKSON CARR

"If Christie was queen of the murder mystery, Carr was certainly its king."

—Village Voice

"First-rate puzzler, with oh-so-simple (once you know it) solution—carefully annotated, with lively talk and interesting people."

—Saturday Review of Literature

"Decidedly one of the better items in stream-lined mystery."

–Will Cuppy
Books

CARTER DICKSON

THE PEACOCK FEATHER MURDERS

A CRIME CLASSIC ®

INTERNATIONAL POLYGONICS, LTD.
New York

THE PEACOCK FEATHER MURDERS

Library of Congress Card Catalog No. 87-82443
ISBN 0-930330-68-4

Printed and manufactured in the United States of
America by Guinn Printing, New York.
First IPL printing October 1987.
10 9 8 7 6 5 4 3 2 1

CONTENTS

CHAPTER ONE

Peacocks' Feathers

THERE WILL BE TEN TEACUPS AT NUMBER 4, BERWICK TERRACE, W. 8., ON WEDNESDAY, JULY 31, AT 5 P.M. PRECISELY. THE PRESENCE OF THE METROPOLITAN POLICE IS RESPECTFULLY REQUESTED.

ON THE surface there would appear nothing in this note, addressed to Chief Inspector Humphrey Masters at New Scotland Yard, capable of giving Masters any uneasiness. It arrived in the first post on Wednesday, that day when the diabolical heat-wave—you may remember it—had reached its height. The note bore no signature. It was typed in the center of a stiff sheet of notepaper. To young Sergeant Pollard, Master's aide-de-camp, it was an additional pin-prick in this day of heat.

"You don't say so," commented Pollard, not without sarcasm. "If they're inviting everybody, it must be rather a large tea-party. What is it, sir? A joke or some kind of advertisement?"

He was certainly not prepared for the effect of the note on Masters. Masters, who always wore heavy blue serge and a waistcoat no matter what the weather, was stewing and sweating at a desk of papers. His big face, bland as a card-sharper's, with the grizzled hair brushed to hide the bald spot, now shone with increasing redness as he looked up. He swore.

"What's wrong?" asked Pollard. "You don't mean to say—?"

"Now, now," growled Masters. When harassed, he had a habit of assuming the air of a parent rebuking an idiot child. "Don't you go making remarks, Bob, before you know what it's all about. When you've been in this game as long as *I* have. . . . Here. Nip out and get me the file marked *Dartley*. Look sharp about it, now."

The file bore a date two years back. Pollard did not have time for a look at it before he returned; but he saw by its heading that it was a murder case, and his boredom was stirred by curiosity. So far Pollard, who had crept into the Force by way of Cambridge, had found nothing but the dullness of secretarial duties. Even his term of service as a uniformed policeman had consisted chiefly of making mesmeric passes at the traffic and arresting just 1,322 motorists. But he was interested by Masters's ominous throat-clearings as the chief inspector glowered at the report.

"Anything—exciting?" he prompted.

"Exciting!" said Masters, with rich scorn. Nevertheless, cautious as Masters was, he could not help going on. "It's murder, my lad: that's what it is. We never caught the bloke who did it, and it's unlikely we ever shall. And I'll tell you something else: I've been twenty-five years at this job, and it's the only murder I ever heard of that didn't mean anything at all. Exciting!"

Pollard was puzzled. "Didn't mean anything at all?"

"That's what I said," agreed Masters, and came to a decision. "Get your hat, Bob. I want a minute with the Assistant Commissioner on the phone. Then we're going to pay a little visit to a man you know—"

"Not Sir Henry Merrivale?"

"Why not?"

"For God's sake, sir, don't do it!" urged Pollard. "Not on a day like this. He'll be wild. He'll tear us limb from limb and dance on the pieces. He—"

Despite the heat, a faint grin began to creep over Masters's face.

"Lummy, yes; the old man'll have his back up right enough," he admitted. "He's really been working, too, for a change. But you leave him to me. The thing to do is hook him, Bob; *hook* him. Hurrum. Then, once you've got his interest—"

Masters was his usual affable self when, ten minutes later, he pushed open the door of H.M.'s office up five flights of stairs in the old rabbit-warren of a building at the back of Whitehall. Here the heat was thick with a smell of old wood and paper. From beyond the door a querulous voice was upraised; H.M. seemed to be dictating letters. Masters pushed open the door without bothering to knock, and found H.M. sitting at his desk, his feet on the desk and his collar off, staring vindictively at the telephone.

"Takeumletter," rumbled H.M., with something of the intonation of an Indian Chief. In fact, despite the glasses pulled down on his broad nose, the woodenness of his face gave him much the air of an Indian Chief: an effect heightened by his grimly-folded arms. His bald head showed against the light of the windows, and his big bulk seemed compressed by the heat.

"To the Editor of the *Times*, Dear Stinker," pursued H.M. "I got a complaint to make, I have, about the leprous and hyena-souled b.b.'s who have the dishonor to compose our present Government. How long, I ask you, sir . . . (that's got a good Ciceronian flourish, ain't it? Yes; I like that; you keep it in). . . . How long, I ask you, sir, are free-born Englishmen goin' to stand the spectacle of public money being wasted on trifles, when there's such a blistering lot of things worth spending money on? Take me, for instance. Five flights of stairs I got to walk up every day of my life, and why? Because the dirty, low-down misers refuse to install—"

"Ah, sir," said Masters affably.

H.M., though checked in violent mid-flight, was too weary even to roar. "All right," he said, blinking evilly. "All right. I might have known it'd be you, Masters. My cup of trouble is now full. You might as well come in and slop it over. Bah."

"Morning, Miss Ffolliot," said Masters gallantly.

Lollypop, H.M.'s secretary, is a dazzling blonde with paper cuffs. At their entrance she got up, closing a notebook which Pollard observed to be serenely blank, and whisked out of the room. Wheezing laboriously, H.M. removed his feet from the desk. In front of him lay a palm-leaf fan.

"To tell you the truth," volunteered H.M., suddenly lowering his defenses, "I been looking for something interesting. These diplomatic matters give me the hump. Somebody's been shootin' at our battleships again. Ain't that Bob Pollard with you? Ah, I thought so. Sit down, Masters. What's on your mind?"

This easy capitulation staggered even the genial Masters. But, Pollard suspected, H.M. had actually been compelled to work for the past few days, and he was looking for any way out. Masters pushed across the table the note about the ten teacups. H.M. studied it sourly, twiddling his thumbs.

"Oh, ah," he said. "Well, what about it? Are you goin'?"

"I am," said Masters grimly. "What's more, Sir Henry, I mean to put a cordon round number 4 Berwick Terrace that a snake couldn't get through. Just so. Now look at this."

From his brief-case he took the Dartley file; and, from among the pages of the file, another sheet of notepaper. This sheet was about the same size as the first, and it was also typed. When he put the two side by side on H.M.'s desk, Pollard read:

THERE WILL BE TEN TEACUPS AT NUMBER 18, PENDRAGON GARDENS, W. 8, ON MONDAY, APRIL 30, AT 9:30 P.M. THE POLICE ARE WARNED TO KEEP AN EYE OUT.

"Not quite so gen-teel as the other one, is it?" said H.M. He eyed the two notes, and frowned. "Both houses in the Kensington district, though. Well?"

"This note about Pendragon Gardens we'll call Exhibit A," Masters went on, tapping it. "It came to the Yard, addressed to me, the afternoon of April 30 two years ago. Now, I ask you, sir," growled Masters, overflowing with bitterness, "what could *I* do? Eh? Beyond what I did, that is. But that was the beginning of the Dartley murder case, if you remember it?"

H.M. did not speak, although his fish eyes opened a little. But he picked up the palm-leaf fan, and pushed a box of cigars across the desk.

"I've been too long at this job," Masters went on, squaring his elbows, "not to know there're good tips to be had from things like that. Eh? But, beyond passing on word to the district police-station, there wasn't much I could do. I looked up number 18 Pendragon Gardens. Pendragon Gardens is a quiet, rather posh street in West Kensington. Number 18 was an empty house—only vacated within a week or so, though, because the light and water hadn't been cut off. The only thing I could find out about it was that, for some reason, people seemed to be afraid of the place and didn't live long there. Have you got it straight, sir?"

"You're a model o' clearness, son," replied H.M., looking at him curiously. "Ho ho! I'm just wondering whether your old bogy is goin' to sneak up and bite you . . ."

"Now don't mix me up!" said Masters. "I was telling you. Hurrum. The constable who had the night-beat past there didn't notice anything odd about the place. But next morning, about six o'clock, a sergeant on his way past to the police-station saw that the vestibule door of number 18 was partly open. He went up the steps and through the vestibule, and found that the house-door was unlocked. And that wasn't all.

Though it was an empty house, there was a strip of carpet laid down in the hall; and a hat-stand, and a couple of chairs. The sergeant started looking into the rooms. There wasn't a stick of furniture in any of 'em—except one. This was the room to the left of the door on the ground floor, sort of drawing-room. The shutters were up on the windows, but the sergeant could see it was furnished.

"Just so. It was furnished right enough: carpet, curtains, and all. Even a new bowl of a chandelier. It was all ordinary stuff, except for one thing. In the middle of the room there was a big round table. On it somebody had arranged in a circle ten porcelain teacups and saucers. There weren't any tea-things; just the cups, and all the cups were empty. The cups . . . well, sir, they were a bit odd. But I'll explain about that in a minute, because they weren't the only odd thing in the room. There was a dead man as well."

Masters drew a long breath through his nose. His ruddy face had a smile of skepticism, though he seemed to pride himself on his conscientiousness as well as his dramatic effect.

"A dead man," he repeated, spreading out more papers. "I've got a picture of him here. He was a little, oldish man in evening clothes, with a light topcoat over 'em. (His top-hat and gloves were on a chair at the other side of the room.) He was lying on his face beside the table, between the table and the door. He'd been shot twice from behind with a .32 caliber automatic—once through the neck and once through the back of the head. Both shots had been fired at such close range that the murderer must have held the pistol directly against him: the hair and neck were burnt by it. It looked as though the old chap had been walking up to the table, maybe to look at the teacups, and the murderer had jammed the gun against him and let go. According to the medical evidence, he had been killed between ten and eleven o'clock the previous night.

"Clews? Yes. But there weren't any. There were plenty of fingerprints in the room, including some of the dead man's; *but* there were no prints at all on the cups and saucers, not even a glove-smudge or the mark of a cloth to wipe 'em. Nobody had smoked or taken a drink; no chairs were pulled up; there was no hint of how many people might have been in the room or what they might have been doing. There was only one other indication. A wood fire had burnt out in the fireplace; in the ashes were found the remnants of a very large cardboard box, and fragments of a piece of burnt wrap-

11

ping-paper. However, they were *not* the box and paper in which the teacups had been packed. The container of the teacups, as I'll explain, was much more elaborate, a wooden box. But that wooden box had disappeared."

From the dossier Masters produced a photograph of a thin, mild face, with a hooked nose, a cropped gray beard and mustache.

"It was easy to identify the old boy," Masters went on. "And then—bang! A blank wall if I ever saw one. Lummy, sir, he was the very last person in the world anyone would have murdered! His name was William Morris Dartley. He was a bachelor, very well off, and he had no relatives except an unmarried sister (formidable old party) who kept house for him. It wasn't only that he hadn't any enemies; but he hadn't even any friends. It was true that in his early years he had been suspected of a business deal or two involving something like blackmail; but that was all over decades gone. His sister said (and, by George, I believed her!) that she could tell me what he had been doing every minute for the past fifteen years. Motive? Half his money went to the sister, and the other half to the South Kensington Museum. As the sister was playing bridge, with a cast-iron alibi—we never seriously considered her, anyway—there was nobody to suspect. The last tenants of the house were a Mr. and Mrs. Jeremy Derwent: Derwent being a solicitor of such painfully straight life, and the couple having no more to do with Dartley than the man in the moon, it was a dead wall again. Dartley's only interest in life, then, was collecting all sorts of art objects, with a strong preference for pottery and china. And so we come to those ten teacups."

Masters leaned forward and tapped the desk with an impressive air.

"Well, now, sir, I'm not what you'd call a connoisseur. Objay dart are a little out of my line. But one look at those cups, and even I could tell they were something special. The cups had a design on them like peacocks' feathers, all twisted up; it was in orange and yellow and blue; soft and shiny-like, and it seemed to move. Also, they were very old. You could almost see 'em shine in the room. And I was right about their being good. Here's a report from the South Kensington Museum:

The cups and saucers are some of the finest examples I have ever seen of early Majolica work from Italy.

12

They are from the workshop of Maestro Giorgio Andreoli of Gubbio; they bear his signature and the date, 1525. But these cups, so far as I am aware, are unique. They are not, of course, teacups since tea was not introduced into Europe until the middle of the seventeenth century. I confess that their use puzzles me. At the moment my conjecture is that they were meant for some ceremonial rite, such as in the secret councils once known at Venice. They are very valuable, and at auction would probably bring two or three thousand pounds.

"Uh-huh," said H.M. "It's a lot of money. But it sounds promisin'."

"Yes, sir; I thought so, too. And we traced the cups first shot; they belonged to Dartley himself. It seems he'd bought them only that afternoon, the thirtieth of April, at Soar's, the art dealers, in Bond Street. He bought them from old man Soar himself, making a great secret of the transaction, and paid twenty-five hundred in cash. Now, then, you'd say there was a sign of a motive, even if it was a crazy motive. Suppose some crackpot of a collector wanted those cups, and went through a lot of elaborate flummery to get 'em? It don't seem reasonable, I admit; but what else was there to think?

"It was elaborate, right enough. There were the furnishings, to begin with. We found out that two days before, April the twenty-eighth, an anonymous note had been delivered to the Holborn office of the Domestic Furnishing Company—that's one of those big places where you can equip your whole house, from lightning-rods to curtains, at one go—and the letter enclosed twenty five-pound notes. It said that the writer wanted their very best furniture for one drawing-room and a hallway. It said to get the furniture together in one lump, and it would be called for. Well, it was called for. The Cartwright Hauling Company received another anonymous letter, inclosing one fiver. This letter instructed them to send a furniture-van to the Domestic Stores, pick up a load for 18 Pendragon Gardens (a front-door key was inclosed, too), carry the load there, and shove it inside the door. It was all done without anybody getting a look at the man who'd ordered the stuff. The furniture men simply piled it all in the hall; there was nobody at the house. The chap behind it all must have arranged the furniture afterwards. Some of the neighbors noticed it being put in, of course. But, since the house was empty, they just supposed a new tenant was moving in, and thought no more of it."

H.M. seemed bothered by an invisible fly.

"Hold on," he said. "The anonymous letters—were they hand-written or typewritten?"

"Typewritten."

"Uh-huh. Same machine, was it, that wrote the letter to you tellin' you there'd be ten teacups at the place?"

"No, sir. It was a different machine. Also—what's the word I want?—a different *style* of typing. The ten-teacup note, as you can see, is bumpy and clumsy. The other two were clear, smooth copy. You can always tell a practiced hand at the typewriter."

"Uh-huh. Carry on."

Masters was dogged. "Now, the—hurrum—the inference," he said, "the inference we were supposed to draw is this: the murderer has baited a kind of trap. Eh? He's got an empty house and pretends it's his own; he furnishes the only parts of it a visitor will see. Dartley walks into it with the ten teacups under his arm, and for some reason is murdered. Maybe to steal the teacups.

"So far, it strings right along with Dartley's behavior. On the night he was murdered, he left his house in South Audley Street at half-past nine. His sister had already gone out to play bridge, being driven in their car; but the butler let him out and spoke to him. He was carrying some sort of biggish box or parcel wrapped up in paper, such as might have contained the teacups. But he didn't say where he was going. He picked up a taxi outside his house: we found the taxi-driver later. He was driven straight to 18 Pendragon Gardens." Masters grinned heavily. "The taxi-driver remembered him all right. Bit of luck, that. The fare to Pendragon Gardens was three and six, and Dartley handed the driver twopence as a tip. He seems to have been a bit of a tight-fisted old beggar, for all his money. But here's what isn't luck. The driver was so disgusted that he slammed in his gears and tore off without even noticing where Dartley went. Lummy, if he'd only caught a glimpse of someone opening that door! Bah. All the driver remembers is that there didn't seem to be any lights in the house."

Masters made a broad gesture.

"And that's every bit of evidence we've got. Everything else ended in a damnation full stop. No irregularities, no enemies, no anything. If you say he was, um, *lured*," said Masters, uncomfortable at the melodramatic word, "if you say he was lured into that house and murdered for the teacups . . . well, sir, I dare say that's easiest. But it isn't sense. Like this! Now, the murderer can't be penniless. He certainly went to a lot of trouble and expense to bait his trap: anyhow, he sent a hundred quid to a furnishing company, when my daughter's furnished her 'ole blooming house for that much. If he can afford to chuck it about like that, why didn't he simply go and buy the cups from the art-dealer? 'Tisn't as though they were museum-pieces. Finally, since he'd gone to all the trouble of setting a stage and murdering Dartley, why didn't he pinch the cups? There they were, large as life, on the table. Plainly and literally, sir, they hadn't even been touched: there wasn't a fingerprint on 'em.

"I told you we'd got a fine crop of fingerprints, including Dartley's, but that led nowhere. They all belonged to the furniture-movers. The murderer must have worn gloves all the time. But he didn't take the cups? Why? He wasn't scared off, because there wasn't a sign of disturbance there all night. And there you are. It won't work however you look at it; it won't make sense; and, if there's anything that puts the wind up me, it's cases that don't make sense. For what does this murderer do on top of it all? He don't touch the cups—but he does walk off with the box that contained the cups, and the paper that was wrapped round it! I ask you, now! And this morning, two years later, I get another note about ten teacups. Does it mean more murder? Or what do you make of it?"

CHAPTER TWO

Policeman's Lot

FOR A TIME H.M. remained blinking at the desk, twiddling his thumbs over his paunch. The corners of his mouth were drawn down as though he were smelling a bad breakfast egg. It was very quiet in the room; the dusky light quivered in heat-waves past the windows. Again H.M. reached after the cigar-box. This time he took out a cigar, bit off the end, and expectorated it in a long, violent parabola of a shot which almost reached the hearth across the room.

"If you ask me whether I think it's bad," he said, sniffing; "yes, I do. I smell the blood of an Englishman again. Burn

15

me, Masters, you manage to get tangled up in some of the goddamnedest cases I ever heard of. All we need to do is get another murder with an impossible situation that couldn't have happened, and you'll be right in your element. Yes, I can feel it comin'."

Masters, still suave, knew how to prod his man.

"Of course, sir, I can't expect too much," he said. "It isn't to be expected that you would see any light when our whole organization has been stumped for two years. Excuse me: after all, you're only an amateur. But, even if it is beyond you—"

"You want to bet, hey?" demanded H.M., galvanized. He howled about ingratitude to such an extent that Pollard feared Masters had gone too far; but when H.M. was somewhat smoothed down Masters remained as bland as ever. "It seems to me," said H.M. malevolently, "that people are never happy unless they're tellin' me what an outworn, cloth-headed, maunderin' old fossil I am. It's persecution, that's what it is. All right. You watch. Just to show you this business ain't nearly as opaque as you footlers seem to think, I got a couple of questions to ask you. But there's somethin' else to decide first."

He pointed towards the note that had arrived this morning.

"Look here, son. 'Number 4 Berwick Terrace, at 5 P.M. precisely.' Why in the afternoon, anyway? There's somethin' fishy about the sound of it. I don't mean it's a hoax or a have: only that there's a queer and fishy element about it. That ending, 'The police are warned to keep an eye out,' on the note you got two years ago—that's straight and square. But, 'The presence of the Metropolitan Police is respectfully requested,' —that's unnatural, and I don't like it; it sounds like somebody laughing. I say, I hope you've had the sense to make sure it's not a hoax? I mean, you've found out whether 4 Berwick Terrace really is an empty house, suitable for polite murder?"

Masters snorted. "You can bet I have, sir. I've phoned a request to the divisional inspector for the Kensington district to get me a report on the place, and anything that's known about it. But it reminds me. He ought to have some news by this time. If you'll excuse me—?"

He leaned forward and picked up H.M.'s telephone. Within a minute he was put through to Inspector Cotteril, and Pollard heard the telephone talking sharply. Masters put his hand over the mouthpiece and turned back to them. His face was less ruddy and his eye looked wicked.

"Right," he said to H.M. "It's an empty house. It's been empty for a year or so. There's a board up in the window; Houston & Klein, St. James's Square, are the agents. Cotteril says Berwick Terrace is a little cul-de-sac: very quiet, sedate, hardly a dozen houses in it. Mid-Victorian solidness and respectability: you know. But number 4 isn't the only unoccupied house. Only a few houses in the street are occupied."

"So? What's the matter? Plague?"

Masters consulted the telephone again. "Very nearly as bad, it seems," he reported. "They're extending the Underground, and they mean to run a branch with an Underground station that'll be almost at the entrance to Berwick Terrace. It isn't finished yet, but it's on the way. The inhabitants of Berwick Terrace were so outraged at the idea of their privacy being invaded with a tube station that they moved out almost in a body. Real-estate values have dropped to blazes. . . . What's that, Cotteril? Eh? Yes; that's done it." When Masters turned round again he was very quiet. "A constable on the beat there reports that yesterday some furniture was delivered to number 4 in a van, and put inside."

H.M. whistled.

"It means business, son," he said. "This murderer's got his nerve right with him."

"He'll have to be an invisible man," said Masters, "if he thinks he can get away with the same sort of funny business twice, *and* twist our tails as well. I'll give him ten teacups! Hullo!—Cotteril? This may be the Dartley case all over again; we can't tell yet. Send your two best men, plain clothes, and cover that house front and back. Get a man inside if you can, but keep it watched. I'll get the keys of the place from the house-agents. We'll have men inside and out. Yes: straightaway. But tell the outside men to keep out of sight as much as they can. Right. See you soon. 'Bye."

"Now, now," urged H.M. soothingly, as Masters put back the receiver with some violence. H.M. had managed to get his cigar lighted, and the smoke hung round his head in an oily cloud. "Keep your shirt on, son. It's only noon now. Grantin' that the murderer sticks to his schedule, you got five hours yet: though I admit you'd be pretty simple-minded if you accepted his word without question. Humph."

"Doesn't it bother you at all?" inquired Masters.

"Oh, sure. Sure; I'm bothered as hell. And it's this fellow's method that bothers me, Masters, and why he happens to be so cocky about it. But I'm not very grief-stricken as yet; be-

17

cause, the trouble is, we haven't got the foggiest notion who has been chosen as a victim."

"Excuse me, sir," interposed Pollard, "but how do you know murder is intended at all?"

There was a pause. Both the others looked at him. Masters turned round a lowering eyebrow, and seemed about to say, "Now, now," in that heavy fashion he reserved for juniors: especially any juniors with what he called "your education." Though Masters was easy to work for, he was a terror to speech. But Pollard had been too interested by that queer picture—the ten teacups, painted with a design like peacocks' feathers, ranged in a circle and shining among commonplace furniture.

"Go on, son," said H.M. woodenly. "What's on your mind?"

Pollard reached out and tapped the notes. "It's these. Neither of the notes actually makes a threat or suggests trouble of any kind. What they do say is that there will be ten teacups at such-and-such a place. Suppose the murder of Dartley was only a slip in the plan? . . . Like this, sir. We've got only one indication as to what the cups might mean. That indication is in the report from the man at the South Kensington Museum. Here it is. 'My conjecture is that they were meant for some ceremonial rite, such as in the secret councils once known at Venice.' I don't know anything about secret councils at Venice. But at least it's a lead. I mean— suppose it's a meeting of some secret society?"

"H'm," said H.M. "Sort of Suicide Club, you mean? Only this seems more like a murder club."

"Won't do," snapped Masters. "Now, Bob, we've been over all that before. *All* of it. The idea of a secret society was suggested at the time of Dartley's death. It was some newspaper idea; they printed a lot of high-colored feature articles about secret societies old and new. And it's bosh. To begin with, if it's a secret society, it's so ruddy secret that nobody else ever heard of it."

"I dunno," said H.M. "You got a simple straightforward mind, Masters. Your idea of a secret society is one of the big benevolent orders, which really aren't secret societies at all in the sense I mean it. There are deeper places than that, son. Seems like you can't believe in a secret society that really is secret, and that's run without fuss. Mind you, I don't say it's so in this case. I doubt it myself. But have you got any reasons for swearin' it couldn't be so?"

Masters was dogged. "Yes," he declared. "I'll give you one

good practical reason: Dartley's sister Emma. That woman could have made her fortune at private detective work. I never saw such a nose for snooping before or since. She swears there wasn't, and couldn't have been, anything like that; and —well, I'd back her judgment. If you met her you'd understand. What's more, we had the whole organization after that lead. And there wasn't a scrap of evidence anywhere to support it. All the signs showed that only two people had been at Pendragon Gardens that night: Dartley and his murderer. Now, sir, I don't know whether you can run a secret society without any fuss. But I'm smacking well certain you can't run one without any members."

H.M. surveyed him.

"You're gettin' out of hand," he said. "But let's stick to facts, if you like it better. You brought up Dartley again, and it's Dartley I want to ask about. He had a pretty big collection, had he?"

"A big collection, and a valuable one. Close on a hundred thousand pounds' worth of stuff, the man from the museum said."

"Uh-huh. What was it, mostly? Pottery?"

"Pottery, yes, but a lot of other stuff as well. I've got a list here somewhere. It was a pretty mixed bag: some pictures, and snuff-boxes, and books, and even a sword or two."

"Did he deal much with Soar's in Bond Street?"

Masters was puzzled. "Quite a good deal, I understand. He was friendly with old Benjamin Soar—you remember, the head of the firm who died about six months ago? Soar's son runs the business now. I remember, the man from the museum said Dartley must have been an uncommonly shrewd businessman, for all his mild looks. There was a packet of receipted bills in his desk, and he'd beaten down Soar to a very good price on a lot of the stuff." Masters looked at H.M. shrewdly. "Not, of course," he prodded, "that it's important. . . ."

"Oh, no. Now, when Dartley bought the teacups, how were they packed?"

"Ordinary big teakwood box about two feet long by one foot deep; nothing out of the way. They were packed inside in tissue paper and excelsior. The box was never found, as I told you."

"Just one more question, son; and be awful careful about the answer. Now, I suppose they took an inventory of the collection after his death, if he gave it to the museum. When they went over his collection, was there anything missing?"

Masters sat up, rather slowly. His big face was half-grinning, with surprise.

"I might have known," he replied after a pause, "that you'd pull a rabbit out of the hat like that. How did you know there was something missing?"

"Oh, I was just sittin' and thinkin'. And I thought maybe there might be. What was it, son?"

"That's the odd part of it. If I remember it right, it was one of the few things in the old chap's collection that wasn't valuable. He kept it as a curiosity, like a toy. It was what they call a 'puzzle-jug.' You've probably seen 'em. It's a big jug, porcelain or what-not, with three spouts and sometimes a hollow handle with a hole in it. The spouts are on all sides. The idea is to fill it up with water and challenge somebody to pour it out one of the spouts without spilling a drop from any of the others." Masters paused, and stared. "But what in the name of sense has a missing puzzle-jug got to do with Dartley's murder, and how does it fit in with ten teacups in a circle?"

"I haven't got the foggiest idea, son," admitted H.M. He looked disconsolately at his hands, and twiddled his thumbs again. "At the moment, anyhow. But I sorta thought, from somethin' you said, that there might have been a missing item in Dartley's collection. No, no, don't ask me why! Burn me, Masters, you got work to do. You're a man of action, and it strikes me you'd better get busy."

Masters rose, drawing a deep breath.

"I mean to," he said, "straightaway. But we've got a conference at the Yard on that Birmingham business, and I've got to arrange to get away." He looked at Pollard. "You're the man to handle the first part of this, Bob. Think you can manage it?"

"Yes," said Pollard briefly.

"Right. Hop round to Houston & Klein, the house agents, in St. James's Square. Get the keys of 4 Berwick Terrace, and an order-to-view. Don't let on you're a copper: they may make trouble. Put on your most high-falutin manner and say you're thinking of buying the place. Got that? Find out if anybody else has asked for the keys. Then get into the house, find the room where the furniture is, and don't leave that room no matter what happens. I'll join you as soon as I can. Hop to it."

The last thing Pollard heard before he left the room was the sound of H.M.'s ghoulish mirth, and a noise from Masters like, "Ur!" Pollard admitted to himself that he was excited about this case; he also knew that, if he fell down on it, Masters would have his hide. Over Whitehall a sickly, darkening sky pressed down, as though there would be rain before evening. Pollard walked so fast after a bus that he found himself in a bath of sweat, and had to re-adjust himself. But within ten minutes he was in the offices of Houston & Klein, outstaring an imposing gentleman who bent forward confidentially across a desk.

"Number 4 Berwick Terrace," said the agent slowly, as though the name were only half-familiar to him. "Ah, yes. Yes, of course. We shall be very pleased to let you have a look at it." He regarded Pollard without apparent curiosity. "May I say, sir, that that house seems to have become very popular?"

"Popular?"

"Yes. We gave a set of keys and an order-to-view to another applicant only this morning." He smiled. "Of course, the prior order entails no advantage if anyone cares to purchase—"

Pollard allowed annoyance to show in his face. "That's unfortunate. That's very unfortunate, if it was the person I think it was. Who was it by the way? There's a sort of wager. . . ."

"Oh, a wager," said the agent, puzzled but relieved. His hesitation vanished. "Well, sir, I don't suppose there's any particular secret about it. It was Mr. Vance Keating."

The name unfolded a whole list of possibilities. Pollard vaguely remembered having met Keating at a party, and having disliked him: but the name had a certain notoriety to any newspaper-reader. Vance Keating was a young man with a great deal of money, who too often and too publicly announced his boredom with life. "We belong," he had once said, in a speech which caused some mirth, "to the cult of the Venturers who are as old as chivalry. We ring strange doorbells. We get off at the wrong stations. We penetrate into harems, and go over Niagara Falls in a barrel. Always we are disappointed; but still we believe that adventure, like prosperity, is just round the corner." On the other hand, Keating certainly had performed several very dangerous exploits; though it was rumored that his stamina was not always equal to his ideals, and that, the time he went after the twelve-foot tiger, he collapsed and had to be carried most of the way in a litter. Pollard remembered having read not long ago of his engagement to Miss Frances Gale, the golfer.

Pollard said: "Oh, Keating. Yes, I'd expected that. Well,

you may expect a struggle, but one of us will get the place. . . . I wonder if you could tell me whether anyone else has been looking at the house recently?"

The agent considered. "I don't think there's been anybody within the last six months. I can't tell you offhand, but I can find out for you. Just one moment. Mr. Grant!" He went off majestically, and returned with records. "I find I was wrong, sir. A young lady viewed the house about three months ago: on May 10, to be exact. A Miss Frances Gale. I believe the young lady is—er—?"

"Thanks," said Pollard, and got out quickly.

If Vance Keating were mixed up in this business, then something spectacular was on the way. Keating concerned himself in no placid affairs. Sergeant Pollard went down into a sweltering Underground, rode as far as Notting Hill Gate, and then walked westward through the steep, quiet streets.

It was only a quarter past one, but the whole neighborhood looked dead. A muddy yellow sky pressed down on the heights; sometimes an air would stir like a puff out of an oven, and rattle the dry leaves of plane trees. He found Berwick Terrace easily enough. It was a cul-de-sac leading out of a larger square, a backwater as cut off as though it had gates. Berwick Terrace was about sixty yards deep by twenty yards broad. In it were ten houses, four on each side and two narrow-chested ones facing out at the end. They were solid, uniform houses in graystone and white facings; with bow-windows, areaways, and stone steps leading up to deep vestibules. Each had three stories and an attic. They had darkened to a uniform hue with soot; they were built together, and looked like one house except where railings went up to the front doors from the lone line of area-rails. But stiff lace curtains showed at the windows of only four houses—possibly that was what gave the street its desolate, gutted look, and to Pollard a feeling of disquiet. Nothing stirred there. The only sign of life was a child's perambulator in the vestibule of number 9 at the end of the street. The only sign of color was a garish red telephone-box at the beginning of the street. Otherwise the chimneys stood up dark against an uneasy sky. Once the greater part of its tenants left, Berwick Terrace had begun to decay with amazing swiftness.

Number 4 was on the left-hand side. Pollard walked down the right-hand pavement, and heard his own footsteps echo. He stopped across the road from number 4, leisurely took out a cigarette, and examined the house. There was nothing to distinguish it from the others, except that it was possibly a trifle more shabby. Some of the windows were shuttered, some were dusty, and one or two of them were now open. Just as he glanced across, Pollard thought he saw the attic window move, as someone pushed it up to look out. There was someone in the house now, and that person was watching him.

A very low voice behind him whispered: "Sergeant!"

The house before which he was standing, number 2, was also vacant. Out of the corner of his eye Pollard had seen that a window on the ground floor, beyond the areaway, was up about half an inch. The voice was coming from there, although he could see nothing because of the dust.

"Hollis, L Division," it said. "I've been here about an hour. Porter is watching the back. We've got it taped; there's no way in or out except by the front or back door.—I don't know whether it's the man you're after, but there's somebody in the house now."

Pollard, lighting his cigarette, spoke ventriloquially.

"Be careful; he's up at the window. Don't let him see you. Who is it?"

"I don't know. Young fellow in a light suit. He got here about ten minutes ago—walking."

"What's he been doing?"

"Can't tell, except that he opened a couple of windows; he'd have choked to death if he hadn't. It's hot as hell in here."

"Did you manage to get inside the house and have a look?"

"No; we couldn't. The place is locked up like a strongroom. We couldn't get in without attracting attention, and the inspector said—"

"Right. Stand by."

With a luxurious puff, Pollard strolled across the street, examining the house with open interest. He drew out the keys, to which a cardboard label bearing the agent's name was attached, and juggled them. The bow-windows to the left of the door, he noticed, were heavily shuttered; that would probably be the room where the furniture was arranged. He started up the steps to the front door. Then he glanced towards the mouth of the street, and stopped.

Berwick Terrace lay off a large square called Coburg Place. The trees of the square stood up twinkling in hot, hard light; and it was very quiet except for the sudden beating of a car-engine. A blue Talbot two-seater cruised past the mouth of the street. The driver, a woman, was leaning out of the car and peering down Berwick Terrace: intently, for the car

23

wabbled. It was too far away for Pollard to distinguish her features, yet there was something intent and startled even about the sound of the engine. Then the car whisked away.

Pollard felt that somewhere a wheel had begun to spin, a conductor had lifted his baton, a beginning had been made in the movement of rapid and evil things. But he had no time to consider that. The inner door of the house was dragged open. There was a step on the marble tiling of the vestibule, and the vestibule door opened as well. A man stood just inside, looking at him.

"Well?" said the man.

CHAPTER THREE

Murderer's Promise

THE VESTIBULE was paved with red-and-white marble flags, and it was very dark, so that Pollard had only an indistinct view of the man inside. But he recognized him as Vance Keating. Keating wore a suit of very light gray flannel, somewhat begrimed, and his thumbs were hooked in the coat pockets. He was a thin, wiry, middle-sized young man, with a long nose and a discontented mouth. Ordinarily his expression might have been spoiled or supercilious, but now it was that of excitement; he carried his own atmosphere with him. Excitement, or suspicion. Pollard saw his eyelids move to the gloom. But there was one thing about him which added an almost grotesque touch: in his excitement he had got hold of somebody else's hat. The hat was a soft gray Homburg a size or more too large for him; it was squashed along one side, and came down nearly far enough to flatten out his ears.

"Where's the woman?" he demanded.

"Woman?"

"Yes. The woman who—" Keating stopped, and in that instant Pollard was certain some secret meeting or conclave was to have been held, so that Keating had taken him for a member of it. But Keating's mind worked too; he weighed possibilities suddenly, and the opportunity for pretense on Pollard's part had gone.

"*La tasse est vide; la femme attend,*" said Keating.

Well, there were the old melodramatics again: evidently the password to which he must supply the answer. And he hadn't got the answer. Pollard had determined on his course.

24

"The chickens of my aunt are in the garden," he replied. "What about it?"

"Who the hell," said Keating in a very low voice, "are you? What do you want here?"

"I want to see the house, if it's all the same to you."

"See the house?"

"Look here," said Pollard mildly, "let's get this thing straight. I want to see the house with the idea of buying it, if the price is right. Didn't Houston & Klein tell you? I'm in the market for something like this. So I got an order-to-view, as I suppose you did."

"But they can't do that," cried the other, in a stupid-sounding voice which had a note of incredulity amounting almost to horror. It was evidently the one thing he had not foreseen. "They can't do that. They gave me the keys—"

"There's no reason why we both shouldn't look at it, is there?" asked Pollard, and moved past him into the hall.

It was a good-sized hall, but very dark in the heavy-woodwork fashion of sixty years ago: a dust-trap and a shadow-trap. On the landing of the staircase a round window of very thick multi-colored glass, twisted into dingy reds and blues, gave a crooked light which barely tinted the darkness. It seemed to draw the hall together oppressively. Footsteps on the bare boards went up and were lost in echoes. As though casually, Pollard strolled across to the room on the left and opened the door.

The furniture had not been put in this room.

Though the shutters were up on the windows, he could make out that much. It surprised him, unpleasantly, for he was now looking for traps. Out of the corner of his eye he watched Keating. Granting that something ugly was on the way, the question became this: was Vance Keating the instigator or the victim?

"Sorry, old boy," said Keating suddenly. His expression had altered and shifted like an actor's, as he debated courses; and now he came forward with an air of very genuine charm. "I'm a bit on edge, that's all; late party last night. There's no reason at all why we both shouldn't look at it. I can even show you over the place, if it comes to that. Er—shall you be long?"

Pollard looked at his watch, which said one-forty. It would be three hours and twenty minutes before the threatened coming of the ten teacups.

"I'm afraid I'm early," he replied. "There'll be a lot of

25

time to kill. You see, I arranged to meet my sister here—she keeps house for me, and naturally wants to see the place—at half-past four. But she'll probably be late at that; she usually is. I'd better not be in any hurry. Or, if you like, I can go now and come back about four-thirty or five."

Keating half turned away. When he turned back again, his face wore a look of calm superciliousness.

"I wonder," he suggested politely, "whether you'd just come along with me for a minute?"

"Come along where?"

"This way," said Keating, and marched out of the house.

Undoubtedly he had to go. Whether Keating were instigator or victim, an eye must be kept on him. But, if Pollard had any notion that Keating was attempting to lead him a dance, it was soon dispelled. Keating went no farther than the telephone-box at the corner of Berwick Terrace. Holding open the door so that the other could listen, he dialed a number.

"I want to speak," he said, in a new and supercilious voice, "to Mr. Klein. . . . Hullo: Klein? Vance Keating speaking. I've made up my mind about that place in Berwick Terrace. What was your price? . . . Yes. And freehold. . . . Yes, that's quite satisfactory. I'll buy it, if—just one moment. There's another customer of yours here. Would you care, my friend, to go higher than three thousand five hundred? Ah, I thought not. . . . Klein? Yes, I'll buy. The deal's made now, isn't it, as soon as I make my decision? The house is mine from this minute, even before I get the deed? . . . It is? You're sure of that? . . . Right. Good-by."

He hung up the phone with a certain care, and stepped out of the box.

"Now, my friend," he announced with satisfaction, "I scarcely think the house will interest you any longer. I am accustomed to having what I want, and I have it now. Any further visits to 4 Berwick Terrace, social or otherwise, will be discouraged. You will therefore oblige me by getting to blazes out of here."

The gray Homburg, flattening out his ears, nevertheless sat jauntily on the back of his head. He moved away with a long, free stride, evidently having the business settled to satisfaction. His air seemed to indicate that he could now forget it. Sergeant Pollard, with an un-Robert-like wrath mounting up to his own ears, took a step after him—when he heard a familiar, long clearing of the throat from the other side of the telephone-box. Turning back, Pollard saw the boiled blue eye of Chief Inspector Humphrey Masters looking at him from the direction of Coburg Place. Masters shook his head, and beckoned.

The sergeant waited only long enough to make sure that Keating went back into the house. Then he joined Masters, whose bowler hat was looking sinister.

"We've got to teach you," said Masters, "when in doubt, never fly off the handle. I don't." His eye wandered down in the direction of the house. "Lummy, but *he* can afford to chuck it about! Thirty-five hundred for—what? That's what beats me. Never mind. Report."

Pollard gave a brief summary, and Masters chewed it over.

Was there anybody in the house besides Keating?"

"I couldn't tell. But I shouldn't think so, judging by the way he rushed out to meet—whoever he thought I might be, when I went to the door. He's expecting a woman, and he wants to meet her very badly."

"It's still a lot of money," Masters pointed out, somewhat obscurely. "Hurrum. And no furniture in the front room. Still, that doesn't mean anything. House is covered front and back. I tell you, Bob, nobody can get in there! 'Tisn't possible! Look here: you've got to get in, though. Sneak in, of course. You've got the keys, and you can try the back this time. If he catches you, you're for it, but you've got to see he doesn't catch you. I'll join Hollis in the house across the street."

The chief inspector reflected, rubbing his chin.

"The trouble is, as you say, that we don't know whether he's a victim or a wrong 'un. In either case we can't show our hand. If we went charging in there, and explained who we were—well, he'd simply order us out. As he's got the right to do. This is the only way. Maybe it happened for the best: there's still three clear hours before five o'clock. You get into that house, you find out which room he's in, and you stick outside that door like glue."

From Coburg Place a narrow mews ran up behind Berwick Terrace. Each house had a spacious back-garden, fenced in by a six-foot board wall. Pollard was relieved to see that all the back windows of number 4 were shuttered. As he slid through the rear gate he was challenged by Porter, the plain-clothes constable stationed in a decrepit summer-house there.

"Not a peep out of the place," Porter told him. "I know them kind of shutters; you can't see through 'em even when

27

you're inside. Duck up to the back porch quick, and he won't be able to spot you even if he's at the window."

The back door had an overhanging roof with iron scroll-work. Once under it, Pollard's great fear was that the door would be bolted on the inside, and that his key would be of no use. But the key opened it; and, to his surprise, the door moved almost soundlessly.

He stood in the gloom of a kitchen. The heat of dry timber came down on him like a bag over the head. Though these old floors were solid, the utter absence of life, of furniture, of anything human and moving inside a shell, made every footstep faintly audible. He found himself walking on shaking ankles to keep quiet, and wished too late that he had had a final smoke before he entered. The plan of the ground-floor was simple: at the rear were the kitchen and the butler's pantry; then the central hall with two spacious rooms opening off it on either side. There was no stick of furniture in any of the four rooms, except a potted plant left behind in one. And Pollard, though far from psychic, did not like the look of any of them. He remembered Masters having said that number 18 Pendragon Gardens, where Dartley was murdered, had such an unpleasant reputation that nobody would live in it; and he wondered whether number 4 Berwick Terrace had a similar reputation. The house, so to speak, breathed wrong. Whoever had lived here last, the occupant had a passion for crowding the rooms with very small pictures; the walls were spotted, like a rash, with lines of tiny hooks attached to nails.

He had penetrated as far as the front room on the right, when he heard footsteps coming down the main stairs.

They were rattling, brisk, jaunty footsteps. He knew that they belonged to Keating even before he saw the man. Looking out through a crack of the door, Pollard saw Keating cross the hall, go out the front door—whistling softly to himself—and lock it behind him. Then silence came again.

Pollard put his head out cautiously. It might be a trap: after all the trouble Keating had taken to remain alone in the house, he would not presumably saunter off like this. On the other hand, he might now have devised his trappings and baited his teacups. He might have finished whatever preparations were necessary.

The sergeant risked it, and hurried up the staircase. After a few minutes' waiting, without a click from the front door or a rustle in the vestibule, he was emboldened to make a search of the two upstairs stories. Each floor had five rooms, bed and sitting rooms, and a somewhat primitive bath. The same desolation curtained off each from the world. There had been children here, for the walls of one were papered in nursery designs; but he did not imagine they had been very happy children. And still there was no trace of the one furnished room.

It must be in the attic, unless Keating had led them all neatly astray by the nose. Pollard suddenly had a vivid remembrance of the first thing he had seen when he arrived at the house an hour ago: a figure, supposedly Keating's, peering out of an attic window. At the rear of the topmost hallway he found a door giving on a narrow flight of stairs almost as steep as a ladder. . . .

The attic was "finished." That is to say, you emerged through a sort of trap into a hall which had been formed by wooden partitions built up to the roof on either side. These partitions appeared to form four separate rooms, for there were four doors. But it was gloomy here, and the heat had become strangling: he felt his pores stir to it. This must be the place of the teacups: though why, in sanity, should furniture be carried up to the remote top of the house when every room was vacant? Yet this front attic room—on the left as you stood facing the front—would contain the window out of which someone had been peering an hour ago.

He went to the door and turned the knob. It was locked. And it was the only locked door inside the house.

Probing into the other three rooms on this floor, he found them all open. This one garret chamber, some fifteen feet square, was the one he wanted. The key was not in the lock, and he tried to peer through the keyhole. He got an impression that the walls were of grimy white plaster; and that in the middle of the fifteen foot room there was a table covered with some cloth that looked like very dingy gold; but the rest was a blur. He investigated a faint line of light under the door, with no result except to discover that the carpet was very black and thick. There was, he felt convinced, nobody in the room now. But it stopped him. To pick the lock he found impossible, and he could not break it open without giving the show away when Keating returned. . . .

It was two hours before Keating returned, a time of dreary waiting during which Pollard's stolidity began to wear thin. He spent it in exploring the house, including every nook of the cellar, and making certain there was nobody hidden.

It was fifteen minutes past four when he heard Keating's distinctive step come into the house, and the slam of the front door. And Keating was alone.

Pollard went softly up to the attic, hiding himself in the rear room to the right. Through the crack of the door he had a clear view of the locked sanctuary. Keating's footfalls ascended the attic stairs, Keating's head appeared through the trap, and Keating seemed greedy with expectancy. Taking a key out of his coat pocket, he opened the sanctuary door. He was so quick about going in and closing the door after him that Pollard had only a brief, narrow glimpse of anything inside. Yet he saw the table-cover dull-gleaming, and he saw teacups ranged in a circle—black teacups. Keating did not lock the door behind him; the key remained in the lock outside. The young Venturer made only one other movement when he slipped through into this uncouth shrine; he removed his hat.

Four-fifteen. Four-thirty. Pollard felt his scalp crawl and his wits thicken under the pressure of heat. Still no sound issued from the room, nor was there a sign of any other visitor, while the watcher stood neck-cramped with his eyes on the door. The hand of his wrist-watch crept upwards: a quarter to five. And now good theories began to dissolve when he remembered Masters's words: "I don't know whether you can run a secret society without any fuss, but I'm smacking well certain you can't run one without any members." He was right. Vance Keating sat alone in the shrine, guarded if ever a man was guarded, with police at both the back and the front. Five minutes to five.

Keating screamed, and Pollard heard the first shot, just as the minute-hand of the wrist-watch stood vertical.

Scream and shot were so unexpected, the explosion so muffled as of a weapon pressed into flesh, that Pollard hardly knew what he was hearing. Then there was the slither and crash of breaking china, and a thump. Then there was the second shot, less muffled, and blasting so close at hand that it shook the key in the door. A heavy revolver had been fired twice behind that door; and, while the echoes of the shots were settling, Pollard heard his wrist-watch loudly.

He smelt powder-smoke from an old-fashioned type of cartridge even before he ran across the hall. When he opened the door of the shrine, he saw a low room with white-plaster walls. In the wall to the right was the room's one window.

30

Outside the sky was darkening with storm, and heavy curtains of dark velvet were partly drawn across the window, but there was light enough for him to see the round table on which were ranged the ten teacups. Two of the cups were smashed.

Vance Keating lay at full length on the floor between the table and the door, his head towards the door. He was lying on his left side, his face pressed into the floor and his right leg a little drawn up. He had been shot twice (these were later known to be undeniable facts) with a .45 caliber revolver which lay on the floor at his left side. In the back of his skull there was a ragged black burn where a bullet had been fired into his brain. In the back of his gray coat there was another burned hole, still smoking and showing an ember against the black, where a second bullet had entered. Above the odor of powder-smoke was that of burnt cloth and hair. The weapon had been held against him, Pollard saw; blood began to come sluggishly from the wounds, but very little, for he died under the watcher's eyes.

Standing so as to bar the doorway, Pollard saw these things not as tabulated items, but of a piece. However a murderer had got in here, the murderer must still be in the room. He knew that nobody had gone out by the door. And the one window was forty feet above the street.

He thought: Steady! Take it easy! Take it easy, now. . . .

Wiping his gummy eyelids, he reached outside, got the key, and locked the door on the inside. Then he went round the room, slowly and with senses strung alert; but he found nobody because there was nobody there. In the thick pile of the black carpet were only two sets of dusty footprints—his own, and those that led to the upturned toes of Vance Keating's shoes. Then he went to the window.

Storm was coming on; a puff of cooler air blew in his face. Serene in its doze, Berwick Terrace lay spread out forty feet below. He realized how little time had elapsed between the firing of the shots and his going to the window, when he saw the bowler-hatted figure of Masters pelting across the street towards the door of number 4. Leaning across the sill, he stared left and right along the blank facade of the house, along a large and empty street which would have shielded no fugitive.

"He got out of the window!" shouted Detective-Sergeant Pollard.

Across the street the ground-floor window in the house directly opposite, where Sergeant Hollis was watching, flew up with an unseemly screech. Hollis poked out an angry head.

"No, he didn't," came Hollis's voice in a faint yell. "Nobody got out that window."

CHAPTER FOUR

Lawyers' Houses

AT EXACTLY half-past five, Doctor Blaine, the brisk police surgeon, rose from beside the body of Vance Keating and dusted his knees. Photographers were at work in the room, and flash-bulbs glared. McAllister (fingerprints) stood close to the window to catch the light, with the .45 revolver on his knee, and used the miniature bellows. Doctor Blaine looked at Chief Inspector Humphrey Masters.

"Just," he asked, "what do you want to know?"

Masters removed his bowler in order to wipe his forehead with a handkerchief. Masters appeared to be suffering from claustrophobia. But he tried to achieve lightness, possibly in self-defense.

"Well, I can see he's been shot," he admitted. "But the gun, now? With that gun?"

"That's hardly my job. You'll know before long; but, all the same, I shouldn't think there was much doubt about it." Blaine pointed. "Those two wounds were made with a .45. Also, it was a very old-style gun with old-style ammunition. A modern high caliber, with steel-jacket ammunition, would have sent both bullets smack through him. And you've got the gun that fits right there, with two exploded cartridge-cases in the magazine."

He nodded towards McAllister, evidently puzzled at the black look on Masters's face. Masters went over to where the fingerprint-man was blowing the last dust off the butt, and Pollard followed him.

In its own way the revolver was a fine piece of gunmaking. Though large, it was not cumbersome, and it was much lighter than you might have expected. The silvered steel of the barrel and magazine had been worn almost black, but the handle was inlaid in curious designs with mother of pearl. Into the foot of the grip had been set a small silver plate engraved with the words *Tom Shannon*.

"That name, now," Masters considered, pointing to it. "You don't suppose—?"

"If I were you, Chief Inspector," said McAllister, with a last puff, "I wouldn't send out a bulletin after Tom Shannon. It'd be like trying to arrest Charlie Peace. Shannon has been pushing up the daisies for forty years. This gun was his. And what a gun!" He held it up. "Know what it is? It's the original Remington six-shooter, made in 1894. If you've ever read anything about the Wild West, you'll know what that means. And Shannon was one of the original bad men. I only wonder there aren't any notches in the thing; but maybe Shannon didn't like to chop up his shooting-irons. Where do you suppose anybody got ammunition for the thing, in this day and age? It's loaded except for two shots gone. Also, how did it happen to turn up in England? Probably the answer to both questions is that it belongs to somebody who makes a collection of guns. . . ."

"Collectors!" said Masters. He seemed to meditate on a string of collections which included teacups, puzzle-jugs, and now six-shooters. "Never mind about that. What about fingerprints?"

"Not a print on the whole thing. The bloke wore gloves."

When Masters turned back to Blaine, he made an effort to recover some of his usual blandness.

"Point's this, Doctor. You've been asking just exactly what we want to know. And there's only one question. Is it absolutely certain, could you swear to it, that both those shots were fired with the gun held close to the body?"

"It's absolutely certain."

"Now, now, take it easy," the chief inspector urged. He became confidential. "I'll explain what I mean. This isn't the first time I've come across a situation like this, and each time I learn a new wrinkle in the way of getting out of sealed rooms. It's a kind of nightmare of mine, if you see what I mean. But it *is* the first time when (if your diagnosis is straight; excuse me) it's proved as certain-sure that the murderer must actually have been in the room. It's also the first time the facts could be sworn to by the police, beyond any possibility of hanky-panky. Like this!"

He tapped a finger in his palm.

"Sergeant Hollis, of L Division—and myself as well—we were in the house across the street, watching. Especially, we watched the window of this room. We never left off watching it. You see, this chap who's dead, Mr. Vance Keating, re-

33

turned to the house at a quarter past four. A little later we saw him peep out of this window. It was the only window in the house that'd got curtains up; and we knew we'd spotted the 'furnished room.' Eh? So we watched. At the same time Sergeant Pollard here—" he jerked his head—"was watching the door. And nobody went out either way. Now, then: if you tell me there's the remotest possibility the fellow might have been shot from a distance—well, everything's all right, because the window was open, and a couple of shots might have come through the window. But, if you tell me the murderer must have been in the room (and I admit I think so myself), then we're up against it."

Blaine said, "The rest of the house is dusty—we're leaving tracks all over the carpet—"

"Yes," said Masters. "I asked Pollard about that. He swears that there were only two sets of prints when he broke in—his own and Keating's."

"Then it was Keating who furnished the room?" asked McAllister.

"M'm—no—not necessarily. Broom standing in a dark corner out there. The furnisher could have swept the carpet after him. *That* doesn't prove anything."

"Except," said Blaine dryly, "that there was no one in the room except Keating when he was shot—unless Pollard shot him."

Masters made a strangling noise in his throat, and Blaine went on.

"What about trap-doors or thungummyjigs?" he inquired.

"Trap-doors!" said Masters. "Take a look around."

It was certainly a sort of tank. Two walls of the room, the one facing the door and the one which contained the window, were the solid stone walls of the house itself. Two wooden walls had been built up to the roof in order to form the four sides of the room. All the walls and the ceiling were covered with grimy white plaster, which showed no crevice except a few wandering microscopic cracks. From the middle of the low ceiling descended the short pipe of a dismantled gas-bracket, with a lead plug over the mouth.

On the floor, which was of solid timbers, lay a black carpet of very rich and deep pile. Against the wall opposite the door stood a mahogany chair. Against the wall to the left was a rather dingy divan. But what took the eye was the object in the middle of the room: a circular mahogany table of the folding variety, some five feet in diameter. It was covered by a

34

square cloth of what resembled peacocks' feathers worked in dull gold, and very slightly pulled out of line on the side towards the door. The circle of very thin black teacups and saucers had been ranged on it like numbers on a clock. Two teacups, on the side towards the door, had been smashed; but smashed in a somewhat curious way. The cups remained in the cracked saucers; the pieces had not been knocked wide, and lay in or close on the saucers; it was as though some heavy object had been dropped flat on them.

"The last place you'll find trap doors," said Masters, "is bare plaster. Look here, doctor: we're going to catch ruddy hell for this. Here we are, smack on the scene of the crime like a lot of mugs, and still——! That's why, if you could show the shots weren't fired in this room——?"

"Well, they were," retorted Blaine. "Your own ears ought to have been able to tell you that. Hang it all, didn't anybody hear them?"

"I did," volunteered Pollard. "I wasn't a dozen feet away from the door, and I'm willing to swear the shots came from here."

Blaine nodded. "Now take a look at the head-wound first. The pistol was held about three inches away from the head; it was a soft-nosed bullet, and it split the skull up badly. You can see the ragged singeing of powder-marks from an old-style cartridge. That other bullet, in the back—it broke the fellow's spine, poor bastard. The gun must have been jammed directly against him. You must have been in here pretty quick, sergeant. Didn't you notice any signs?"

"Plenty of them," replied Pollard, facing vivid memory. "The cloth was still burning; I saw sparks. And there were smells. Also smoke."

"I'm sorry, Masters," said Blaine. "There's no doubt whatever."

There was a silence. The photographers had gathered up their apparatus and had gone out. From the street ascended the murmur of a crowd, and the voice of a policeman ordering them on; the halls of number 4 Berwick Terrace were alive with trampling feet, where Inspector Cotteril had charge; and in the center of the web Masters prowled round the room pounding at the walls with his fist. He addressed McAllister, who was also prowling.

"Finished?"

"Just about, sir," said the fingerprint man. "And it's the barest den of iniquity I ever got into. There's not a print in

35

the place, bar a few blurred ones on the arms of that chair and a few clear ones on the window-frame—but I'm pretty sure they were all made by the dead man."

"Nobody touched the table or the teacups?"

"Not unless they wore gloves."

"Oh, ah. Gloves. It's the Dartley case all over again, with fancy trimmings. Lummy, how I hate cases that aren't sense. Right, McAllister; that's all. You might ask Inspector Cotteril if he'll come up here a moment. And thanks, Doctor; that's all for you. I'd be glad if you'd do the p.m. as soon as possible; we want to be sure about that revolver. But I don't want the body removed for just a minute yet. First I want to go through the pockets. And then there's a gentleman coming here presently . . . hum . . . name of Sir Henry Merrivale; and I want Sir Henry to see him."

When Blaine had gone, Masters prowled once more round the table, peering.

"Flummery," he said, pointing to the teacups. "Flummery, all got up for the express purpose of hoaxing us, somehow. What price secret society now? I know; you thought Keating gave a password. But you can't tell me there was a *meeting* here, and that ten members vanished out of here instead of one murderer. Ah, well. Cheer up; don't look so glum. We were had for a prize parcel of mugs, right enough, but I don't see what else we could have done or had a right to do. Besides, the old man should be here before long. He'll arrive mad as fifty hornets, but I don't mind telling you I'll be pleased to show him the one closed circle he won't be able to get out of." Masters studied the body. "This chap Keating, Bob. Know anything about him?"

"Nothing beyond what I told you this afternoon, after he'd bought the house and tossed us out—"

"Yes. He was fair set on dying, wasn't he?" asked Masters quietly.

Pollard looked at the limp body in gray flannel, its spine broken and its straw-colored hair blackened into the brain.

"He's got a lot of money," the sergeant said. "And he likes to call himself 'the last of the Venturers.' That's why I thought he'd be interested in any secret society, if it were sufficiently mysterious or sufficiently lurid. What he wanted, he said, was thrill. I believe he lives in a flat in Westminster; Great George Street, I think."

Masters looked up sharply. "Great George Street, eh? So that's where he went!"

"Where he went?"

"Yes. Today. You haven't forgotten he left here this afternoon at ten minutes past two o'clock, and didn't return until a quarter past four? Just so. I know where he went," Masters announced, with satisfaction, "because I tailed him myself. But that's neither here nor there, at the moment. What about his relatives, or friends? Know anything about them?"

"No-no, I'm afraid not. I know he's got a cousin named Philip Keating. And he's engaged to be married to Frances Gale. You've probably heard of her; she's the one who seems to have been winning all the golf tournaments."

"Ah? I've seen her picture in the papers," said Masters, with interest. He ruminated, evidently turning the picture over in his mind. "*She* wouldn't be mixed up in games like this, I'll bet you a tanner," he decided. "Never mind. Here: lend a hand, and let's turn the poor chap over on his back. Easy now. . . ."

"God!" said Pollard involuntarily.

"So he wanted thrill," observed Masters after a pause, during which there was no sound but Masters's asthmatic breathing. "Not pretty, is it?"

They had both risen. No damage had been done to the face which was now exposed, except a spiritual damage. But mind, as well as life, had gone out of it; and the reason for its witless look was fear. Pollard had read much of faces supposed to be distorted with the fear of something seen. During his term as a uniformed constable he had seen a man fall to death out of a high window, and a man get the charge of a shotgun full in the face. The feelings such sights inspired were of physical things like pulp and angles; yet they were of the same cold quality as those inspired by this undamaged face, whose pale blue eyes were wide open and whose straw-colored hair was neatly plastered down. Quite plainly, he did not care to look at it. Keating, who wanted thrill, had evidently seen something more horrible than that which comes into the homes of harmless men.

"I say, my lad," put in Masters gruffly. "How would you like to spend a night in this room?"

"No, thanks."

"Just so. And yet what's wrong with the place? It's ordinary enough, you'd say. I'd rather like to know who was the last tenant." After a somewhat sharp glance round the room, Masters squatted down by the body and began to turn out the

37

pockets. "Stop a bit! Here's something. What do you make of this, for instance?"

"This" was a thin and polished silver cigarette-case. It was not in Keating's pocket; it had evidently been lying under the body, partly inside the fold of the coat. Masters snapped it open, finding that it was filled to capacity with Craven A cigarettes; but Masters handled it very gingerly, by each end only, for on the polished surface there were several clear fingerprints.

"It's got a monogram in the corner," said Pollard. "Do you make out the letters? *J.D.* That's it: J.D. It isn't Keating's. It may be what you're looking for."

"If the old man were here," said Masters, with a heavily ruminative air, "he'd say you'd got a simple straightforward mind, my lad. This murderer is much too canny a bloke to smear up the best fingerprint-surface in this room. We'll see; but I'll make you a little bet that these prints are Keating's, and that he's been carrying somebody else's cigarette-case." He folded up the case carefully in a handkerchief. "Point is, what's the thing *doing* under his body? He didn't smoke at any time—nobody did; just like the Dartley case. At least, there aren't any cigarette-ends in the place, and the case is full. If he was carrying somebody else's case . . . here, that reminds me! Whose hat was he wearing? I shouldn't think it was his own. And where's the hat now, by the way?"

Pollard crossed the room to the divan, which was pushed out a little way from the wall, and felt down behind it. He fished up a gray Homburg somewhat crumpled. It had been lying on the divan, he remembered, when he had made his first search of the shrine. He turned it over, handing it to Masters and pointing to the band inside; on the band was printed in gilt letters the name *Philip Keating.*

" 'Philip Keating,' " repeated Masters. "Oh, ah? That's the cousin you mentioned, is it? Yes. It's a good thing for Mr. Philip Keating we all know his cousin was wearing the hat, or he might find himself with a lot of questions to answer. This is a very casual sort of young gentleman, Bob. He wears somebody else's hat, and he carries somebody else's cigarette-case—we think. Ur! I know that type. Can you tell me anything about this Mr. Philip Keating?"

"Well, sir, he'd probably sail up to the ceiling and bust if he were ever involved in a murder case. He's a stockbroker, I think; very pleasant, but respectable as the devil."

Masters looked suspicious. "All right. We'll go into that.

38

But is there anybody connected with either of 'em whose initials are J.D.?"

"I can't tell you that."

"Let's see what's on him, then. Put all that stuff out in a line. Now, then: wallet. Eight pound ten in notes, and a couple of his own visiting-cards. (Yes, that's the address: number 7 Great George Street.) Nothing else in the wallet. Fountain-pen. Watch. Bunch of keys. Box of matches. Handkerchief. Six and four-pence in coppers. That's the lot, and not much to go on. Except that he was a heavy smoker: every pocket's got tobacco in the lining."

"Unless he's wearing somebody else's suit," said Pollard. "He was a heavy smoker, but he didn't light up during a three-quarters-of-an-hour wait. Look here, sir, do you think it was to be some sort of—religious service?"

Masters grunted noncommittally. "No, the tailor's label's all right. It's his own suit. *You* think you're making jokes, my lad, which aren't funny. But I don't. I go at it. I've seen queerer things . . . ah, Inspector! Come in."

Divisional Detective-Inspector Cotteril was a long lean man with a long melancholy countenance, which he balanced by an affable manner. But he saw the upturned face of Vance Keating, and whistled.

"Cor! There's a sight for you," he said. "The house has been searched, every inch of it. I can tell you now that there isn't, there wasn't, there hasn't been anybody else in it; but you knew that already. We're at a dead end. But here's what I wanted to ask you, Chief Inspector. Do you want our division to go on with this, or will the Yard take over? The Yard, I suppose?"

"I suppose so. But that'll be decided this afternoon. You can carry on with finding out what hauling company brought this furniture here two days ago, where they got the furniture, and trace it back as far as it'll go. I think we'd better take charge of this revolver: it's a curio, and there's no registration number. But I'd like to get some information. Do you know anything about the last tenants of this house?"

Cotteril reflected. "Yes, I can tell you myself. I remember, because the people came round to the station once to report a golden cocker spaniel being stolen; and I own one myself. Now, what in blazes was that name?" demanded Cotteril, and knocked at his temple. "Mr. and Mrs. . . . But I don't think you'll find much there. As I remember him, the old man was a solid solicitor; you know, old and crusted; elderly.

Had a very pretty wife. Damn it, what *was* that name? I can remember everything except that. They moved out of here about a year ago. The name was something fancy; I think it began with a D. Mr. and Mrs.—I know: got it! Mr. and Mrs. Jeremy Derwent!"

Masters stared at him, his color changing a little. "You're sure of that, now?"

"Pretty sure, yes. Certain. The dog's name was Pete."

"Man, listen! Don't it mean anything to you? Don't you remember the Dartley case?"

Cotteril opened one eye, and spoke drily. "Not personally, thank the Lord. I was shifted here from C Division just after all the rumpus. I know about it, of course. I know how it's repeated—here."

"Dartley got it through the back of the head at 18 Pendragon Gardens. The last tenants of 18 Pendragon Gardens moved out less than a week before the murder. They were Mr. and Mrs. Jeremy Derwent. They were so plain downright respectable, it was so clear they'd got nothing to do with Dartley, that we never bothered much with them. But now they turn up as the last tenants of 4 Berwick Terrace. And under Keating's body is that cigarette-case marked with the initials J.D." Masters pulled himself together. "Just so. I'm a bit curious to know what Sir Henry Merrivale will make of that, my lad."

CHAPTER FIVE

Dead Man's Eyes

"YOU WANT to know what I think?" said H.M. "I think you got a goddam nerve, that's what I think. You insult me into comin' here, after it's you that bungled the business. Three flights of stairs you drag me up—as though there wasn't enough stairs in my life—to a goddam Turkish bath that'll probably give me pneumonia after a walk out of it. And now you got the incredible, staggerin', stratospheric cheek to suggest that, since we're goin' out to pay calls on polite and refined people, I'd better be dignified and put on my collar. Oh, my eye. That's the end. I'm through."

"Now, now," urged Masters soothingly. "I only suggested—"

H.M.'s arrival, at a little past six o'clock, had been attended by some difficulty. This, it was learned, was due to his secretary's persistent attempts to make him put on his collar, which he refused. He had been in such a fettle of triumph after winning this argument that he resorted to the dubious and almost unheard-of course of driving his own car; with the result that, sweeping majestically out of Horse Guards Avenue the wrong way, he had very nearly contrived to knock Mr. Geoffrey Madden-Byrne, the Minister of Transportation, clean over the fence of the Royal United Service Museum. H.M. is very proud of his skill as a driver, if only he *cared* to drive: and it is true that he reached Kensington in safety. He sat now collarless on the couch in the attic, and groused.

Masters did not mind. On the contrary, it was as though all the grousing Masters wished to do, and could not do, was transmitted through H.M.: so that Masters's mind was eased of a great weight, and he could become his affable self again. The body of Keating had now been removed, which was also the easing of a weight.

"—I only suggested," pursued Masters, "that you might find it more comfortable to wear a lower collar than the kind you usually do. I didn't think about it. I only threw it off, casually. But you picked it up and made it the whole point of what I was driving at. Now the thing I do want to know, sir, is what you think of this case?"

"You mean your notion about the Derwents? Ghoulish idea, ain't it? Elderly solicitor and his pretty wife move from sedate house to sedate house; and wherever they go, just *after* they've left the house, murder comes in and camps. Shivery, that. Just you think it over. It's artistic, Masters; I like it."

"Thank you," said the chief inspector gravely. "I'm not usually accused of being artistic; far from it. But I didn't necessarily mean about the Derwents. I mean about the murder."

"Murderer disappearin' in thin air?"

"Yes. Do you believe somebody could have stood here in the room beside Keating; could have shot him twice at close range; and then could have disappeared?"

"I got to believe it, son," replied H.M. quite seriously, "by what you tell me. I warned you this murderer was awful cocky about bein' able to slide through any nets you set for him. That was what worried me. You talk about master criminals; but honestly, now, nobody outside Bedlam is deliberately goin' to make an appointment with the police—

41

unless he's quite certain there's not a rag of a chance he'll be caught."

"Or unless he's a real lunatic, of course."

H.M. scowled malevolently. "Not even then. No loony except a political assassin is ever loony enough to want to be caught. Jack the Ripper was a crackpot if you like, and he wrote to the police; but he never warned 'em beforehand where he meant to use his razor. Besides, there ain't a tinge of flavor of lunacy about this case, as I hope to be able to explain to you. No, Masters. This feller knew he was safe, safe and cozy to do his murder, no matter how you tried to stop him."

"That's all very well, sir; but look at facts! Do you know of any safe method of committing a murder?"

"No, son," said H.M. "And I only hope to God we haven't found one here."

Again Sergeant Pollard was conscious of uneasiness. Outside, the early evening was still thick with promise of a storm that never came. H.M.'s small eye moved round the room, measuring.

"Well, now, we'll just go over the evidence, as far as I've been able to follow it from the gibberish you've been tellin' me. There are a couple of questions I'd like to ask you, and then we're goin' to reconstruct the crime. But let's take it from the beginning. You, son." The small eye fixed rather disconcertingly on Pollard. H.M. moved his glasses up and down his nose, rumbled to himself, and went on. "Ah, I got it. You went to Houston & Klein. They told you that Vance Keating got the keys of the house this morning. They also said that the last time anybody viewed the house was three months ago—and the person who got the keys then was Frances Gale, the gal who's engaged to Keating. That right?"

"Yes, sir."

"Meaning what?" asked Masters softly.

"Oh, not necessarily anything. Only we've heard that a haulin' van came here yesterday, and the men delivered some furniture. Well, they had to have a key to get in. I was only wonderin' where they got the key, if Keating didn't get his until today. . . . Don't interrupt me, dammit! Now, son. As you were walkin' up the front steps of the house, a Talbot two-seater went past up at the head of the street; there was a woman in it, and she seemed to be lookin' in a marked sort of way at this house. Right?"

"Yes, sir."

"Uh-huh. Would you know the gal, if you saw her again?"

"I think so. She was young, and she certainly wasn't bad-looking; but it was some distance away, and the car shot past. I got the number-plate, though. It was MX792."

"It's being traced," said Masters.

"Now we'll take your story," pursued H.M., turning to the chief inspector. "After Keating went to all the trouble to buy the house and shut everybody out of it, he went out himself at ten minutes past two. Where'd he go?"

Masters took out his notebook, cleared his throat, and began to recite. "Person in question went looking for a taxi. Walked down as far as Kensington High Street before he got one. Found a cab-rank there. Taking next taxi, I followed—"

"I know. You leaped into the cab hissing, 'Scotland Yard! Follow that car!' Ho ho. I can see you doin' it, son."

"Excuse me, I didn't do anything of the kind," said Masters equably. "You must never tell 'em beforehand you're a copper; otherwise they start to argue about whether or not they'll get their fare, and you lose your man. Hurrum!" He resumed his official manner. "Person in question was driven by way of Piccadilly, Haymarket, Cockspur Street, and Trafalgar Square to the Galleon Tavern in Whitehall. Had two drinks there, speaking to no one. Left when bar closed, at three o'clock. Did not seem to be in any hurry. Walked down Whitehall, crossed to Great George Street, and entered block of flats called Lincoln Mansions. (He lived there.) Went upstairs in lift. I approached, and was about to speak to hall-porter when person in question came down in lift again. He said to hall-porter, *'Don't let Mr. Gardner leave,'* and went out—"

"Stop a bit. What'd you take that to mean?"

"I've got no idea," acknowledged Masters, becoming human again. He smiled wryly. "Except it's another name for our list. Frances Gale. Philip Keating. Mr. and Mrs. Jeremy Derwent. And somebody called Gardner. I hope it's the lot. But about Keating. He wasn't in the flats more than three or four minutes. After that he walked out and fooled about on the street for a minute, looking round. At 3:20 he called a cab, and was driven to Coburg Place here. There was a traffic block, and we didn't get back for nearly an hour. He walked across Coburg Place, down Berwick Terrace, and back to the house. Not much in it, is there?"

"No. Nothin' very spectacular, anyhow. You thought he was just out to kill time, hey? Yes. Well, now, let's see what

43

we can do about reconstructin' the crime. We may not be able to tell how the murderer hopped it. But let's imagine Keating is lyin' there now, with the gun by his left hand and the cigarette-case under him. Let's see where he might have been standin' or sittin' when he was hit; and which of the shots was fired first, and why; and what he might have seen, to give him that look. I say, Masters—have you found out yet whether the fingerprints on that cigarette-case were Keating's or somebody else's?"

"Not yet. McAllister had gone when we found it. But it's been sent to the Yard, and we should get a report any time now. Also a post-mortem report, I hope."

With great effort H.M. heaved himself off the couch, muttering, and blundered to the middle of the room. The peacocks'-feather design on the gold table-cover gleamed in evening light; the black teacups had a somber richness; and these, with the mahogany chair, made a sort of core and lure for the heart of a commonplace attic-room. H.M. stopped by the table. For a time he remained staring owlishly at it.

" 'And all King Solomon's drinking vessels were of gold,' " said H.M. suddenly, " 'and all the vessels of the house of the forest of Lebanon were of pure gold; none were of silver; it was nothing accounted of in the days of Solomon.

" 'For the king had at sea a navy of Tarshish with the navy of Hiram; once in three years came the navy of Tarshish, bringing gold, and silver, ivory, and apes, and peacocks.' "

It was one of those abrupt changes of mood which could still make Masters jump. Then H.M. opened his eyes wide and grinned.

"Ho ho! You surprised to hear the old man quotin' First Kings? My eye, Masters, what literature! I was just thinkin' of the recurring design of peacocks' feathers in this case. Dartley's shot by the side of ten teacups painted with peacocks' feathers. Keating also goes down by a table, in just about the same way. . . . What's it suggest? Burn me, I dunno. You got classical mythology: the peacock was the favorite bird of Juno. Also, in the Middle Ages, one of the solemnest oaths of the code of chivalry was taken 'on the Peacock.' Chivalry! Chivalry! Now I wonder?"

Masters regarded him curiously. "Where do you pick up all this stuff?" he asked.

"Oh, I dunno. I just browse round, and it comes flowin' in somehow. Besides, I hate modern novels like hell, except detective stories, so my readin' time ain't unduly cluttered up. But I'll tell you something that's not out of books, Masters."

He reached out and fingered the table-cover.

"That's real gold. I remember tellin' you, at the time of that Red Widow case, how I'd been to Rome over that business of Briocci, the collector who got himself poisoned in his private museum. Uh-huh. I also remember, somebody showed me one of these cloths: not peacocks' feathers, but some religious pattern. This thing's worth a lot of money. It's medieval Italian work in gold leaf woven into cloth. Point number one: there wouldn't be many people in England who'd own one of them, and only a very few dealers who might handle 'em—like Soar in Bond Street, for instance; point number two: somebody can afford to chuck it about as much as Keating did. Then there's the furniture. It don't look like museum pieces, of course; but still it's good stuff and must have been pretty expensive. Finally, there's the teacups—"

"Ah. The teacups. And what might they be worth?"

"Well . . . now," said H.M. He picked up one of the thin black cups and turned it over. "At sixpence apiece, that's five bob for the lot."

"Sixpence apiece?" shouted Masters.

"Yes. For the cup and saucer together," explained H.M., after a curious pause while Masters got to his feet. "They come from Woolworth's. You can see stamped on the bottom, 'Elephant; Made in England,' and a Woolworth's stock-number. Whoever arranged this has carefully set out expensive furniture and an almost priceless table-cover—on the top of which he also carefully places cups costing three pennies. And there you are. I tell you, Masters, somebody is laughin' at us, and I don't like it."

"I'm beginning to be certain," said Masters, "that we're chasing a real lunatic after all."

"No, we're not, son. Everything here means something: which is the trouble. But we started out to reconstruct the murder, and let's do it. As a startin' point, we might begin with the cups—I mean the two smashed ones. Take a look at the cups, and tell me what you make of 'em."

Masters pulled himself together. Assuming the round table to be a clock facing the door, with the cups roughly as numbers on a dial, the two broken cups were in the position of the figures 6 and 7. Masters studied them.

"Yes, I'd thought of that," he said grudgingly. "The cups are broken in a very rum way. They're not knocked about,

45

as they'd have been in a struggle; they're not even moved off the saucers, though the saucers are cracked. There aren't any pieces all over the place, as though they'd been hit with a bullet. Just so. It looks as though a dead, heavy weight had dropped flat on them. Like a loaded valise, or something."

He looked up at the ceiling, and hesitated.

"What about the dead man?" inquired H.M. "That's what happened, son. A .45, especially at such close range, has a power like a horse's kick. Now looky here. Keating was walkin' up towards the table—like Dartley. He was walkin' from somewhere in the direction of the door, or at least from the side of the room where the door is, towards the table. Otherwise, d'ye see, he'd have smashed or dislodged more cups when he fell; and they're still in a neat circle. So. The first bullet hits him. He goes over *flap,* either with a broken skull or a broken spine, in a dead weight on his face across the table."

H.M. brought the palms of his hands together sharply, and Masters nodded.

"I daresay," muttered the chief inspector. "Oh, ah. It's got to be, because there's nothing else that could've broken the cups. But in that case how did he come to be facing the other way when we found him—lying at full length with his head towards the door?"

"Because the first shot was through his back, d'ye see. If the first bullet had been the one that hit him in the head, he'd never have moved off that table; he'd have been dead. He'd never have moved unless he slid off, and the cloth's not rumpled enough for that. The cloth's rumpled just enough to show that he . . . aha! Got it, have you?"

"That he tried to pull himself up on his feet and look round behind him," suggested Pollard.

"Exactly, son. But carry it further; watch the genie form out of the bottle." Again the little eye fixed him disconcertingly. "I see you got an inspiration. Quick, what were you thinkin' of?"

Pollard stared at the table.

"It wasn't an inspiration, sir. Just the opposite. There's another big contradiction here. Keating saw something terrible enough to give him that look on his face—*yet* at the same time he was shot twice from behind! If he first saw the sight, how did the murderer get round close behind him to fire without Keating making an uproar or a run or a fight? The whole thing seems to have been over too quickly. Hold on, though:

I believe I've got it! The murderer comes up behind Keating unseen, and also unheard on this thick carpet. He jabs the gun into Keating's back, possibly intending to shoot him through the heart. But Keating jerks, and starts to look round. . . ."

"And screams, I think you said," supplied H.M.

There was a pause.

"Oh, it's ugly enough, my lads," he continued blankly. "For I'll just ask you what Keating saw when he looked over his shoulder, that gave him the look on his face. Then our 'somebody,' our Old Man of the Mountain, pulls the trigger; and Keating is knocked forward on the teacups. But he won't stay there. He'll try to get up, and turn round, and get away: maybe even attack what's behind him. He's got the use of his arms, but his spine's gone and his legs won't hold him. So, when he gets on his feet and turns round to the left, he loses his balance again and simply tumbles forward the other way. And the murderer leans down and gives him another one through the back of the skull, while he's still lyin' helpless on his left side."

"Ugh," grunted Masters, after another silence.

"Oh, no; it ain't pretty; I admit that."

Masters nursed his chin. "It's all very well for you, Sir Henry, to go as fast as that. But I'm a bit more cautious. And, while I admit it all *sounds* reasonable . . . By the way, in your reconstruction what about the cigarette-case that was found under the body?"

"I don't go quite as fast as that, son. Depends on what fingerprints are on it. Depends on whether they're Keating's own, or somebody else's. I'm not goin' hurtling away to explain something before I know what it is I got to explain." He sniffed, and considered. "That thing seems to be hagridin' you, but I also admit it may be a bit of a puzzler before we get through with this business. What's the good of a cigarette-case if nobody's smoked? What's the point of it?—Hey? Yes; what is it?"

Rapid footsteps had tumbled up the attic stairs and along the hall. Sergeant Hollis, who had been left on guard downstairs along with two constables, came in with a slip of paper in his hand.

"And this, if I mistake not, is our client now," said H.M. with relish. "Speak up, son. Got some information from headquarters?"

"Yes, sir. But that wasn't what I wanted to see you about. We—"

Masters took the slip of paper from him, and the chief inspector spoke grimly.

"Ah! There we are. Settles two points, anyhow. First, about the fingerprints on the case. There are two sets: Keating's own, and a woman's. I suppose you'd call that suggestive. Next, about the blue Talbot two-seater number MX792. It belongs to Miss Frances Gale."

"That's what I wanted to see you about, sir," Hollis put in hastily. "About Miss Gale. She's downstairs. She's been here ever since we took out Mr. Keating's body; she saw us put it in the van. She isn't making a row, but she's pretty cut up in a quiet way; and all she's doing is asking us questions we can't answer. Could you see her? I know you said you weren't to be disturbed no matter what happened, but all the same I thought maybe—?"

CHAPTER SIX

In Which Six Persons Are Found Near a Revolver

WHEN FRANCES GALE was brought into the attic room, Pollard expected to see a girl somewhat on the large and muscular side. He was surprised. Miss Gale was not more than twenty years old, rather under the medium height for a woman; and, though she was clearly radiant with health, her appearance of very soft slenderness gave no hint of any athletic capacity. She was the same girl Pollard had seen in the car earlier that afternoon. She had brown bobbed hair, somewhat light and fluffy; darker brown eyes with black lashes; but, in contrast, a very determined chin. Though she was not pretty in any conventional sense, health and vigor made her seem so. She wore a close-fitting hat of white straw, and a white silk dress with a vivid scarlet buckle at the belt; also, she appeared to be trying to twist her white handbag in two. But her emotion now seemed less grief, or fear, or nervousness, than a miserable perplexity as at too many things on her mind at once.

"I—I—" she said, and stopped.

Masters was in his element. The chief inspector rose with that suavity, that humble persuasiveness as of one seeking information from wiser heads, which he had always found so useful.

"Please don't upset yourself, miss," he urged. "We must apologize for bringing you upstairs here, but there's nowhere else to sit down; and if you *would* care to help us out—eh? Just so. Will you sit down on the couch here? Ah, that's better. Now—"

"But what on earth is all this?" she said, nodding towards the furniture. Some new emotion was so strong that it rushed up among those she was already feeling: a conflict so strong that for the first time tears came into her eyes. "And who are you? And what's happened? And everything? I know I've seen you before." She stared, winking, at H.M. "I've seen you, and my father said something about you. He said you wore funny hats, or something; but I don't know what you're doing here—"

"Now, now," rumbled H.M. with surprising gentleness. "Sure you know me, and I know your old man. You're Bokey Gale's daughter; he was the great rugger captain in '06. So you see you're among friends. But if you're Bokey Gale's daughter there'll be no use in tryin' to smother you with rose-leaves and glue: you can face it, my gal."

"I've been trying to," she answered, after a pause. "But it's pretty awful just the same. For what was he *doing*, and why? I saw them carry him out, but I didn't even know how he died. And then I asked questions, and all they'd tell me was that there had been an accident."

She clenched her hands, and looked from one to the other of them, while Masters shook his head.

"I'm afraid it was no accident, miss. It was deliberate murder."

"Yes. I thought so."

"Oh, ah? Why did you think so, miss?"

"Oh, do be sensible! What else could I possibly think, the way things were? How was he—hurt?"

"He was shot: shot in the back." At the last few words, Pollard saw an even worse shadow of perplexity come into her face; she hesitated, and moved her shoulders a little, as Masters went on: "Did you have any reason to think anyone might kill him?"

"No. No, not really. That is—"

" 'Not really.' Hurrum!" said Masters, smiling paternally. "That's a bit difficult to understand, Miss Gale. I know it's probably not important, but you mean somebody threatened him?"

"Not really. I said that before I thought what I was saying. Apparently Ron threatened him, or said he'd shoot him, when he was in a temper; I don't know quite what it was, because I wasn't there." She raised candid brown eyes. "I tell you that because you'll probably find out all about it anyway. And you'd better hear it from me, because I *know* it was nothing serious. In the first place Ron would never kill anybody; not really. In the second place I do know jolly well he'd never shoot anybody in the back."

"Who is Ron?"

Frances Gale looked surprised. "Why, Ronald Gardner. He's a great friend of Vance's. I know it doesn't sound much like it, but he is. I thought you might have heard the name. He does a lot of things Vance does, only with not so much—so much splash about it." Suddenly she flushed, and went on in a rapid tone as though she were talking against time: "I mean, I thought you'd have read a book Ron wrote, a grand book, about a voyage up the Orinoco. Also, Ron's got a ranch in one of the western states of America; Arizona, I think; only I can never keep the states straight because there are so many of them. Ron—"

Masters had already made a gesture to Pollard, who was sitting at the table taking this down in shorthand. Now the chief inspector interposed.

"Just one moment, miss. You say Mr. Keating and Mr. Gardner had a row? Now, when was this?"

She looked doubtful. "The night before last, I think. Let's see: this is Wednesday, isn't it? Yes, it must have been Monday night. At least, that's what Philip said. Philip is Vance's cousin, and he was the one who told me about the trouble."

"And what was the trouble about, miss?"

"I haven't the least idea! Truly."

"But didn't you inquire, or try to find out? After all, when someone threatens to shoot your *fiancé* . . . eh?"

Again she was on the edge of tears. "If you'd only let me explain! It was like this. I didn't know there was supposed to be any trouble until yesterday. Last night, you see, there was to be a big party. Vance and I were going; we arranged that a week ago. Well, yesterday afternoon I rang up his flat to find out what time he'd be round to call for me in the evening. Out of a clear sky he said he was sorry, but some business had come up unexpectedly which made it impossible for him

50

to go to the party; and that the business might occupy him for a couple of days; and that he'd let me know when it was finished."

Masters was staring at her a little crookedly, and stroking his chin. The chief inspector concealed his eagerness.

"Did he state the nature of the business, miss? Hum! That is, did he mention a quarrel, now?"

"No. But I suppose he wouldn't. He spoke in that cold, stiff, kindly-polish-my-boots way he uses sometimes. First I wondered whether I'd done anything to offend him. And then I was furious. I don't know whether you care for a direct snub, but I don't. So I thought: Very well, then; I'll go to the party by myself. Of course they all asked me where he was. Even Ron Gardner had the colossal cheek to inquire after Vance, and ask why he wasn't there. Finally I got Philip Keating aside, and asked him straight out whether he knew what this 'business' was that kept Vance away. Philip hemm'd and haw'd . . . he prides himself on his tact . . . but at last he admitted there had been a row between Vance and Ron, and that it was probably the reason why Vance hadn't cared to come. He couldn't or wouldn't say anything more."

"Just so. Did you speak to Mr. Gardner about it?"

Her eyes narrowed. "Oh, yes, naturally; and it's so silly! Ron pretended to be surprised. He swore to me, he gave me his word of honor, that there hadn't been any row of any sort between him and Vance. He even pretended to wonder where I'd got such an idea. But I suppose he felt he had to lie like a gentleman, too, especially since—"

H.M., who had been sitting back in a corner of the couch hunched up like a Buddha, at this point opened one eye. He had got out his black pipe.

"Well . . . now," he murmured in a dubious sort of tone. "That might stand amplifyin', you know. Especially since what?"

"I—I don't know."

"Masters will tell you," pursued H.M., "that I got a nasty suspicious mind. But if you're old Bokey Gale's daughter, I wouldn't like to see you tangled up in any more of a mess than I'd have to explain to him. Looky here, now: did you have any reason to believe that this quarrel might have been about you?"

She turned slowly round to face him, and put her hands flat on the divan.

"Certainly not!" cried Frances Gale. After a pause she said: "What makes you think that?"

"Well, now, there's only one subject concernin' which a man lies like a gentleman," said H.M. rather apologetically. "On any other subject he just lies like a plain, human, everyday cuss. And there seems to have been rather an agonizin' attempt to hide matters from you. It sort of occurred to me that to judge by what you've been saying you must be rather more struck by this feller Gardner's qualities and abilities than you were by Keating's. Are you fond of Gardner, or is he fond of you?"

"I like Ron, yes. Naturally. But I happen to be engaged to Vance. And I can't stick much more of this. You bring me right up to the very room where Vance was *killed*, and I don't know how or who by and you won't tell me anything, and then you begin to b-bully and badger—"

Masters's suspicious gaze moved from H.M. to the girl. Then Masters cleared his throat, and struck in with soothing effect.

"You mustn't mind the old man, miss. That's only his way. Why, miss, we're quite ready to tell you anything you'd like to know! Like this. For instance, you tell us Mr. Gardner has a ranch in America?"

"Yes, he has."

"Ah. Then you might be interested in knowing the kind of gun Mr. Keating was shot with. I can't show it you, because it's been sent to the Yard. But it's a Remington .45, with a pearl-inlaid handle, an old style of gun with the name *Tom Shannon* engraved on the handle; and they tell me Tom Shannon was a bad man of the old days out there. Eh?"

"Oh, God," said the girl unexpectedly. She looked at him with a steady, shining regard. "You're not lying to me, are you? I mean, this isn't one of those things you read about, where they get you to admit something and then they say, 'Ha ha, we didn't know that before but we know it now?' "

"No, miss, it is not."

"You needn't be so stuffy about it; I only asked. And I hope it isn't, because I know that gun prefectly well. Unless there are several of old Tom Shannon's guns knocking about over here, and I shouldn't think that was likely. It belongs to Ron. He's got a collection of pistols, and he's very proud of it. Why, I've seen that .45 a hundred times! And that's not all. You remember that party I was telling you about, last

52

night? I saw the gun then. We were using it to play Murder with."

"Murder?" exploded Masters. Then he rubbed his chin, and stopped. "Play Murder? Oh, ah! I see. Do you mean that game where you draw cards, and the ace of spades is the murderer, and then you put out the lights—look here, miss: you didn't use a real gun in the game, did you?"

"Yes. Loaded with blanks, of course. It was got up terribly elaborately. There was a piece of thin rope done into a strangler's noose. And a tin dagger with a blade that would go up into the handle, and a little bottle labeled with skull and crossbones for poison. And the gun. They were a part of the hazard, you see. They were all ranged out in a line on the mantel-piece in the living-room, and the murderer had to pinch one of them without being seen. . . . It was a Murder Party, really, with a lot of improvements on the ordinary game. It was Mr. Derwent's idea. He gave the party. He said he'd always wanted to give a Murder Party."

Masters spoke with great care, lowering his head a little. He said: "Ah? That would be Mr. Jeremy Derwent, the solicitor?"

"Yes. Do you know him? He's Vance's solicitor."

"I've heard of him, miss. He was—ah—socially friendly with Mr. Keating, was he? And you?"

For some reason her rather too expressive brown eyes slid round towards H.M. She spoke in a colorless voice.

"*I* didn't know them particularly well. Only for about six months or so, anyhow. But Vance did. Mr. Derwent has always handled his family's affairs, and he's a charming old boy really. They live not very far away from here, by the way: in Vernon Street. I went to the party because . . . well, you know. And then it wasn't just an ordinary binge; it was a farewell party. They're leaving Vernon Street next month, and moving into a house in the country."

Sergeant Pollard looked up from his shorthand. Chief Inspector Masters walked to the window, his hands clasped behind him, and stood looking down into the darkening street. So intense had been the heat of the attic that now, as it gradually lessened, the place felt almost chilly.

"Miss," said Masters, turning back abruptly and seeming to stare at her fluffy brown hair rather than at her face, "I've got to thank you for the way you've kept your nerve today, and the way you've answered our questions fair and straightforward—it 'ud seem. But I don't want you to conceal anything about that party. There was where somebody stole the gun that killed Mr. Keating: unless Mr. Gardner took it away with him, as may be. First, what people were at that party?"

"With Vance, there were to have been seven," she told him promptly. "We were using the whole house for the game, of course; but if you have too many people they get in each other's way. There was Mr. Derwent. There was myself, to get me out of the way. There was Philip Keating. There was Ron Gardner. There was Mr. Soar—"

"Soar? That's an unusual name. Do you mean by any chance Benjamin Soar, the art-dealer?"

"Y-yes, I suppose so." She frowned. "But I'm not sure. I met him for the first time last night. He was nice; I liked him."

"Miss Gale, can you tell me that even now the words 'ten teacups' *still* don't mean anything to you?"

For the first time she really looked at the table, at the teacups, and at the chair. Then her glance flew back to the divan again, as though she were fascinated by it.

"You don't mean," she said slowly, and Pollard was willing to swear it was the first time the idea had entered her head, "that man—I don't know his name—he was killed—and there were ten teacups on the tab—I mean, the case I've heard them talk about?"

"Come, now! Honestly, Miss Gale: you don't think rooms in empty houses are usually fitted up like this, do you? Do you expect me to believe you didn't notice, or didn't connect it with the Dartley case?"

Her white handbag spilled out of her lap. She bent to retrieve it; and, when she faced him again, her face was pinker and more puzzled.

"I don't know what you believe, I'm sure. I *saw* it, yes. But this makes it all the worse, because I don't see. . . . No, Inspector; nothing important. You're straying off the fairway. I had just given you a list of the people at the Murder party, and quite suddenly you jumped all over me. 'Come, now' yourself!"

Masters hesitated. "Just so," he agreed, going back to business. "However, I don't think I've got a complete list. I have Mr. Derwent, Mr. Philip Keating, Mr. Gardner, Mr. Soar, and yourself. Even excluding Mr. Vance Keating, that's only six. Where's the seventh? Um—what about young Mrs. Derwent?"

"I don't quite know what you mean by 'young Mrs. Derwent.' The age of the present Mrs. Derwent is forty-five. I believe they have a son, aged eighteen or so, away at school somewhere."

"But I understood—"

"Oh, quite righty-ho, Inspector," agreed Miss Gale, with sudden heartiness. "Most people do understand that she is rather younger, from her looks. But I was going to tell you. Yes, she *was* a member of the Murder party. But not for very long. About half-past nine she told us she had a splitting sick headache, and begged to be excused. After she had gone the Murder party became a most awful frost. In the first place there were too few of us for a good game. In the second place—there it was. All of a sudden it seemed rather silly to be wandering about in the dark."

"So you didn't play the game after all?"

"Yes, we had one very short game before Mrs. Derwent went upstairs. She was the corpse, come to think of it. The strangler's noose was used—I think I told you all the weapons were laid out on a line on the mantel in the living-room—and she was strangled on a sofa in Mr. Derwent's den. Mr. Derwent was the detective. (And did it jolly well, too!) Philip was the murderer. He got caught in about fifteen minutes. For a member of the Stock Exchange, poor Philip is a dreadfully bad liar."

"Always a recommendation, miss, from the view-point of the police," Masters observed affably. "Now I don't care about play-murders, but I want to know about that gun. Everything about it! When you last noticed it; who might have taken it; what you saw; everything."

She regarded him steadily.

"I can't tell you anything about it. That's the absolute truth. I've been racking my brains, and I simply don't know. The only thing I can say positively is that it was on the mantel at the beginning of the game: Ron put it there. He had been showing it round very proudly. As for who went near it, I don't remember anybody picking it up afterwards. But I can't swear nobody did, because I didn't notice it at all."

Masters's eye grew almost hypnotic. "Now think, miss, think! You must have!—At least you noticed it at the end of the game. Didn't you? If it was Mr. Gardner's property, he'd pick it up and take it home with him, wouldn't he? Or he'd say something if he found it was missing?"

"I don't know that, either." She was thinking hard now. "I went out to my car a little ahead of the rest of them, because by that time I was feeling a bit low and headachy myself, and I wanted to *run*. But one thing I'm absolutely positive of. Ron Gardner didn't take the gun home with him."

"How can you be certain of that?"

"He drove home with me in my car. Ron doesn't run a car now. He—lost a lot of money, or most of it. So I gave him a lift home."

"Well, miss?"

"You needn't snap my head off, you know. Well, he was wearing a light summer suit. You know, no lining and no waistcoat. And on the way back in the car he took off his coat. If you've seen that gun, you know nobody could possibly conceal it if it was being carried."

Masters studied her with heavy doubt. "That's that, then," he said, like one making a snap-decision. "You might think it over, miss. But in the meantime I should like to clear up a little point or two on which you're better informed. Let me see. When you drove past here in your car (MX792) early this afternoon, why were you so interested in this house?"

"I didn't drive past here this afternoon."

Her questioner glanced round at Pollard who, though he disliked doing it, nodded definitely. "Come, miss, we can never get anywhere if you go on like that," Masters urged with great cheerfulness. "You were seen by a police-officer, you know. So let's just have it out. I repeat: when you drove—"

"I didn't!" cried Frances Gale, and went into a tantrum so exactly like a schoolgirl that Masters blinked. Yet there was genuine violence behind it. "I wasn't anywhere near here this afternoon. I didn't I didn't I didn't I didn't! And you can't make me say I did."

"Right you are, then, if you say so. You never had any interest in this house? You never saw it before, to your knowledge?"

"No, I never did."

"We can't have that, you know. Three months ago and less (on May 10, to be exact) you got the keys of this house from Houston & Klein in St. James's Square. Now that's an absolute fact."

Though this statement did not appear to rouse such unexpected and apparently unreasonable fury as the first, it had its own effect. She did not so much rise as slide to her feet, deftly, so that you thought of someone preparing for fight. But her eyes were miserable.

"I didn't," she said. "I didn't do that, either; and you can't say I did. And I'm going home, and you can't stop me. All you've done is ask me questions that don't mean anything. You've never once told me anything about poor Vance, or who would have killed him or—except that it must have been Ron, and I know it wasn't. I wish my father were here. I wish I had a piece of brick or something, and I'd—I'd—" She lifted her hand.

She paused once in the doorway of the room, whipping round with a whirl of white silk skirt.

"And as for your Mrs. Derwent, you can tell her from me that she's a great big b-blowsy old—"

The close-fitting white hat had become slightly askew; she pressed it down hard on her head, as though to give some outlet for emotion in her hands. Then she disappeared, but they heard her sobbing as she went scampering and tripping away down the stairs.

Masters expelled his breath in a slight whoosh.

"Gawd lummy," he said, like one making a philosophical observation.

"What brought her on like that, all of a sudden?" he went on, staring. "She's a child, I admit. Worse'n my own kids, though she seemed sensible enough up to that last minute. And yet, all the time she was flaring out like that, she somehow managed to make me feel *I* was in the wrong. H'm. . . . And I must say, Sir Henry, *you* haven't been much help. All you've done is to sit there like a mummy and make noises with that pipe."

H.M. murmured: "I was just sittin' and thinkin'. And it struck me you didn't need any help; you needed a brake. You don't want to get your pores clogged with too much information at the start, son." Hoisting himself up, he let one hand fall on the dingy brown cloth of the divan. A puff of dust rose from it, and H.M. blew the dust away. "As for the girl . . . h'm. I got an idea she'll be round to my office tomorrow morning and tell us All. My eye, but don't she hate Mrs. Derwent, though! 'The incense that is mine by right, They burn before her shrine; and that's because I'm seventeen, While she is forty-nine.' I think we'll find Mrs. D. something buxom and languorous-eyed and mysterious. Poor old Keating would have liked that."

"You think there may have been something between Keating and Mrs. Derwent? And the Gale girl knew it? Yes. I thought of that."

"Oh, anything's possible, though Mrs. D. sounds very canny to me. In any case, after we've had a bit of grub, I think we'd better pay a little visit to the sinister solicitor in Vernon Street: the solicitor who's movin' house *again*, next month."

While H.M. blundered down the gloomy stairs, swearing, Masters remained for a moment behind in the room. He stared at the ceiling. He looked down at the place where the body had lain, and then he bent over to scrape at the carpet. When he followed H.M., who was bellowing from below, Masters's face wore the smile of one who has scored.

CHAPTER SEVEN

Lady's Limousine

THE HOUSE of Mr. Jeremy Derwent, where they found Mr. Derwent in his garden, was called The Gardens. It was a square, solid place behind a gate in a high wall. But they did not reach it until some time afterwards: not until the lamp-lighter was hurrying with his pole in the high streets, and little yellow flames were springing up against blue dusk.

H.M. stood the dinners to his two companions; he handsomely (ghoulishly, an outsider might have thought) offered to drive them in his own car to the tavern. The experience was not as bad as might have been expected. Despite H.M.'s taste for speed, their pace was moderate, even partaking of a mysterious jerkiness which startled traffic-policemen; but in justice to their own necks Pollard refrained from pointing out that the car would function better with the hand-brake off. They jumped along the streets like a mechanical toy, H.M. with a sort of wooden sneer in his own pride, and a good dinner restored them all. On the way back to Vernon Street, when the car was smoothly jerking, Masters got down to business.

"You say," he began, producing the silver cigarette-case that had been sent for, "that the girl will be at your office to-morrow and—um—get it off her chest. Perhaps. But in any case what did you make of her, exactly? Parts of it are pretty plain. . . ."

"What, for instance?" demanded H.M., eying a pedestrian-crossing.

"I read it like this. We assume Miss Gale and Keating

were fond of each other: they were engaged, anyhow, if that means anything in this day and age—"

"You gettin' cynical?"

"I've never been anything else, since I was a little baby," admitted Masters. "At the same time, she seems a bit fond of this Ronald Gardner. When she hears of a quarrel between Keating and Gardner, she assumes it's about her. But is that *all* she assumes? Follow me, sir? Suppose Gardner has said to Keating, 'Look here, you're engaged to Frances Gale, so stop hanging about Mrs. Derwent.' It doesn't intimidate Keating, for this 'business' he speaks of on the telephone—the business that will take him several days—is really some kind of appointment with Mrs. Derwent. And Miss Gale suspects it. She suspects it still more when, at the Murder party that same night, Mrs. Derwent leaves the party at half-past nine. What do you say to that?"

"I say it's eyewash."

"Well, now, sir. . . ."

"Eyewash," repeated H.M. firmly. He rolled round a moon-face of fantastic jollity. "It strikes me in passin' that you—you, of all the prophets o' caution—are now flying at theories without ever having met any of these people. Never mind. You want reasons. Right.

"You suggest that Vance Keating and Mrs. Derwent might have been plannin' an assignation for last night. But, in all your wide and cynical experience, did you ever hear of anybody who planned an assignation in quite such a fatheaded way? Look what they've done. They've chosen the night of the Murder party, the one night when their absence together is bound to be noticed, the one night when attention will be focused on 'em, without makin' a ghost of an excuse to anybody. To the contrary, Keating makes a point of insultin' his fiancée. And on top of that Mrs. Derwent walks out of the house while a party is goin' on. Even if she isn't seen on the way out, she'll have a tolerable lot of explaining to do to her husband when she gets home."

Masters shook his head.

"I don't see that, sir. Suppose they didn't care, because they meant to go away together? Suppose they planned it as—hurrum—a kind of dramatic gesture, like? Keating said he would be occupied several days. It sounds to me like an elopement, or a deliberate challenge about an elopement. What about that?"

"Uh-huh. The only trouble bein' that they didn't elope;

59

they didn't do anything last night. Just think of Vance Keating's behavior today, and tell me whether you believe he was already embarked on the venture. Hey? It won't fit in. At one o'clock this afternoon, serene and unaccompanied, he's foolin' about an empty house over his teacups. He kills time, goes for a cab ride, has a drink, stays in a fever of excitement all afternoon—because he's *expecting* something to happen. He's expectin' what? A woman."

There was a pause.

"Do you begin to see what I'm drivin' at, my fatheads?" inquired H.M. "If you had said to me somethin' like this: Keating intended to meet Mrs. Derwent this afternoon at 4 Berwick Terrace. Their meeting was with or without the intention of funny business, but at least concerned ten teacups. Frances Gale properly believed there was somethin' up between those two; and therefore she followed Keating in her car when he went to Berwick Terrace. That's why the Gale wench went into screamin' hysteria when you brought up the subject: because she wouldn't admit she was jealous enough to be snoopin' and spyin' after him." H.M. punched the horn. "There's my case. If you had said that to me, I'd have believed you. I think it's pretty much what happened. H'mf. All I want to point out with most awful sincerity is that (so far as we know) there was nothin' like a meeting between Keating and Mrs. Derwent last night."

Masters was puzzled. "The next turning is Vernon Street," he pointed out, "and Derwent's number is 33; I got it out of the telephone directory. But this other thing? Lummy, I don't see what you're getting at! What difference does it make?"

"What difference does it make?" roared H.M.

"Exactly. It's a quibble. If there was an affair, let's say, between Mrs. Derwent and Keating, the whole point is that there *was* an affair, and that they arranged to meet at Berwick Terrace this afternoon. I don't see that it matters a curse whether they did or did not meet last night."

"Oh, Masters, my son," said H.M. with some despondency. "After all the trouble I've taken—look here. I've been tryin' to lead you slowly and delicately along the path, so that you'll see what to me is the real contradiction, the essential contradiction, the great blazin' query of the whole case! And it's this. Why did Keating refuse to attend the Murder party last night?"

The chief inspector stared at him.

"Contradiction?" he repeated slowly. "Where's the contradiction? I'm not what you'd call imaginative, but I could think of half a dozen good reasons off-hand. Out of all the flummeries and queer sides of this case, I don't for the life of me see why you pick on that one. Why, for instance—" Masters never got any further.

Number 33 Vernon Street was on the right-hand side. A mottled dusk, swept blue and black as though with a brush, made a background for the warm sparkle of gas-lamps. One street-lamp was just outside the house. A high garden wall of smooth stone, with arched double-doors painted dull green, showed tree-tops above it. To the right of the doors a name, *The Gardens,* was painted in small black letters beside a bell-pull. And at the curb before the house was drawn up a Daimler limousine, with only its sidelights burning, and a chauffeur standing beside it.

The green doors opened, and a woman came out. The chauffeur stepped up to her, touching his cap.

"Mrs. Derwent, ma'am?" he inquired.

"Out you go, Masters," said H.M. softly.

She was standing under the street-lamp, her head a little turned towards them, and there could be no denying her extreme if somewhat overblown beauty. Though she was not overly tall, she appeared so. Masters later swore that she must have weighed over eleven stone, but this is libel. Equally libelous, Pollard thought, was Frances Gale's statement as to her age. She wore an evening-wrap of black velvet, with a high collar. It was the expression of the eye which caught you. You thought of graciousness and mournfulness; but the Old Adam intervened with thoughts of hansom-cabs and frilled rooms and Mademoiselle de Maupin. She had, like that which has been vulgarly attributed to a certain *danseuse,* a glance that could open an oyster at sixty paces.

Yet, even while this overpowering bundle was turned loose in a suburban street, Sergeant Pollard felt certain doubts. It is all very well to be mysterious, and yearning, and even soulful; but, carried too far, a male observer sees in this the deceptive coyness of those ladies who talk about their souls on sofas. The far-away heat of that eye must have been shrewdly controlled, or she would have bumped smack into the lamp-post. But these were vague doubts, which sheer feminine appeal drowned out or even flooded out.

Chief Inspector Humphrey Masters approached her, taking off his hat, and got it like a pail of water in the face.

"Hurr-um!" said Masters. "I beg your pardon, ma'am."

"Yes?" she said. Her voice was a low contralto. Pollard observed her very heavy and very rich blonde hair, which gleamed as she turned her head; it was arranged at the nape of the neck in a heavy and old-fashioned style of dressing, and it was probably this that brought notions of hansom-cabs or New Arabian Nights. "Yes?"

"I beg your pardom, ma'am," pursued Masters, like a clockwork talker, "but am I addressing Mrs. Jeremy Derwent?

"Yes, that is I," replied the large blonde melodiously. She looked at Masters, and her eye seemed subtly to warm to him. "You—er—wished to speak to me? Or to my husband, perhaps? You will find him in the garden."

"I should like to see Mr Derwent all in good time, ma'am. But for the present I must inform you that I am a police-officer from Scotland Yard, and I should like to have a few words with you, if quite convenient."

The announcement did not seem to startle her greatly, although the pale blue eyes, with very heavy lids, opened a little. There was also a pucker on her classic brow.

"I'm terribly afraid it isn't convenient, you know," she said gently. "I have a most urgent appointment. Oh, dear. I suppose it's about that tiresome Dartley business again. I did so hope that we had finished with it. Er—it is about Dartley, isn't it?"

"Partly, ma'am."

"Yes, of course: Dartley."

"No, ma'am. I said—" Masters pulled himself up, and cleared his throat. "I am bound to tell you that I have no authority to detain you, but it would be greatly to your advantage. *Greatly,* ma'am."

She hesitated. "But I don't see how I can. Unless—" she bent forward sweepingly, her half-lowered eyes fixed on his face, and smiled—"unless, of course, you would care to ride along in the car with me?"

It is a sober fact that the back of Masters's neck went brick-red.

"Just so, ma'am," he agreed gruffly. "If you please."

"I am afraid that I cannot take more than one of you. But if you will follow me—"

It is probable that, as with a swishing of black lace she made a stately and graceful bend into the car, some part of her joggled Masters's arm. Something flew out of his hand, flashing brightly in the lamp-light, and the silver cigarette-case clattered round on the pavement. Mrs. Derwent gave a little ladylike scream as she turned her head; she saw it before Masters scooped it up; and for about a tenth of a second there was a certain quality in her expression which gave Pollard a cold shiver. Yet she smiled.

"Why, wherever did you get my cigarette-case?" she asked.

"You identify this as your cigarette-case, ma'am?"

"I believe so. May I see it? But of course. That is my monogram there in the corner, as you see in the J.D. figure. My Christian name is Janet. But please, if you will come in after me—?"

The chauffeur slammed the door of the limousine. As the car swept past them, the watchers had a view of a richly cushioned tonneau, and Mrs. Derwent bending forward towards Masters with great smooth marbly coyness, and Masters with his bowler hat slightly tilted over his eyes.

From H.M.'s car Pollard now heard a low, unmelodious, strangled noise which he soon identified as mirth. Though H.M.'s expression hardly changed, he was rocking back and forth in a kind of wooden ecstasy. On and on went the mirth. There did not actually occur to Pollard the younger Weller's comment, "Well, I never see sitch an old ghost in all my born days. What are you laughin' at, corpilence?" But he was thinking something of the sort, and what he said was:

"Great suffering snakes! Do you think he can take care of himself?"

"Oh, he'll be all right, son," grunted H.M. soothingly. "He'll do his duty; and, when he does, that woman's goin' to be in for a very uncomfortable quarter of an hour. But, burn me, that I should ever 'a' lived to see this! She had him scooped into that car before you could say hocus-pocus-allagazam."

"I suppose solicitors do own Daimler limousines," the sergeant considered. "But where was she going, do you think?"

With some difficulty H.M. crawled out from under the wheel. "That car? It was hired. There's a company that rents 'em out for the evening when you want to impress your friends. Humph. Come along, son. You and I are goin' in and have a little *causerie* with Derwent. Orders? Never you mind whether you got any orders; I'm the one who's got the authority, curse you, and don't you forget it. I'm glad to hear old Jem Derwent is at home. I rather like the feller."

"You mean you know him?"

"I know everybody, son," replied H.M. wearily. "Sure I know him, but that's why I was pretty careful to keep my head shut about it in front of Masters. Jem Derwent is a good man, and a thunderin' clever man. Now I wonder—?"

He pushed open one of the green doors. Inside the high wall, a neglected-looking front garden was shadowed by green leaves. The house was square and unadorned, showing no lights. Instead of going to the front door, H.M. lumbered round to a side path which took them to the back. London seemed shut out altogether. Through a deep garden at the rear, a straight path ran down to a summer-house. And from the summer-house a faint light was shining. On moist air they could smell the smoke of a cigar.

A shaded lamp burned on a table in the summer-house. Beside it, leaning back in a basket-chair, sat a long lean man in a dinner-jacket. His long black legs were crossed; he seemed to be looking at something far away. Moths fluttered round his lamp, and a large brown one beat in zig-zags about the summer-house; but he did not stir an eyelid. Even when he lifted the cigar to his lips, the movement was so slow that the long ash did not flutter. In this complete immobility there was something disquieting and a little (the word occurred again) sinister.

But the first close sight of him dispelled it, when he rose. Jeremy Derwent might have been a few years past sixty. His manner was reserved to the point of dryness, but there was humor in it. It expressed him: even his white hair—what little he had left of it—was of a wiry dryness. His temples were hollowed, his close-shaven chin pointed, and his look betrayed no secrets.

"That can't be Merrivale?" he said, in the same sort of dry voice. "I believe it is, though. My good sir, this is an unexpected pleasure. Please come in."

H.M. lumbered into the summer-house, wheezing.

"Hello, Jem," he said. "Jem, I got an awful lot to get off my chest, and I hope there'll be time for it. This is Detective-Sergeant Pollard, from a place you know of; and the Assistant Commissioner has roped me into it. Jem, I'm afraid we're here on business."

Nothing in Derwent's countenance seemed to change. He greeted Pollard with great courtesy, pushed two chairs towards the table, and remained standing until the others were seated.

"Now, I'm not goin' to lay any traps for you, or hide behind hanky-panky so I can jump out and say, 'Boo,' " H.M. went on. "You're a lawyer, and you know exactly how far you can go. If you wanted to start evadin' we could sit here all night. But I'm goin' to lay the facts out in front of you, and ask you questions to which Bob here will write down the answers. You know a feller named Vance Keating, don't you?"

Derwent's eyes narrowed slightly. "Yes."

"Jem, he was murdered this afternoon in a room with the police guardin' door and window. Somebody shot him twice through the back at close range, and somehow flew away without bein' caught or seen. Point is: the house where Keating was killed is number 4 Berwick Terrace—where you used to live. And there were ten teacups on the table again."

Derwent trimmed the ash off his cigar, laid the cigar carefully on the edge of an ash-tray, and for a time he remained staring at the floor with his hands clasped together.

"That is shocking news, Merrivale," he said. "That is really ghastly news." He looked up. "But what do you want me to say?"

"Yes, it's shockin'. But does it surprise you?"

"It does, most decidedly. That is a mild way of putting it. Keating, of all people! Why, I was to have seen the poor fellow only last night. And then, frankly, this coming on top of that business at Pendragon Gardens—"

"Uh-huh. Let's begin with that," suggested H.M. soothingly. "I won't ask what seems to be dogging you, so that as soon as you move out of a house somebody dies there. I'll be more practical. I'll ask what in the unholy blazes you mean by movin' house all over the shop as though the bailiffs were after you. You're a solid citizen. In your position you got to be. But in a little over two years you've lived at 18 Pendragon Gardens, 4 Berwick Terrace, and 33 Vernon Street; and now they tell me you're movin' again next week. Why?"

It would not be true to say that Derwent smiled: the effect was more that of a slight sardonic loop at the corner of his mouth, though his manner remained formal.

"My wife," he said, "my wife, I fear, is very sensitive to atmosphere."

"Oh, now, son! You can't mean that. Do you mean that, every time she got fed up with a house, she insisted on movin'? And you agreed?"

"Yes. My wife has great powers of persuasion.—I fear you misunderstand me," he added dryly. "I referred to the power of speech. The power of speech can be a formidable

65

weapon to any man who desires a quiet life, although I believe I am not the first man to make that discovery."

"And that was the only reason?"

"That was the only reason."

"In that case," said H.M., sleepily regarding the moths that fluttered round the lamp, "you better hear the rest of the story." He told Derwent fully, and almost succeeded in rattling his host's composure. Towards the end of it the solicitor rose and began to pace gravely round the summer-house; at times Derwent would rub the scanty, wiry white hair at the back of his skull, but it was his only nervous gesture. "You see what a narrow circle we have," H.M. concluded. "Excludin' the possibility that an outsider wandered in (as I suppose you can), we can be pretty sure that the gun was pinched, and Keating was shot, by one of the six people who were playin' Murder here last night. Add to this the fact that your wife's cigarette-case was found under the body—"

"It does not follow as a logical proposition," said Derwent dubiously, "though I admit there is strong contributory evidence. As for Mrs. Derwent, I can assure you that such a notion is fantastic. Or so I believe. The cigarette-case means nothing, even if it should be found to be covered with her fingerprints. Vance Keating was a young man addicted to the practice of casually picking up things. You yourself tell me that he was wearing his cousin's hat. If I found his pockets full of my cigars, or half a dozen bottles of my port in his wine-cellar, it would not surprise me. What I cannot understand, what seems to me the real deviltry in this affair, is the repetition of the—the teacups! It would amost seem, as you suggest, that something is dogging me."

"H'm. It would, wouldn't it? But let's talk about Keating. I hear you were his solicitor; so you knew him pretty well?"

Derwent considered. "Put it, if you like, that I was well acquainted with his legal and financial interests."

"That'll do to start with. Wealthy feller, wasn't he?"

"Most of the world knows that."

"Tell me, Jem: I don't suppose he ever made a will, did he?"

The other came back to his chair, picked up the cigar, and settled his lean body as though luxuriously.

"Yes, it is to his credit that he did. You may recall that the poor fellow was forever going off on some hazardous expedition, with no object, so far as I could see, but to gain some notoriety and a great deal of discomfort. Mr. Philip Keating and I prevailed on him to make a will. You will ask me about its provisions." He was silent, while the big brown moth battered in circles round the room. "Since Keating is dead, I have no objection to telling you. Aside from some minor bequests, his estate was equally divided between his cousin, Mr. Philip Keating, and his fiancée, Miss Frances Gale."

"You don't usually give—humph—gratuitous information, son," said H.M., opening one eye. "Have you got any purpose in tellin' me that?"

Derwent frowned thoughtfully. "Your purpose in asking, I take it, was to find a possible motive. Well, I cannot see one there. It is true that Miss Gale's parents are not wealthy. It is also true that Mr. Philip Keating, like all of us, has at times encountered business reverses. But, honestly, Merrivale, the idea of either of them as a murderer is—most unlikely. Besides . . ."

"Besides? I think we're comin' to it."

"The will is no longer valid," replied Derwent gravely. "And here I confess I am in difficulties. I cannot tell you how I came to learn of the existence of a new will; it occurred over a debate on a matter of legal ethics, and I received the news through underground channels. I need scarcely say that *I* did not draw up the new will. But I am informed on reliable authority that poor Keating did make a new one less than a week ago. Its provisions are simple. His entire estate is left to my wife."

CHAPTER EIGHT

An Absence of Moths

For a TIME H.M. remained staring at him with an expression as wooden as Derwent's own, staring up at him over glasses pulled down on his nose. Presently something like animation, or even a grunt of admiration verging on a chuckle, crept into H.M.'s look.

"Gor," he said. "Burn me, son, I always regarded you as rather a tough walnut to crack. The crackin' isn't so difficult; the trouble is to pick the pieces out of the shell. Here! Was the existence of this will pretty well known?'

"It was not. Aside from Keating and the friend of mine who drew it up, I believe I am the only one—"

"What about Mrs. Derwent?"

"Ah! That I cannot tell you, since I never asked her. But," said the other dryly, "I should think it likely that Keating mentioned the matter to her."

"I'll bet he did. You can see what this brings up, son. It gives her a whackin' motive, but you can see it gives *you* a motive too?"

"Of course. That was why I told you about it," explained Derwent. "It will be common knowledge in a day or two. And I prefer to thrash the matter over with you, and hear what you think of it, rather than risk your possible interpretation behind my back. Kindly attend me, now." Again he put down his cigar and bent forward, his pale, shrewd gray eyes fixed on H.M. "I am not a rich man. Certain wishes and caprices of my wife have at times cost me a great deal of money. I should not care to tell you, for example, what it cost me to send her, this evening, to visit two maiden aunts in Streatham in a hired limousine, so that she might impress them suitably—"

"Two maiden aunts," said H.M. "Poor old Masters. Well?"

"—but Merrivale, I assure you I did not kill Keating, if that is what has entered your head. I do not think I would kill any person . . . for money. And I had no grudge against the boy. Quite to the contrary, I wished him luck."

"You wished him luck," repeated H.M. in a somewhat hollow voice. "This case is openin' up all sorts of possibilities. Right, then: was Keating makin' advances to your wife?"

"To the best of my knowledge, he was."

"And was there anything between them?"

"Unfortunately, no."

Sergeant Pollard looked up from his shorthand. "I didn't quite catch that last, sir. Did you say 'unfortunately' or 'fortunately?'"

Derwent turned on him with dry indulgence. "Did I say 'unfortunately?' Tut! A regrettable slip of the tongue, sir, I meant, of course, 'fortunately.' After all, we are informed that virtue is the fairest jewel that can adorn the fair. The poets unanimously agree on this point, and some of Shakespeare's heroines carry it to an almost gruesome extent. No, Mrs. Derwent is virtuous. For one who is beyond any doubt fond of men, she is the most virtuous woman I have ever known. Fortunately I am able to recall a passage or two early

68

in our married life. Otherwise I might even now wonder to what obscure biological process—more suitable, perhaps, to a limerick than to real life—our son Jeremy owes his own existence."

He faced them with a smile of sober charm.

"You find me, gentlemen, in a mood to speak frankly. I am not often in this mood. It has been brought about during the past few minutes by the clear realization that this affair, when it becomes public, means professional ruin for me. I am too old a man to feel any undue bitterness, but I had hoped for a quiet life. Even apart from the revelations that must come out concerning my wife, the fact remains that I have been the late tenant of two houses where two odd and brutal murders have been committed. Therefore I feel inclined to tell you curtly what the situation was between Keating and Mrs. Derwent.

"There has never been any infidelity, I regret to say, or I should have had grounds for divorce. My wife was aware that I would give her a divorce if Keating would consent to marry her. But when it came to the actuality I knew—and she knew—that Keating would never marry her under any circumstances. For the other side, Mrs. Derwent's native prudence has prevented her from accepting him on any other grounds. She is the last woman in the world who would throw her bonnet over the windmill; of that I can assure you. And there the matter has rested."

"I see. Did you ever speak to Keating about it?"

"Never," said Derwent with some distaste. "And, if it is convenient, I should prefer not to discuss the matter further."

H.M. leaned forward. "Take it easy, Jem. I'm goin' to ask you just one last question. Don't you honestly believe that your wife was goin' to 4 Berwick Terrace this afternoon to meet Keating?—Wait, now, dammit! Stop a bit before you answer. I'm not suggestin' an assignation of the kind you mean. I don't think there was any such thing. People makin' an assignation don't usually choose tea-time in a dusty attic hole where the temperature is 105. It looks to me like a rite of some kind, though I dunno what. But if there were some mysterious crystal-gazin' or secret-society hocus-pocus concerned with the teacups, would she have been intrigued by it and apt to go? If she isn't interested in love-makin', is she at least interested in tomfoolery?"

Derwent reflected. "Yes, I concede that. Janet loves mystery as lesser women love sweets: though I should not deprecate her own love for sweets, since she consumes a five-pound box of chocolates in a week. But she is more interested in her soul. Therefore—"

"Well?"

"Therefore I am certain she was not invited to Berwick Terrace, or she would probably have gone. You see, Merrivale, I know what she was really doing this afternoon. A moment ago I mentioned her two maiden aunts, and the expense of sending her to visit them in a private limousine. For an evening's entertainment it might not have been so expensive. But this has been a gala day. She wished to give the aunts what she called a treat: a matinee, a tea—"

"You're not goin' to tell me," H.M. interrupted sharply, "that the car was hired for all day?"

Derwent inclined his head. "Since early this afternoon, yes. She was in the company of her aunts all afternoon. The sergeant will want their names and addresses: they are the Misses Alice and Lavinia Burkehart, 'The Dovecot,' Park Road, S.W. 18. They went to the Shakespearean revival at the Shaftesbury Theater. They had tea at Frascati's, and I am instructed to say that they had tea at five o'clock." He raised his eyes. After a pause he went on: "This evening she changed into evening splendor and visited them to meet some of their friends. Since this outing has been planned for a week or two, I hardly think her arrangements for this afternoon can have concerned ten teacups."

"It's awful neat, son," said H.M. He regarded Derwent with a strange, fishy, malevolent look. "I don't want to carp about terms. But is this what you actually know to have happened? Or is this what she told you?"

"That, my dear Merrivale, I must leave up to your own decision."

"Oh," said H.M.

He lumbered up from his chair. He wandered in his near-sighted way to the door of the summer-house, and stood sniffing like an ogre at the warm night. Though the moths banged past him, none of them touched the upright, rather elegant old solicitor. The man, plainly, was indecipherable. Yet Pollard, as their host's eyes stole sideways towards H.M., thought that he had detected Mr. Jeremy Derwent in at least one lie. When they had arrived at 33 Vernon Street a while ago, Pollard remembered how the chauffeur of the limousine had approached the woman who came out of the door and inquired, "Mrs. Derwent?" But if the car had been hired all day the chauffeur must have known who she was already. Well?

"Jem"—H.M. spoke offhandedly, to the night—"we've managed to obscure a lot in this little conversation; but, whatever else is obscured, I suppose you don't deny that somebody killed Keating. Got any ideas about it?"

"Yes. I should suggest that you look for the link."

"Link?"

"Exactly. The only factor that is common to the cases of both Dartley and Keating." Derwent spoke with a touch of impatience. "I suggest, my boy, that in the sensationalism of Keating's death you are in danger of forgetting Dartley altogether. What is the obvious common factor? In Dartley's case, there occurs the name of old Benjamin Soar, who has since died. In Keating's case, in the list of the six people who were here at my home last night for the entertaining if rather stupid game of Murder—"

"Yes. I was comin' to that.'"

"—there occurs the name of young Benjamin Soar, who was closely associated with his father in their business for some years before the old man's death."

"I dunno that it's the only common factor. There's your wife and yourself too. It just depends on which end you start at. H'm. What are you conjurin' up, son? Visions of the murderous art-and-curio dealer prowlin' among his bric-a-brac? I say, has it ever struck you that there's somethin' a bit spooky about those places? It's fascinated everybody who's written about it. Think of Markheim standin' with his dagger among the clocks, and the little shop where Gautier bought the mummy's foot, and—"

"Nonsense," interrupted Derwent, eying him sharply. "Mr. Soar junior is an able and competent business man, who is putting what I believe they call 'ginger' into his trade. I am far from even intimating that he would kill either Dartley or poor Keating. And his presence at my house for the Murder party last night is not a coincidence. I know him well. I have known him ever since we were thrown together at the time of the Dartley affair, as—ah—common factors in the sum."

"Where's the coincidence, then?"

"It is this," answered Derwent with a new intensity. It seemed to Pollard that he was trying to conceal this intensity; but his finger-nails scratched slightly on the table. "You may remember that Dartley, on the afternoon before

71

he died, was alleged to have bought from old Benjamin Soar a set of Majolica cups painted with a design of peacocks' feathers?"

"Yes."

"And that he bought these cups under circumstances of secrecy: I may say of *great* secrecy?"

"Yes."

"Then it may interest you to know that yesterday, on the afternoon before *he* died, Keating bought a certain article from the firm of Soar. *He* bought it under terms of some secrecy. *He* did not actually visit the shop, as we are informed that Dartley did not visit the shop either. The article Keating purchased was a Milanese cloth or shawl, of great beauty and evident antiquity, worked in gold leaf with a design of peacocks' feathers.—I should not be surprised if it were the table-cover you found in the room of the teacups."

He sat back, smiling humanly and luxuriously for the first time. But if he expected to produce a sensation, or gall H.M.'s wits with a new puzzle, he was disappointed. H.M. only shook his head.

"To tell you the truth, I was expectin' something of the kind. It may be important; but, all the same, I'm much more interested in that Murder party of yours. Did you get any details about Keating buyin' the shawl?"

"Unfortunately, no. The fact alone."

"How'd you come to hear about it at all?"

"Mr. Soar happened to mention it to me, in passing, at the unfortunate Murder party you speak of." Derwent's reserve drew over him again, and his voice became smoothly dry. He put his finger-tips together. "I should not have permitted that—that damned piece of childishness, Merrivale, though I confess the idea attracted me. You've heard that Mr. Keating did not appear. We wondered why, and Mr. Soar—"

"Aha, now we're gettin' down to it!" rumbled H.M., with his first sign of life. He turned round fully. "So it surprised you when Keating didn't turn up for the party, did it?"

"It surprised us very much. Keating had been particularly enthusiastic about the game; I believe he suggested the idea himself. He was anxious to try his hand at being the detective. But may I ask why you take so much interest in it?"

"Steady, son. Didn't you try to find out why he wasn't there?"

Derwent frowned. "Oh, here, Merrivale! I had expected him to escort Miss Gale. She arrived alone, somewhat flustered, and evidently reluctant to speak of it. I supposed there had been a tiff between them. Under the circumstances I hardly wished to press her."

"Sure. But did you hear anything about a row between Keating and a feller named Gardner, possibly over the Gale girl herself?"

"No, I did not."

"You seem surprised. Certain, now? Let's omit the old-school stiffness and chivalry. The trouble was supposed to have taken place the night before your party: Monday night. Gardner threatened to kill him."

Their host studied the past. "It is news to me. I can only tell you that I think it highly unlikely. Good Lord, man! Ron Gardner! Besides, I saw Keating himself on Tuesday morning. I had business in Westminster; and, since there were—certain business matters to discuss with Keating himself, I called on him at his flat. He certainly said nothing of any trouble. On the contrary, he seemed in excellent spirits, and was looking forward to the game at my house that night."

"On Tuesday morning," said H.M. with laboring care, "he still expected to come to your party. Hey? And so something between Tuesday morning and Tuesday afternoon, when he told Frances Gale he couldn't go, made him change his mind. Oh, my eye. I told Masters it might be the blazin' query of the case." He brooded for a moment. "Let's get back to what Masters thinks is the blazin' query of the case. Jeremy Derwent. Janet Derwent. Philip Keating. Ronald Gardner. Frances Gale. Benjamin Soar.—Jem, which one of 'em pinched that revolver from your house?"

"Henry, I don't know," said Derwent.

There was a silence.

"I was afraid you were goin' to say that," admitted H.M. "The little joker in this case is much too subtle to be seen whiskin' a big .45 from under your noses. Still and all, you were the host. You ought to have been more observant than Frances Gale."

Closing his eyes as though in concentration, Derwent tapped his fingertips together very slowly.

"I agree. Let me see if I can recall it. At about half-past nine my wife retired from the party, having a headache. At this time I remember distinctly that the revolver was lying on the mantelpiece in the drawing-room at the front of the house. We played no more games of Murder after my wife

73

left us. We sat in the drawing-room, chatting. At about half-past eleven Philip Keating suggested that it was time for him to be going. The others also wished to excuse themselves. I asked the men whether they would not drink a nightcap with me in my study at the rear of the house. They agreed, and Miss Gale accompanied us. I was the last to leave the drawing-room. I then noticed that the pistol was still lying on the mantelpiece, and I reminded myself to call Ronald Gardner's attention to it so that he should not forget it when he left. Am I clear so far?"

He opened his eyes sharply at this point, and closed them again.

"We went to my study. Four of us took a whisky-and-soda, and Miss Gale a light sherry. None of us left the room during this time. Miss Gale, as I told you, had been under some strain that night. After barely tasting her sherry, she suddenly showed signs of discomposure if not actual tears; she excused herself, and almost ran out of the room. We were surprised. Ronald Gardner finished his drink and followed her somewhat hurriedly after she had gone, explaining that she had offered him a lift home in her car. I walked with Gardner to the front door. He did not go near the door of the drawing-room: which was, I think, closed. I reminded him of the pistol. He answered me something to this effect—I quote from memory —'Oh, that's all right; it'll be in good hands.' At this time I took the words to mean that he was leaving the pistol behind, since he wished to catch up with Miss Gale and did not care to be bothered with it at the moment. Miss Gale was then in her car. I walked with him to the gate and saw them drive away.

"When I returned to the house Mr. Soar was standing outside the front door. Philip Keating was getting his hat from a coat-closet in the hall. I do not know whether either of them had gone into the drawing-room. Philip Keating had his car, and Mr. Soar chose to walk to the Notting Hill Gate Underground station. It was only when I began to lock up the house and turn out the lights that I noticed the revolver was missing. Then I did not know what to make of Gardner's words. I still do not. That's all."

Though his cigar had long ago gone out, he chose to emphasize the end of his story by a turn of his bony wrist in stabbing out the cigar on the ash-tray. Again his eyes moved sideways towards H.M., showing a twinkle of agile intelligence. Pollard always remembered him at that moment:

the scanty white hair that was a trifle ruffled, the faint smile, the wrist poised above the ash-tray as for a move at chess. Outside the summer-house a breeze stirred, and the garden frothed with white blossom.

"No questions, Henry?"

"No questions. You've said all you mean to say," H.M. informed him. H.M. pulled himself together. "Well, now, I expect we'd better be gettin' along. I got a whole lot to sit and think about tonight."

"Is your curiosity satisfied?"

"My curiosity? You know it ain't," H.M. returned rather sharply. "I sort of think that's on your mind right now. I appreciate your courteous and old-school attitude. I appreciate how you won't whisper evil of anyone by speculatin' as to who might 'a' pinched that gun, or who might 'a' committed an impossible crime at 4 Berwick Terrace—"

"That is not courtesy. That is caution."

"I know. They often amount to the same thing. But what I can't quite understand, d'ye see, is why you should be courteous about speakin' of a piece of furniture."

"I beg your pardon?"

H.M. squinted down his nose. "I got a friend named Masters. His particular bugbear is things that couldn't have happened but did happen: like this murder today. To the outward eye, that attic-room miracle of a murderer who vanished is the most bewildering thing in the whole case. Yet it don't bother you; it don't even interest you a flicker; you never even mention it casually. I'd like to know why. Even the room don't interest you. I tell you all about a load of furniture that the movin' men have brought there—a mahogany chair, a mahogany table, a nice carpet, a divan. And you don't speak up and say: 'I don't know about the rest of the stuff, but the movin' men never brought that divan.'

"Because the movin' men never did bring it, Jem. That ain't subtle deduction; everybody noticed it. It was an old and dingy-lookin' piece of furniture. When I hit it with my hand, the dust came up in a cloud. So it'd been left behind in the house, probably by the last tenants when they moved out. And I was just wonderin' . . ."

"Why I never mentioned it? But, man!" protested Derwent humorously. "Of course I never mentioned it. I fail to see its importance. Yes, it belonged to us, and we left it behind. Er— it was always a favorite of Janet's. I daresay it gave her a feeling of Oriental luxury. Even when it became somewhat decrepit, it was relegated to the attic instead of being thrown out or given away."

"Yes; it does seem to have a special fascination. Frances Gale was mighty interested in it too. She was so interested in it that she didn't have eyes for anything else and didn't even notice the teacups. So I was just wonderin', that's all. Well, we won't keep you any longer. Sleep well."

Derwent rose and went with them to the door of the summer-house.

"Thanks. I will say only à bientôt, gentlemen, for I feel sure the police will see me again. I feel sure they will want to know what I myself was doing this afternoon." He spoke with sudden seriousness. "Believe me, I am honestly grateful for this visit. I can't say more. I am sorry we could not have met to discuss the art of murder more amicably, over a cigar and a glass of port, rather than in a moth-ridden summer-house. However, one thing at least it will have taught you to observe."

H.M. turned round.

"You will have observed," said Derwent, smiling gravely, "that no moths have settled on me. Good night, gentlemen. Goo-ood night."

CHAPTER NINE

Stockbroker's Conscience

AT A LITTLE PAST nine o'clock on the following morning, Sergeant Pollard was mounting the dingy flights of stairs to H.M.'s office overlooking the Embankment. He had been told to go there when he had taken leave of H.M. on Wednesday night, and this morning he had been at the Yard since eight o'clock. Acting in a sergeant's capacity as a sort of secretary to his chief inspector during a murder-investigation, it was his duty to collect any information which might have come in over-night and prepare it in the form of a report for Masters. His report, containing a few more ugly facts, was ready now. But still there was no sign of Masters.

Nor of H.M., as he discovered when he reached H.M.'s office. The big, dingy room was as quiet as though there were no typewriters downstairs, and seemed shut away from Whitehall. Everywhere there were traces of H.M.'s untidy presence, from scattered papers to cigar-ends. The day was hot, and Pollard raised both windows. He prowled round the room. He inspected the Mephistophelian portrait of Fouché over the mantelpiece. Finally he sat down at H.M.'s desk, lit a cigarette, and began to read over what he had written.

Post-Mortem Report: Deceased was killed by two bullets fired from a .45 caliber revolver. One bullet pierced the supra-occipital bone and lodged against the frontal bone over the left eye. The other bullet entered the back between the third and fourth lumbar vertebrae, severing the nerves of the spinal cord, took an oblique upward direction, and lodged near the right lung. Both shots were fired within an inch of the body.

Firearms Report: Both bullets taken from the body were, beyond any doubt, fired by the Remington . 45 revolver presented for inspection (no registration number).

"And that is that," Pollard said aloud. He turned over the other sheet, which was the gist of the report from the divisional-inspector.

Furniture: On Tuesday morning, July 30th, the manager of the Atlas Furnishing Co., Oxford St., received a typewritten letter asking for one folding mahogany table, two light chairs of same, one plain black carpet size 10x12, one set black velvet curtains, with curtain rods, for window 4x5½. (This is not the same company which supplied furniture in Dartley case.) Ten £10 notes were enclosed. The furniture was to be called for in the name of "Grant."

On same date, Cartwright Hauling Co., Kensington High Street, was instructed by letter to pick up furniture and deliver to 4 Berwick Terrace. No key was enclosed, but door was to be open. The furniture was placed in front lower hall. Due to error at the Atlas Stores, only one of the chairs requested was delivered. (Cartwright Ltd. was the company which delivered furniture in Dartley case.)

At this point Pollard, who had been subconsciously listening to slow footsteps on the stairs outside the open door, glanced up from his notes.

"Excuse me," said a voice rather coldly; it may have been from nervousness.

In the doorway stood a plump, bustling-looking man with a

77

bowler hat cradled over his arm. His round face, in spite of a somewhat hard gray eye, had an expression of good-living and good-nature. His thin brown hair was brushed and polished, like his well-cut black suit. But he was plainly disturbed. He entered in some suspicion, as though he expected to find a bucket of water poised over the door; then he pulled himself together. Pollard knew him at once.

"You can't be Merrivale?" he suggested, with tentative friendliness. "They—er—told me to come up here. I thought anything in the world could be wangled, but I never had to pull so many strings in my life as to get any information from the police. And I'm the man's relative, mind you. Bloody awful, I call it. My name is Keating, Philip Keating."

"Yes, sir. Come in. Sir Henry Merrivale will be here soon."

"Here, don't I know you?" asked Philip abruptly. "Of course I do; I've met you somewhere. No, don't tell me—I never forget a face. I'd have had your name like a shot if this infernal business hadn't put me off."

He seemed a trifle dashed at the news that Pollard was a police-officer; but he dug after details of their acquaintance, expertly; he established friendliness on a sound footing, and he seemed to feel that there were compensations. Then he hitched a chair close to the desk, lowering his voice. If Pollard had been going to talk business with him, the sergeant would have been very wary.

"This business," he said; "it's pretty rotten, isn't it?"

Pollard agreed that it was.

"And in a way," Keating went on slowly, "it makes me feel such a swine."

"What does?"

"Oh, having a little argument with Vance just before he went out yesterday. Say what you like, Vance has always played the game with me; and I've tried to play the game with him. It's not important, but you know how these things affect you. It leaves a nasty taste, and you blame yourself, to think that the last time you saw a man alive you said—"

Philip Keating's confidential air was interrupted by the gusty entrance of H.M.

He was an apparition. With a peculiar perverseness whose reason Pollard could imagine, H.M. did not today refuse to wear his collar. On the contrary, in addition to his ancient top-hat, he was tightened into full resplendent morning costume: morning-coat, striped trousers, wing collar, and gray cravat, over which he glared and perspired. He came sweeping round the corner of the door like a hansom-cab, a truly impressive figure. He looked like What The Government Wants. The effect was somewhat marred by his getting out a corn-cob pipe, lighting it with manifest relish, and putting his feet up on the desk.

Philip Keating greeted him with subdued heartiness. "Any other time, Sir Henry, I'd have been pleased to have made your acquaintance," he confided. "But this thing—well, it's jolly rotten, as I was telling Sergeant Pollard. Vance and I were more like brothers than cousins."

"Thanke'e, son. Yes, it must have been a oit of a shock," said H.M., looking sideways. "Old Boko gave you all the facts, didn't he? I asked him if he would."

"The Commissioner? Yes. But it isn't only Vance's death. You see, this thing will have—repercussions," Philip confided, looking over his shoulder to make sure the door was shut. "I've often told Vance, it was all very well for *him* to be unconventional. He hadn't got his living to make. Call me respectable and psalm-singing. It's not that. Play the game, and no damn nonsense; that's my code. See what I mean? Besides, I don't violate a confidence when I tell you that I'm engaged to be married to Lady Prunella Aberystwyth—the Earl of Glambake's daughter, you know," he added, somewhat self-consciously. "And old Glambake—"

"Not to interrupt you, son," said H.M., taking the pipe out of his mouth, "but would you mind tellin' me just exactly what you're talking about?"

"Don't you know who killed Vance?"

"Not just yet. Do you?"

"I can't tell you who it was, exactly. But I can tell you *what* it was. It was a secret society called the Ten Teacups."

There was a pause. H.M. laid down his pipe. Philip Keating regarded him with such heavy sincerity, and such worry on his round good-natured face, that H.M. appeared to hesitate.

"That's very interestin', son. What do you know about this society?"

"Not very much, I'm afraid. Only a hint or two Vance has dropped, and something I saw—well, never mind. I believe it's a sort of religious society."

"Religious society?"

"Not in any good sense. They worship something: I'm not certain what. Magic, or perpetual life, or transporting themselves into another age, or some such ruddy rot. Anyway, one of the subsidiary laws is that any man who is allowed to become a member can take as his Bride, by an oath or something, any woman in the group he wants. Now, we're men of the world; and I don't say I object to stepping out with something nice myself; if it's done discreetly. But this flummery! ... And here's the point. I'm pretty sure that Derwent woman is a member."

"Yes, that'd be understandable," H.M. conceded. He examined his shoes. "But a lot of questions come along with it. How big a society is it? How old is it? Where does it come from? What do the teacups mean? And does it bring about perpetual life by whackin' its members through the head with a bullet?"

Philip shook his head.

"I can't tell you that, I'm afraid. What I've told you has been pieced together, if you know what I mean. I think Vance was to have been initiated into it, and I think that Derwent woman is a leading spirit."

The curious part of it, Pollard was reflecting, was that this story of the Ten Teacups, which should have been so fantastic, did not sound fantastic in the least. It confirmed his original idea. And it was also *right*. The characters of Vance Keating and Janet Derwent suddenly fitted into that peacock pattern. He himself could testify how Keating, going into the place of the teacups, had removed his hat. He himself could testify that there was an atmosphere even in hot afternoon. And whatever you might think of charlatanism, one practical and obdurate fact stood out: that Keating had bequeathed to Mrs. Derwent a fortune of several hundred thousand pounds.

Pollard had time to consider several possibilities, since H.M. said nothing for quite some time. Then H.M. picked up his pipe as though dismissing the subject.

"You've brought us a load of dynamite, my lad," he said, "and I want time to think about it. D'ye see, that ain't the only surprise. I had your story prophesied all wrong. When you said, 'Don't you know who killed Vance?' I thought you were goin' to give us an entirely different explanation. I thought you were goin' to say it was a feller named Gardner."

Philip opened his mouth, and shut it again. For some reason he seemed uncomfortable.

"No. No. Hang it all! There wasn't much in that. At least, I don't see—"

"Look here, we seem to have got the wires crossed. At that Murder party on Monday night, didn't you tell Frances Gale that there'd been a row between Gardner and Keating, and that Gardner had threatened to shoot him? I been a long time gettin' to the bottom of this, and I want to know the truth."

"Good Lord, no!" exclaimed the other, in plainly genuine astonishment. "Here, I say! It's you who've got the wires crossed. It wasn't Ron who threatened to kill Vance. It was Vance who threatened to kill Ron, and blooming well nearly did, at that. I know, because I was there. Vance was raging on about killing him, and how he'd got Ron into a corner and was going to make him confess. Then he shot at Ron—but I don't suppose he meant to hit him, really, because the bullet went wild and smashed some glasses that Bartlett, Vance's valet, was carrying in on a tray."

"Well, I'm glad to hear there was no trouble," said H.M. "Just a nice little social evening, hey? When did this happen?"

"At Vance's flat, on Monday night." Philip frowned, but he did not seem nervous. "Still, I shouldn't take too much stock in it, if I were you. Vance had a devil of a temper when he got started; *he* called it artistic temperament, or some such rubbish. And I'll tell you a little secret. Vance was a good man, and in most things he'd got twice as much guts as anyone else; but secretly—right down in his heart—he was afraid of firearms. I don't know why. He'd have died rather than admit it, and ever since we were kids he's been trying to conquer it. He may have lost his head in the excitement, having the gun. . . ."

"It don't look like a small thing to me, son. Let's hear exactly what happened."

"If I've got to—?" Philip hesitated, and examined a well-polished shoe. "It happens that I've got a flat in the same building as Vance, two floors higher up. We were constantly walking in and out of each other's flats. On Monday evening, about eight o'clock, I went up to see Vance. I didn't bother to knock; the door is always on the latch. Inside there's a long hall that runs through the flat." He stopped. "Unfortunately, I'm not one of those fellows who can overhear a quick-fire conversation and then repeat it word for word. I've often wondered how they do it in the trials. It was all over too dashed quickly. Anyhow, I was in the hall, and I heard Vance in the living-room going hammer-and-tongs, ending with, *'Now I've got you cornered, so just admit it!'* or something of the sort. Then Ron said something, and Bartlett—Vance's valet—shouted, *'For God's sake, sir, look out!'* Then, bang! the gun, and a sound of glass smashing all over the show. For a second I didn't know what to do. Then I . . . er . . . went pretty quietly to the living-room door, and looked round it. There was Vance, with a revolver in his hand, facing me; and Ron looking grim; and Bartlett at a side-table with a tray and a bottle, and some glasses smashed to blazes. Over at the other side of the room, Hawkins—that's the waiter who serves the meals—was poking his head through the door. All like a ruddy wax-works."

"I see. What'd you do then?"

"The fact is," Philip began impressively, and stopped. "You can see my position," he went on, altering his tone to a sort of cherubic growl. "It's all very well for Vance to be unconventional. But for me to be mixed up in any rows—fights —lawsuits—what Prunella's father would say—"

"You mean you turned round and tiptoed out of there as fast as you could cut?"

"To put it briefly, I did. You can see my position. I decided not to inquire into the business. None of my affair. Least said, soonest mended. At least, that's how I look at it. So I decided," he spoke with complacency or shrewdness, "to be a jolly good fellow with everybody concerned, and not to mention it unless anybody mentioned it to me. And nobody did. Of course, I felt bound to drop a hint to Frances Gale. That's a wonderful girl, Sir Henry. On the night of Derwent's party I felt bound to give her a hint, to explain why Vance wasn't there—"

H.M. regarded him with fishy eyes.

"And scared the blazin' daylights out of her," he commented. "I got an idea her romantic soul saw pistols at twenty paces in Hyde Park. You're a model o' tact, son; I heard her remark on it. Then this row *was* over Frances Gale, was it?"

"That's what I gathered," said Philip stiffly. "I certainly heard her name mentioned when Vance was talking."

"Cousin Vance was jealous, then? He wanted Gardner to 'confess' somethin' about Frances Gale?"

"I didn't say that," returned Philip calmly. "I don't know what it was. I only mention her name at all to show you it was another example of Vance's 'temperament.' Frances is a jolly decent girl, and nobody will tell you any different." He sat back, tapping his fingers together. "No. You don't want to confuse the issue with quarrels like that. You go after the Ten Teacups. *If* you can find 'em. This Disappearing Murderer trick: that's the worst of it. I couldn't believe my two ears when I heard about it. I was at a cocktail party this afternoon, at the Dorchester, when it must have been happening. That disappearing murderer is some flummery, tied up with this teacup business. If you ask me, it's some mechanical device hidden in there. It—"

"Again not to interrupt you," said H.M., "but I don't think we can duck out of the quarrel as easy as that, son. Humph, no. By your statement, Gardner is beginnin' to take on highly sinister colors—"

"Don't get the wrong impression," Philip urged, as though eager not to speak ill. "Ron's a decent sort. He'd have been a great cricketer if he'd been willing to keep in condition. But I've told him like a Dutch uncle, you can't drink whisky and expect to have a good eye. Stands to reason. He's even written a good travel-book, or at least they tell me it's good; though —" Philip smiled jovially—"I've often asked him who wrote it for him. And I'm afraid he's an utter ass about money. That's why he's lost most of what he had. But there it is. I can't honestly see him concerned in this. There's just one thing that bothers me. . . ."

"The gun, hey?"

"So you noticed that," said the other, in a slightly altered tone. "Well, yes—the gun. Sir Henry, the revolver that Vance used to take a shot at Ron, on Monday night, was the same one that was used to kill Vance himself."

"You're sure of that, now?"

"Positive. I've seen that revolver too often at Ron's, and it's too distinctive. When I looked in the living-room at Vance's flat, I knew it immediately. There wasn't a great deal of light, a lamp or two on the tables; but Vance was standing near one and the light was on it. Good gad, you can imagine the start I got when I saw the same gun turn up again on Wednesday night at Derwent's party! —Ron bringing it, mind you. In fact, he seemed more concerned about a tin dagger that he brought than about the gun. Of course, I didn't say anything. And I can't say I'm much impressed by it. Even Ron wouldn't be such a chump as to kill Vance with his own gun. But, after all, I should think it calls for questioning. It *was* Ron's gun. He did bring it to Derwent's house. He did take it away with him, and he's the last person known to have had it in his possession. . . ."

"Hold on!" roared H.M., straightening in his chair with such abruptness that Philip started. "Think what you're sayin', son. Take a deep mental reflect, and don't get this tangled up no matter what else you tell us. Are you certain

Gardner took that gun away from Derwent's house on the night of the party?"

"Yes, of course. —Ask young Ben Soar, if you don't believe me."

On H.M.'s desk the telephone-bell rang sharply.

H.M. wasted only a moment in blank staring before he picked up the telephone and groused at it. His expression became wooden again; he put back the receiver, and got up.

"Son," he said to Philip in a colorless voice, "I got a little favor I'd like to ask you. I wonder if you'd mind waitin' in a room downstairs for about ten minutes before I fetch you up again? It's a nice room. All the top-hats from the diplomatic bunch wait there; I got *La Vie Parisienne* there, and *Snappy Sketches,* and all the readin' matter they like. Thanks. *Lollypop!"*

A genial but somewhat suspicious Keating was edged out of the room, after which H.M. turned to Pollard.

"It's Masters," he explained, not without a certain expression, "back from his evil joy-ride to Streatham. And that ain't all. He's got Frances Gale with him; and it seems she wants to tell us something—about a divan, d'ye see."

CHAPTER TEN

The Burn on the Carpet

IT WAS an almost majestic chief inspector who entered alone: brisk, freshly shaven, and bland. In one hand he had a briefcase and in the other a small valise.

"Ah, sir," he boomed, either not at all abashed or pretending not to be. He put his hat on the desk with great nicety. "Bit cooler this morning, don't you think? Morning, Bob."

"Ho, ho," said H.M. "Come off it, Masters. You don't fool me. Burn me, I been lookin' forward all night to the story of your interview with the Kurse of Kensington; and you're not goin' to deprive me of a syllable of it now. Come on: let's hear it."

For a moment Masters glowered.

"Well, sir, just between ourselves, I don't mind admitting—"

"So that's how it is. Masters, confess! You were scared of her."

"No, sir, I was not," replied the chief inspector with dignity. "It's not that, exactly. But I don't mind admitting, just between ourselves, I kept thinking: Lummy, suppose Mrs. M. should poke her head into the car now! And it—hurrum! It's that woman's manner, like." He got out a handkerchief and mopped his forehead. "But that's not all. If anybody'd told me, Sir Henry, that after twenty-five years in the Force, a—a blooming plaster Venus could make a fool of me . . . ur! I *beg* your pardon, Bob. Do you happen to see anything funny in this?"

"Yes, sir," said Pollard.

"You just attend to your notes, my lad," said Masters darkly, "and you leave other things to them that know better. As I was saying, Sir Henry. I don't mean make a fool of me in the way you mean. I'm a copper, and I know my duty. But —suppose we get down to business. Whatever I did or I didn't find out—" he tapped the desk impressively—"two things I did establish.

"First, the fingerprints on that cigarette-case—the woman's fingerprints—aren't Mrs. Derwent's.

"Second, for the whole afternoon of the murder Mrs. Derwent has a cast-iron alibi. Eh?"

H.M. nodded. "Yes, we got an inkling of that," he grumbled, looking at a corner of the ceiling. "We been gatherin' some information too. Now, now, Masters, nobody's trying to pull your leg. What happened?"

Masters hesitated. "I suppose I'd better get it over with. But mind!" He mopped his face again. "We got into the car, as described. First I tackled her about that cigarette-case: where did she last see it, and so on. First she only laughed and sort of—hurrum. Then all of a sudden she remembered. She said, of course, she had given it to a friend of hers on Monday afternoon. The friend was Mr. Vance Keating. It seems that she and Keating *and* her husband (got that, sir?) had been having tea together on Monday afternoon. Keating had borrowed the case and forgot to return it. That gave me a handle. I went on the assumption that, if Keating intended to meet her yesterday, he might have taken the case along to give it back. Then I let her have the news about Keating's death."

"Well?" prompted H.M.

"I don't mind admitting I wasn't quite prepared for what happened. For a second she just looked at me—queer; I don't know how to tell you. Then she leaned back and screamed. Yes, screamed. Gawd lummy," said Masters in an awed voice, "that lady's a one. I never heard such a screech in all my born days. The car swerved over and nearly hit the curb. The chauffeur turned round, looking like thunder. Then he stopped the car and got out and opened the back door. By this time that woman was leaning back in a corner, breathing soft-like, with the tears coming out of her eyes, and her hand up sort of shading her eyes—

"Well, sir, blowed if that chauffeur didn't grab my arm. He said I know what games you're up to, my bucko; out you get. I said I was a police officer. He said horseradish; and then blowed if he didn't haul off and try to paste me one. I tell you, it's a kind of atmosphere that woman's got. It makes everybody act like that—"

"Lord love a duck," breathed H.M., his eyes opening. "And what did you do?"

"There was nothing for it but to paste him back. Then I nipped behind him and got his arm locked so he wouldn't move; but *he* was yelling by that time. And the crowd started. And—now, we needn't go into that. The point is," growled Masters, "that all the time the commotion was going on, either out of devilment or to give her time to think what she was going to say, that woman was lying back pretending to cry, and laughing at me through her fingers.

"I knew it. She knew I knew it. But *she* was the one who quietened the row. Ah. By leaning out, all handsome and overcome, and saying please, it was all right. But she did it in such a way that everybody in the crowd (the copper included) thought she was only trying to avoid scandal. Cor, the things they said about me made my ears—!

"We got started again. But she wasn't through with me yet, and she kept patting my knee. She started off about how terrible it was, and how everybody knew how fond Mr. Vance Keating was of her, though it was all innocent. She said they might even suspect her, eh? I said yes, they ruddy well might. Then she said the only thing to do was to take me straight to the people who could prove her as pure as whatnot. You mightn't believe it, but she took me straight to—"

"I know," said H.M. drowsily. "To 'The Dovecot,' Park Road, S.W. 18."

Masters peered at him. "Here, now! You didn't put up this thing on me, did you? So help me, if I thought you had—"

"No, no. Carry on."

"To, as you say," agreed the chief inspector grimly, " 'The Dovecot,' Park Road, S.W. 18. Home of two maiden aunts. *And* there was a sort of bridge-party-swaray going on. Before

I knew what she was up to, or I could grab her alone, she walked me straight into the middle of it, proclaiming the news. Blowed if the 'ole shoot didn't gather round her like a tragedy queen, or the like; and then they all set about my ears. Oh, Mrs. Derwent had it all her own way, she had. She's the cleverest lady I ever met. Instead of me asking her questions, it was me that couldn't fight through the mob. They said how exciting it was—ur!—to have a real Scotland Yard man there. They asked me was it true or not that we went about in disguise, and what about the Bournemouth trunk-murder, and the rest of it. Oh, I fought through 'em, all right. But all I got for my pains was a corporate alibi as big as a house, and the proof that her fingerprints weren't on the case."

Masters's account of Janet Derwent's movements on Wednesday afternoon tallied exactly with Derwent's own account of the night before.

"For a second," he explained, "I thought I might have caught her out. I mean, that business of having hired the car all day. The chauffer who was waiting for her in Vernon Street (you noticed it?) didn't know her when she came out of her house to get into the car. But that wouldn't wash. In hired cars of that kind, they've got afternoon and evening drivers. It was a different one who drove her in the afternoon. Well, this morning I nipped round to the Mercury Motor Services, and saw the man who drove her in the afternoon. At five o'clock, when Mr. Keating was shot, she was just walking out of a restaurant in Oxford Street with two aunts and three other people who'd been to the theater with 'em. Alibi. Solid." Masters drew a long breath of tigerish resonance. "And now you know as much as I do."

"Yes, you had quite a night," H.M. acknowledged. "You need a drink, and you're goin' to have one. Maybe you'll be a bit cheered by what we've got to tell you. But give me an impression first. What did you make of Mrs. D.? Aside from the fact that she's clever?"

"A wrong 'un," said Masters promptly. "Cold as ice, and something more. I know the sort. Nesta Payne, that we hanged eight or ten years ago, was like it; only she hadn't got the abilities or advantages of this lady. That sort don't commit murders, as a rule. But they stand by and watch murders being done—ah, and they never break down afterwards, like the more human kind. I admit this alibi is sound, but I don't like it. Sounds too arranged and well-prepared beforehand. If Mrs. Derwent stood to gain anything out of Keat-

87

ing's death, I'd begin to look for the man behind her. . . ."

"She does stand to gain by it," said H.M. "I dunno how much Keating left, but it must be a couple of hundred thousand at least. And she bags the lot." Briefly, and with surprising conciseness, he told of the interview with Derwent. "Now draw whatever deductions suit your whiskers. But for the love of Mike, Masters, don't go jumpin' to conclusions before you've even met Jem Derwent. Hey?"

"You ought to know, sir, that I never jump to conclusions," declared Masters. H.M. looked at him, but Masters was dogged. "Though that gives me several ideas, which I'll keep to myself—like you. But Derwent! Derwent! Why, I heard something about that gentleman only this morning."

Masters was now clumping up and down the room with a curiously pigeon-toed walk. He shook his head as he glanced at H.M.

"No, nothing to Mr. Derwent's discredit. Quite the contrary, it makes him look more like an honest man. I heard it from the Assistant Commissioner this morning, when I was being officially put in charge of this case. The fact is, Mr. Derwent has been trying to reopen the Dartley case. Just so. He's got a theory, it seems. He's been at the Yard three or four times in the past month trying to get our file on Dartley. Something to do with an idea that a few times in the past the very respectable firm of Benjamin Soar & Son have been suspected of selling fake antiques."

From the way in which Masters looked at H.M., Pollard suspected that this was bait. But H.M. made no response, except to say:

"And they also told you, doubtless, that they were shovin' Philip Keating down here to me. Interestin' study, Philip. I say, Bob, you might read out to Masters a transcript of the more salient points in Philip's story." While Pollard read, H.M. watched the chief inspector with sour amusement. "I don't think you're going to jeer so much at the idea of the Ten Teacups as a secret society now; eh, Masters?"

"That's as may be, sir."

"Meanin' nothin'. Oh, well. You see the intriguin' part?"

"Too many of them, and all questions," Masters decided. "Either there is a secret society called the Ten Teacups, or there isn't. Either Mrs. Derwent is a member, or she isn't. Either Gardner had a row with Keating, or he didn't. Either Gardner took the gun away from Derwent's house on Tuesday night, or he didn't. . . ."

H.M. was disturbed. "Either it'll rain tomorrow, or it won't. No, no, son. You can make a problem out of anything on earth if all you do is make a statement and then give the converse of it. This business surely ain't as complex as all that. No, I meant the interesting part: the character of Philip Keating. Don't you agree, Bob?"

"Keating?" said Pollard, surprised. "You mean Derwent, don't you?"

"So you don't agree? Well . . . now," said H.M., muttering. "For the sake of argument, suppose you give me your impressions of him in a thumbnail character-sketch."

The sergeant considered. "I'd call him more of a type than anything else. Pleasant, at least on the surface. Cautious. Likes to be thought of as a Friend of the Family. Prides himself on brusque manners, but probably a little indecisive. He might swindle you, but I doubt if he'd murder you. Loyal to the people he likes. He's clearly fond of Frances Gale, and just as clearly he hates Mrs. Derwent—"

"Yes. Then why," said H.M. obstinately, "did he murder her?"

There was a silence. The other two stared at him, while H.M. stirred with ghoulish mirth.

"Why did he murder Mrs. Derwent? No, my lads. I don't mean in real life: I mean in the one Murder game they did play at Derwent's house on Tuesday night. You remember, the Gale gal told us they did play one short game at the party, before Mrs. D. complained of a headache and went upstairs? Uh-huh. Philip Keating was the murderer, and the corpse was Mrs. Derwent. He caught her on a couch in Jem's den, and strangled her with the noose. —I say, Masters, did you ever play that parlor pastime called Murder?"

The chief inspector intimated that he had better things to do than to fool about like that. He plainly thought H.M. was off on another digression. "And speaking of Miss Gale," he pointed out, "hadn't we better have her up here? She's downstairs, and she won't talk to anybody but you, for some reason—"

"Y'see, I got a childish mind," explained H.M., ignoring this and staring into space. "I do like playin' it. And there's one thing about it I've always observed. If you're the murderer in that game, you never murder anybody except someone you like or that you're pretty intimate with. Why it is I dunno; I'm just statin' the fact. There don't seem to be the same homely, happy feeling about murdering somebody that you dislike or

89

that you don't know. People shy away from it; I never knew anybody in a game who bumped off a person he didn't get on with in ordinary life; and they'll shuffle round half the evening before they do it. Say I'm wool-gatherin' again, if you like. You probably will. But if Philip Keating honestly dislikes Mrs. D., then why, burn me, *why* did he murder her?"

Masters grinned.

"Bit too subtle for me, I'm afraid. Maybe it's one of these repressed desires you read about in the papers. Come, sir! If you've got anything more practical—?"

"No. Just one more kink, son. Why is our friend Philip so certain his cousin Vance was murdered with some kind o' mechanical device?"

This struck Masters, in the phrase, where he lived.

"Mechanical device?" he demanded. "What about a mechanical device? What mechanical device?"

"Ho ho. Your old hobgoblin with the thirty-nine tails, ain't it, Masters? *I* don't know. It only struck me as very, very rummy that right in the middle of Philip's talk he should come out with the statement about a mechanical device. It didn't seem to fit into the smooth run of his character. It didn't seem like him. But, of course, I may be wool-gatherin' again. Hey?"

"But, blast it—! Look here, Bob, have you got that postmortem report?" Masters hesitated. He took the report, studied it, and returned it to H.M. Something in the report appeared to interest H.M., so that Masters eyed him dubiously. "Any leads? So far as I'm concerned, it looks as though the thing's settled. He *was* shot with that .45. Mechanical device! You mean some sort of gun-trap that might have been rigged up, so that he pulled a string or something, and shot himself? But would it shoot him twice? Would it shoot him in different places? And where in lum's name is it?"

Again the chief inspector looked at H.M. suspiciously.

"Odd, sir. Very odd that you should mention mechanical devices. I don't mind admitting it'd occurred to me. Now, I don't go in for fiction much; but I once saw a trick in a play —practical as paint. It was a gun-mechanism concealed in a telephone receiver. The bell rang; victim picked up the receiver; receiver opposite the side of his head; bang! Shot over the ear, and not a sign of a murderer. Just so. Consequently, I admit I've been thinking a bit about that gas-bracket. . . ."

"Gas-bracket?" roared H.M., sitting up. "What gas-bracket?"

A very faint grin began to creep over Masters's face, though he tried to keep an air of bland innocence.

"Hadn't you noticed it? Hum! I should have thought you'd have noticed it—"

"Masters," said H.M., "you been holdin' out on me, just the same as you always do. So you're up to your old tricks again, hey? Burn me, I'm not goin' to stand for this! Nothin' delights your soul more than to do me in the eye—"

"Well, it's what you always do to me," Masters replied philosophically. "Now, sir, no call to go off the deep end like that! I'll just call your attention to that attic room, if you please. You remember it's got a low ceiling; eight or nine feet at the most?"

"I suppose I got to listen to this. Well?"

"And you saw," pursued Masters, "that there sticks down from the ceiling a straight length of gas-pipe, without a fixture or anything, but ending in a lead plug? Just so. Now, this pipe isn't in the center of the room. It's more towards the door, like. Fact is, it's very close over the exact spot where the body was lying." Again the chief inspector eyed him keenly. "I like to keep these little things to myself, until I've got some sort of case. But there it is. Rum fact, sir, but the size-round of an average gas-pipe is about the same as the barrel of a .45 revolver. Eh?"

H.M. looked at him with real curiosity. "I say, son. Were you so burnin' eager to do me in the eye that you didn't pull the thing out of the ceiling and have a good look? 'The Gun in the Gas-Pipe,' by H. Masters. You got a romantic soul. Also, if there was any trap like that, who obligingly shoved the lead cap back on the pipe after it was used?"

"Oh, Cotteril's attending to that today," Masters grinned, and then became serious. "Mind you, I don't say it *is* true. Especially as it's upset by the report that the .45 really was used. But I'll give you another tip that you mayn't have noticed. Smack under that gas-pipe there was a powder-burn on the carpet. Eh?"

There was a sharp and rather angry knock at the door. The door opened, and Frances Gale came in.

CHAPTER ELEVEN

Nobody's Hat

THE SUBJECT was closed as quickly as though someone had shut down a lid, and Masters became his bland self again. Frances Gale stood looking from one to the other of them, her chin up. Though she seemed willing to meet apologies half way, still there was about her a certain defiance which might have been embarrassment. Today she looked older, and paler, and curiously more swashbuckling: possibly because of a tilted blue hat.

"If this is another kind of third-degree," she said coolly, "I don't like it. I won't wait any longer. You promised to play fair, Mr. Masters. My father told me that *you*—" she looked at H.M. accusingly—"would play fair. He—he was going to bring me here with a whole crowd of solicitors, or something. But I couldn't stand that. I ducked out of the house while they were still arguing."

"I sorta thought Bokey would send you round here," admitted H.M., who for some mysterious reason seemed uncomfortable under her eye. "But if you'd like to get a few things off your mind—"

"I think you're beasts, all of you," said Miss Gale. "But I'm ready to tell you what you want to know, if you must know it."

"Now, miss, if you don't mind my saying so, that's the real spirit!" applauded Masters, with broad and deceptive heartiness. Masters bustled round to get her a chair. At the same time he casually took Janet Derwent's cigarette-case from his pocket. "Sorry to have kept you waiting so long, but you understand how these things are." He extended the cigarette-case. "Will you have a cigarette, miss?"

She regarded it coolly, but with a heightened color.

"Oh. That's the case you found under poor Vance's body, isn't it?"

"Straight in the eye, son," observed H.M. drowsily. "The women are unlucky for you today."

"Now might I ask, miss," pursued Masters, pulling himself up, "how you know that? I didn't say anything about the case to you yesterday. The report isn't in the papers this morning."

"My dear friend Mrs. Derwent phoned all her friends about it this morning. Even including me." For the first time since they had known her, a twinkle of life and amusement, almost an impish look, appeared in her brown eyes. "What's more, Mr. Chief Inspector, you don't scare me any longer. That's one I've got on you. I know all about how you tried to make violent love to her in the car last night—"

"Honest to God, Masters, did you?" inquired H.M., turning his head with interest. All Masters's iron self-control was required now.

"No, sir, I did not," said Masters, with bursting calmness.

"I don't suppose you did, really," the girl conceded. "Poor Mrs. Derwent says that about everybody, whether they do or whether they don't. Even about poor Philip. But all I've got to do is just to *think* of you in that car, and what you were supposed to have done and all, and—well, you don't scare me any longer. I know what you want to know. You want to know whether my fingerprints might be on that cigarette-case. Yes, I should think maybe they are."

"Ha ha," said Masters. "You intend to confess to the murder, miss?"

"Don't talk like that, even as a joke." She looked at him sharply. "One part of dear Mrs. Derwent's story is true, anyway. Vance certainly had the case on Monday afternoon, after he'd had tea with her. I know, because I saw him afterwards, and I handled the cigarette-case."

"That's a bit odd, miss. I seem to remember reading in one of the papers my wife takes—*The Christian Family Guardsman,* or the like—that you were one of our finest young lady athletes because you didn't either drink or smoke."

Again she looked at him.

"I don't, usually. Though I have wine sometimes. But it wasn't to smoke. I found the mirror in my compact was broken. (And it *did* bring bad luck, as I told my father.) I was fussing about it, and Vance handed me that polished cigarette-case that's as bright as a mirror, and said, 'Here, use this.' When I saw whose case it was, I thought he'd done it deliberately, and I was going to throw it in his face. Oo, I was furious! But he didn't mean anything by it. Vance was just—like that."

At the mention of the cigarette-case in this capacity, a curious expression changed the wrinkles in H.M.'s forehead. He reached over and took the case from Masters. He studied it. But he did not speak.

"Now, miss, let's get down to it," the chief inspector went on. "I asked you two questions yesterday, and you chose to fly off the handle. Kindly answer them now. First, you denied that you were driving past Berwick Terrace yesterday afternoon in a blue Talbot, and looking at the house where—"

"Of course I denied it. You know why, don't you? Since you've talked to dear Mrs. Derwent, I suppose you know it all. I was spying, that's what I was doing."

"You followed Mr. Keating to Berwick Terrace?"

"Yes. That is—I hadn't intended to, at first." She looked miserable: less, Pollard thought, from grief than from humiliation. Her finger-nail dug at the arm of the chair. "I drove round to Lincoln Mansions, where Vance lives, to—see him, and find out what was wrong. He was just going away in a taxi. When I saw him go to that house in Berwick Terrace, I didn't know what to think. So I drove round a few more streets, and came back. Some other man—" she glanced briefly at Pollard—"was just going up the steps, and I *couldn't* make it out."

"Did it surprise you to see Mr. Keating going to an empty house?"

"No."

"Why not, miss?"

She made her fingers walk along the arm of the chair with some concentration. "You had another question, Mr. Masters. You asked me yesterday why I got the keys and viewed that house three months ago. I didn't *want* to view the beastly place. I never even wanted to go near it. But saying that was the only way I could get the keys from the agents, so I could get in. Because of course I couldn't explain the real reason—"

"What was that?"

"Mrs. Derwent sent me," replied Frances Gale, her jaw growing mutinous.

"I told you I'd only known her six months," she went on, after a pause. "And I didn't know her quite so well then. But I knew why she'd sent me directly after I went there, the old cat! You see, about every three months or so she gets a spell when her—her soul grows sick, or something—" Frances made a face—"and she lies up in bed, very queenly, and tries to hypnotize herself, and talks about her lovers. Well, once when I was there she suddenly sat up, as though she'd fallen into a trance, and began talking about letters. She said she'd just remembered. She said that in the house where they'd moved from (Berwick Terrace, you know) she remembered that she had left behind some letters in a secret hiding place. She said she couldn't bear the thought of someone moving into that house and finding the letters. She said—oh, she went on *awful!*

"I was a bit frightened. Yes, I was. She made me promise to go and get the letters for her immediately. At first she thought she had the keys to the house, which she'd never given back; but she found they weren't there. So she asked me to go to the house-agents. . . .

"And do you know why she did it? I got the letters, all right. It was because several of them were from Vance. Of course she knew I would read all of them, the old cat."

She brooded on this; but, all the same, she seemed relieved to tell it at last. H.M. laid down the cigarette-case.

"Uh-huh. Quite a wench. But that's not the part of it we're most curious about. You say these letters were tucked away in a secret hidin' place of some kind. Have I got any reason for a belief that this hidin' place was somewhere in or around an old brown divan in the attic?"

"Yes, you have. It was rather a favorite of hers. She told me she used to lie on it and have—all kinds of dreams. There was something about it, she said." The girl floundered. "Anyhow, the letters were in the divan. You see, it's hollow."

"Hollow?" repeated Masters, getting very slowly to his feet.

"Not exactly hollow. But half of it opens on a hinge. I don't mean it opens out like a bed, because it's big enough for a bed anyway. But it opens just that way, and there's a space inside where you can store pillows or blankets or anything like that. You'd never know the hinges were there, either. . . . I say, what's wrong?"

"Now just one minute, miss!" urged Masters, waving his hand at her like a mesmerist. "Do you mean there's a space big enough for somebody to hide inside that divan?"

"No, I don't think so." She looked startled. "That is, not unless the person was very tiny and as thin as—as a pillow. No, it wouldn't do. Besides, the person would smother."

Nevertheless Masters, with a muttered oath, had already reached after the telephone to ring up Inspector Cotteril. H.M., undisturbed, continued to pull at his corncob pipe.

"I don't think it's as easy as that, son," he said. "I'm like the gal; I don't think any murderer could have slid away inside there. But there might be somethin' interesting in it. . . . I say." He contemplated Frances Gale. "You've been answerin' a lot of questions you refused to answer yesterday. Now that we're all gettin' along well and smoothly, would you like to take anything back?"

"Take anything back? I don't understand."

"For instance," said H.M., making a drowsy gesture, "you told us that, from your certain knowledge, your friend Gardner didn't and couldn't have pinched that Remington revolver out of Derwent's house on the night of the Murder party."

"Well?"

"Does it stand?"

"It does, absolutely!" cried the girl, clenching her hands. "I wish you'd stop! You're making Ron a kind of—of dummy, or scapegoat, or something. He didn't, I tell you. He didn't, he didn't! Why don't you go and ask him? He's at Lincoln Mansions this morning. He . . . who says he did take it?"

"Philip Keating. By the way, Masters, I think we'd better have Friend Philip back up here."

Masters had finished his telephoning, and H.M. gave the necessary instructions. The girl remained quiet and defiant. Studying her, Masters opened the valise he had brought in. On H.M.'s desk he put down the soft gray hat inscribed inside with Philip's name, and the .45 revolver. Though she flinched a little at the sight of the pistol, she made no comment. Keating, entering a moment later, was plainly surprised to find her here, and showed some traces of apprehension.

"Frances, old girl," he said with subdued heartiness, "I haven't had a chance to see you and tell you how sorry I am for you in your great—"

"Oh, bah," she said, and turned on him, flaming. "Philip Keating, I want to know what's got into you recently. You don't seem like yourself. You seem queer. You seem funny. Did you tell these people that Ron Gardner took that gun—" she pointed at it—"home with him on Tuesday night? Philip Keating, you know perfectly well he didn't. I should think *you* at least ought to tell the truth—"

"So that's what it is," observed Keating, suddenly alert. Again Pollard noticed his rather cold eye. "Well, gentlemen?"

Masters introduced himself, while Pollard could have sworn H.M. was asleep. "Now, sir," said the chief inspector, "we appreciate your suggestion about—hum—a mechanical device killing Mr. Vance Keating."

He paused here, as though waiting for the bait to take effect; but Philip only nodded with polite watchfulness, and Masters had to go on.

"But to the best of our knowledge it was done with this gun. *This* gun." He held it up. "Can you identify it, sir? Just so. Now, you have stated that Mr. Gardner took it home with him on Tuesday night."

"Just one moment," said Keating. "I don't see that all the blame for this should be put on me. To the best of my belief and knowledge, he did."

"Did you actually see him take it?"

"No. But Mr. Benjamin Soar told me he did, and why should Ben Soar lie?"

A slightly altered tone had come into Keating's voice, and also into the proceedings. It may have been that he wondered what they had been talking about in his absence; or it may have been some other reason. Philip Keating no longer wore his manner of confidential heartiness. The round, honest-shining face was polite: no more than that. He had taken a small penknife out of his pocket, and was mechanically opening and shutting the blade as though to find work for his fingers.

"Suppose, sir, we confine ourselves to things you saw for yourself," said Masters briskly. "When did you last see this revolver?"

"At the Murder party, on Tuesday night. About eleven-thirty. Or thereabouts."

"How can you fix the time?"

"The party was breaking up. We were going home. Derwent asked us all whether we wouldn't take a quick one for the road. We said we would, and so we went out of the drawing-room, and back to his den. I can tell you this: at that time the gun was lying on the mantelpiece. I saw it."

So far, Pollard noted, Philip Keating's story of Tuesday evening agreed with Derwent's. Again the blade of the pen-knife clicked.

"Just so. And who was the last out of the drawing-room?"

"Derwent. I think he closed the door. —Well, dash it, I see you're looking at me; but there's not much else. We went back to Derwent's den and *had* a drink."

"Yes, sir. And then what?"

"Well, in the middle of it, Miss Gale got upset, or something, and went out to her car. Ron Gardner followed her."

"Just one moment. While you were all in the den together, did any of you leave the room before Miss Gale left?"

"No. We were only there a couple of minutes."

"How long after Miss Gale had gone did Mr. Gardner follow her?"

Keating looked puzzled. "I can't say. Half a minute, or a

97

minute, maybe. I advised Ron not to go. I said, 'Look here, old boy, when they get like that, the wisest policy's to let 'em alone.' Let sleeping dogs lie. But he went."

"Alone?"

"No, Derwent went with him out to the front door."

"So that, if Mr. Gardner took the gun, he must have taken it between the time he left you in the den and the time he went out of the house with Mr. Derwent?"

"I suppose so. I didn't see them." Keating hesitated; he seemed to find Masters's heavy, impersonal relevancy somewhat disturbing after H.M.'s wanderings. "Do you still want more? Yes, of course. That left Soar and myself in the den. Soar went out after Derwent and Ron; he was leaning in the doorway. I followed him, to get my hat. I thought I'd left my hat in the dining-room, so I went to the dining-room after it. But it wasn't there. When I came out into the hall again, Soar was just coming out of the drawing-room door up at the front of the house. That was how I knew."

"Knew, sir?"

"Yes, knew. Soar said to me, he said, 'Confound that fellow Gardner; he's taken the pistol after all.' I asked him what he meant. He said that earlier in the evening Ron had promised to lend him the gun for some sort of display, and Ron said he could take it along with him that night. And then Soar said, 'But he's taken it with him, after all. I wonder if he's trying to insult me?' He pointed into the drawing-room. And sure enough, the gun was gone off the mantelpiece. That's all I know. Soar went out the front door, and I went to the coat-closet in the hall and found my hat at last. Soar was pretty mad about it, I can tell you that."

Masters considered. Philip Keating shut up the penknife with a final click, and put it away in his waistcoat pocket.

"You tell us, Mr. Keating," Masters went on, clearing his throat, "that Mr. Soar said, 'I wonder if he's trying to insult me?' What did he mean by that?"

"Oh, no, that's all right. That's Soar. He's Welsh, you see. Touchy. Proud as Satan. Full of this imagination-stuff. —Not but what Ben hasn't got his head screwed on the right way, mind you! He must have a little gold-mine in that business of his. He's got a manner that would float any company in the City: inspires confidence. Fine head and nose; that sort of thing."

Masters suddenly took on an attitude of broad tolerance.

"Lots of meat in your story, sir. You'll admit—from what you've said—that Mr. Soar himself could have nipped up to the drawing-room and taken that revolver himself while you were looking for your hat in the dining-room. Eh?"

"I suppose he could have. Not that I think he did, mind you."

"Just so. About this dining-room, sir: is it on the same side of the hall as the drawing-room?"

"Yes. Oh, I admit I couldn't see the drawing-room door. But—"

"Has it a communicating door with the drawing-room?"

"Yes. Why?"

"Only a suggestion, Mr. Keating, at which I know a gentleman of your intelligence won't take offense," Masters told him with assurance. "But if you couldn't see Mr. Soar, he couldn't see you either. You might have nipped into the drawing-room and got that revolver before he got there."

For a moment Philip stared at him. Then the convulsion of a chuckle began in his plump stomach, traveled up the ridges of his waistcoat, and animated his plump face to such mirth that tears came into his eyes. He opened one eye, and chuckled. He shut both eyes, and guffawed. But all he said was:

"Well, I didn't. I was at a cocktail party yesterday afternoon; I can give you names and addresses, if you like. At least, I hope I can prove I was there."

"I'll have those names and addresses in just a moment, *if* you please. But may I ask, sir, what it is you find so funny about the question?"

"Me being a murderer," said Philip.

"Often difficult to realize, of course. Now, Mr. Keating, I understand you eventually did find your hat at Mr. Derwent's? Exactly. Was it this hat, for instance?" inquired Masters, lifting the gray one from the desk.

"No."

"You'll have heard from the Commissioner that this hat was worn by Mr. Vance Keating shortly before he was shot. As a matter of form," said Masters, handing it over, "will you identify it as yours?"

Philip turned it over in his hands. He looked inside it. He put it down on the desk.

"I'm afraid I can't identify it, my lad," he said in a worried tone. "It certainly doesn't belong to me."

99

There are certain things, H.M. argues, that investigators have a right to expect in a case, and therefore they are led into error. For example, they do not expect truisms to collapse or chairs to run away from them when they try to sit down. But H.M. also says that it was at this moment he learned his lesson, a lesson that aroused his torpid wits and did something to put him right. Chief Inspector Humphrey Masters, however, was not concerned with philosophical ideas just now.

"I can't help it," insisted Philip Keating, replying to the Now-then-let's-have-no-more-of-this-nonsense look on Masters's face. "It's still not my hat."

"You admit it's got your name in it?"

"I couldn't very well deny that," said Philip, grinning. "But what of it? When you go into a shop to buy a hat, they don't ask you for your ruddy birth certificate in order to print the name you give 'em. What's more, I never had my full name printed inside a hat in my life. Just initials. That's all. Somebody's trying to put up a game on me: you can see that for yourself."

"Can you explain how anybody could have been putting up a game on you, when Mr. Vance Keating himself was wearing the hat earlier in the afternoon?"

"No."

"And you admit that this hat fits you?"

"It's my size, if that's what you mean. But if you'll come over to my flat with me, I think I can prove it never belonged to me." He appealed to the girl. "I say, Frances, you can confirm me. You've known me a long time. Did you ever know me to wear any kind of hat except a bowler?"

"No, I never did," she declared emphatically. "Except a top-hat, that is. It's quite a joke among us, Philip and his bowler."

Masters tapped the desk impressively.

"Come, now, sir! I'd like to remind you that finding this hat in the same room where your cousin was shot does *not* mean any suspicion attaches to you. Please understand that. We've heard he lived in the same building as yourself. We've heard he borrowed things—"

"Thanks. I know all that," said Philip. "Now listen! When I heard a hat of mine had been found in that room, it didn't surprise me. I told the Commissioner so. I thought it must be mine. So use your common sense. You yourself admit that

100

no suspicion attaches to it. Well—if the hat really belonged to me, why in blazes should I deny it?"

They looked at each other blankly. H.M. said it was time for a drink.

CHAPTER TWELVE

Valet's Mishap

LINCOLN MANSIONS, Great George Street, was a new and craggy block of flats showing white against the green trees and gray dignity of Westminster. Overpowering heat made it look still more somnolent when H.M., Masters, Philip Keating, Frances Gale, and Sergeant Pollard arrived there. But clouds were piling up: Masters enlivened the journey with speculations as to possible rain. And they had more luck than they anticipated. As they entered the foyer, the hall-porter saluted Philip.

"I hope it's all right, sir," he said. "Mr. Gardner and Mr. Soar are waiting for you upstairs. I thought you wouldn't mind—"

Philip said it was all right. But he looked uncomfortable. That Mr. Gardner and Mr. Soar were actively awaiting him became evident when the lift took the visitors up to Philip's flat on the fourth floor, and Philip opened the door. A long and rich hall ran through the flat. From an open door on the left they heard someone speaking to a telephone.

"—she said he did that?" inquired the voice. "Yes, but look here, Derwent, with all due respect, you know Jane. . . . Yes, I admit it'll give us all a fair chance to state our cases. If we have a council of war here, and then go on to Scotland Yard in a body. . . . But what else did the fellow do? . . . He put his hand under her—*W-h-a-t?* Go on! I don't believe it. The old rip. What was the fellow's name? Coster? Oh, Masters. Chief Inspector Masters. Yes. Well, if he—"

In the somewhat dim hall, Pollard could see only the back of Masters's neck. But Pollard was beginning to feel some sympathy for the man. Masters might well feel that a final point of bedevilment had been reached. That his superior officer did not swell and burst Pollard simply remembered as a fact. But Masters went with a heavy-footed clumping down the hall, and looked through the doorway.

There were two men in the room. One sat at a telephone

table, the other on a sofa looking up with interest from a magazine. It was a polished hardwood shell of a room with concealed lighting, and sharp-angled chairs covered in blue cloth. Both men glanced up as Masters appeared in the doorway; and Pollard had a look at them as though they had been caught by a camera.

At the telephone sat a burly young man in his late twenties, as of an athlete run slightly to fat, with a square and rather handsome face, and a friendly looking jaw. His cropped mustache was of a darker color than his light brown hair, both having what can only be called a woolly effect despite close cutting. He was deeply tanned; and a light, amiable eye looked up over the telephone. His sports hat was old, and his flannels disreputable. Pollard—correctly selecting him as Ronald Gardner—began to understand why most people had difficulty in connecting him with murder. But that, the sergeant reminded himself, meant nothing.

As for Benjamin Soar, Pollard could understand why Philip Keating had spoken of him as inspiring confidence. You could trace it to no individual look or feature. As a matter of detail he was short, he was thick, he had dark hair and wore rimless glasses: it was even marred by a sensitive quality behind reserve. But it was there. Though he seemed to enjoy the telephone conversation as much as Gardner, his amusement was internal, and showed in a slight alteration of the mouth, a slight shift of the eyes behind the thin glasses, rather than in Gardner's chuckles. But at Masters's appearance he became quiet again, and the eyes narrowed.

"Hullo!" said Gardner.

"Ur!" said Masters, or some indistinguishable noise of the same sort. "Good day, gentlemen. I hope I don't intrude. I have to inform you that I am a police-officer from New Scotland Yard—"

It was plain that Gardner's nimble brain divined Masters's name even before the chief inspector had spoken.

"—and that I am Chief Inspector Masters, that you were speaking of a moment ago—".

"What a man!" said Gardner, in quite genuine admiration.

"—and I should like to warn you, sir, that I must ask you some questions which I *squick*, which I—"

"Well, you don't waste any words, anyhow," said Gardner. He had got up from his chair, but he sat down abruptly again. "Hey, what's the game? Keep off, can't you? You're

102

crowding me into the wall. Will somebody take this lunatic away before he gets violent?"

"Easy, son," interposed H.M.'s heavy, sleepy voice, with such sudden authority that everyone turned to look at him.

"Hello, boys," continued H.M. "He'll be himself in just a minute, but *I* got to warn you that even the patience of the police has its limits, and that this story about Mrs. Derwent has gone far enough. By the time you've finished tellin' it, you'll have Masters chasin' Mrs. Derwent down Piccadilly in her garter-belt. If we're goin' to do any lying, as I expect we all are, let's do it fair and square."

At the entrance of Frances Gale, with Philip behind her, Benjamin Soar had got to his feet. Soar showed himself as a squarer, stockier figure, with a curiously bristly look: if you could imagine the popular conception of a Wild Man shaved, scrubbed, and civilized, with hair-oil on his black hair, and rimless eyeglasses, and a gravity of good manners—that (Pollard thought) would convey the impression.

"You will be Sir Henry Merrivale," said Soar pleasantly, in a heavy baritone voice. "Derwent told us to expect you. Yes, that seems a fair enough proposition. At least this little encounter has had the effect of breaking the tension, and that's something to be said for it. We needn't begin by telling you how bad a business this is, or how we feel about it. Any friend of Mr. Keating knows how we feel. Maybe the best thing would be to get down to business at once."

"That suits me, sir," agreed Masters, who was himself again. He turned round. "Ah—maybe I pressed it a bit too hard. But am I right in assuming that you're Mr. Gardner?"

"Yes," said the burly young man with the woolly hair. "And look here: it's my fault, Inspector. I shouldn't have given you the raspberry like that. But you caught me off-guard. What's more, you didn't need any fire and thunder in my case; if you don't think I've got the breeze up already, you're not the detective I take you for. What in the name of hell am I supposed to have done?"

"If you people will just make yourselves comfortable, and excuse me," interposed Philip Keating, "I'll see about getting some drinks—"

Masters held up the valise he was carrying.

"Just a moment, Mr. Keating. We shall want you for this." While Masters established his tribunal, H.M. lumbered over to the sofa and sat down beside Soar. H.M. fiercely shushed Frances Gale, who seemed about to speak, and sat her down

103

on the sofa beside him. Masters opened the valise. "Now, **Mr.** Gardner—this revolver. It belongs to you. Eh?"

Gardner took the gun somewhat quickly, as though he had been waiting for it. But he opened the magazine, took out one of the cartridges, and examined it.

"Come along, sir! You don't have any doubt about it, do you?"

"No, it's mine all right. Derwent says this was the one used to— But it wasn't the gun I was looking at: it was the ammunition. These are the old Remington 'ducks.' You can't get 'em anywhere. The last time I saw this thing, it was loaded with blanks."

"Oh? But it was not loaded with blanks on Monday night, was it?"

"*Monday* night? Yes."

"Suppose I tell you, sir, that we know there were real bullets in this revolver on Monday night?"

"Then you're a cock-eyed liar," said Gardner, with deplorable lack of manners, but with flat candor. "Because that's when the blanks were put in. I bought a box on my way over here. Was that when you mean?"

"I mean last Monday night, when you and Mr. Vance Keating had a row about Miss Gale down in Mr. Keating's flat; when he threatened to make you confess; and when he shot at you with that pistol."

"So that's it," said Gardner abruptly.

He remained looking at the past: his shoulders a little hunched, his powerful wrists hanging out of his sleeves, his hand running along the barrel of the gun.

"Believe it or not, I thought of everything except that," he went on. "Of all the wild, crazy, twisted interpretations—" With a sudden quick gesture he put the pistol down and added: "Poor devil."

There was a pause. In those last two words there had been such bitter sincerity (or it may have been irony as well) that even Masters hesitated. It compelled belief.

"I say, gents, let me butt in here," growled a heavy voice from the sofa, where H.M. had been inspecting each person in turn. "Unless I tell him what really did happen down in Keating's flat, Masters ain't goin' to believe you, son—and you know it. Let me see if I can lead you a little way along the road. You came here to see Keating on Monday night. He probably invited you to dinner, hey?"

"Yes, that's right."

"But *was* it about me?" said Frances Gale from the sofa, and caused a little sensation. It pulled Gardner up short; but he winked at her jovially.

"If people hereabouts will kindly shut up—" said H.M. with austerity. He looked at Gardner malevolently. "You and Keating had already arranged to go to a Murder party at Derwent's on Tuesday night. And at this party Vance Keating was goin' to act as the detective? Uh-huh. Don't interrupt. And Keating, whatever else he was, was a lad who liked to show off. If he was goin' to be the detective, he meant to take jolly good care he pulled off a brilliant and accurate piece o' detection. Burn me, how they'd gasp! Wouldn't they? Especially Mrs. Derwent. *So he was goin' to cook the whole thing up in advance.* It's human, Masters. It's awful human. . . .

"I dunno the exact details of the scheme. But I've got a suspicion that the cards were to be hocussed so that you—" he looked at Gardner—"were to be the murderer. You—" he turned to Frances Gale—"were to be the victim. The finale was to be somethin' spectacular, like a play. 'And when I've got you in a corner, I'll make you confess,'—by some means or other. Say what you like, Masters; but I repeat, it's awful human. . . ."

Masters turned round slowly.

"Are you trying to tell me, either of you—" he said.

"A rehearsal," grunted H.M. "Sure. Y'see, Masters, it didn't seem at all likely that a man would carry on a denunciation of somebody, involvin' his own fiancée, while his valet was peacefully servin' drinks from an adjacent side-table, and the hotel waiter was standin' interestedly in the doorway waiting to tell 'em both that their dinner was ready. It didn't even seem likely that Keating would ring up Gardner, and tell him to step over to the flat and bring an out-of-date .45 revolver, just so that Keating could threaten his life with it. That fancy pistol looked like a stage-property. So did the whole general excitement."

"Thanks," said Gardner. "That's just what happened. Don't take my word for it. Ask Bartlett and Hawkins. What I can't understand—"

"I'll remind you, sir," persisted Masters, "that—at least, according to our information—a shot was fired and a glass was smashed by it just the same."

"Just a minute." Gardner went to a house-telephone and spoke briefly to it. "Now, Inspector. It was like this. We hadn't any intention of using the gun in the actual Murder.

I was to kill Frances with a tin dagger. Vance rang me up on Monday afternoon. He said to come over here for dinner, and bring my fanciest-looking pistol with some blanks. When I got here he explained the great scheme, and showed me the dagger.

"I suppose you've heard how elaborate this game was to be. It wasn't merely the where-were-you-at-such-and-such-a-moment sort. According to our rule, the murderer *must* leave a material clew which, properly interpreted, would lead straight to him. . . ."

H.M. opened his eyes.

"That's interestin'," he said. "I say, son, I find the background of this thing more suggestive than the explanation of it. H'm. The murderer must leave a material clew—Who suggested that little frill?"

"I did," answered Benjamin Soar.

He spoke with a sort of grave amusement, and he did not elaborate.

"Yes, but that'd take a whole heap of ingenuity, wouldn't it? I mean, leavin' a clew that would point to the murderer with proper thinkin'-out, and yet wouldn't blow the gaff the minute the detective saw it?"

"Oh, we're ingenious people," said Gardner with a disarming grin. "Judge for yourself. This was to be another 'left-handed' murder. Now, I'm not left-handed in real life, and everybody knows it. The point was for the detective to *prove* left-handedness on somebody. When I 'killed' Frances, she was to be lying down with her hands holding the dagger against her at such an angle that the detective would deduce left-handedness. That, of course, didn't prove anything. He tests all the suspects—and finds they appear to be all right-handed. He gets to the climax slowly, after long questioning. Then . . . well, I'll show you. Inspector, I see you're wearing a collar-pin?"

Masters was fuming. "I don't see the point of all this, and that's a fact. Collar-pin! What about a collar-pin?"

"You know: like a glorified safety-pin under your necktie. You stick the point of the thing in one side of your collar, and pass it through, and fasten it on the other side." Gardner spoke with lumbering earnestness. "Look at your own! You're right-handed, aren't you?"

"Yes, sir, I am right-handed. But—"

"Right. That means you'll always shove the point, when you put it on, through the right-hand side of your own collar.

And the *head* of the collar-pin (put your hand up and feel it) will always be on your own right side, while the *fastening* is on the left. Anybody could see it. But that was the point of our game. The collar-pin I was to wear at the Murder party was to have its head on my left and its fastening on my right; turned just the wrong way round—proving that I was left-handed, and that I committed the murder."

Nobody spoke, while Masters fingered his collar.

"I know I shouldn't be talking like this," Gardner said, rather shamefacedly. "But a garbled version has got round, and I've got to show you how Vance was working up to a sky-rocket ending. That's how he came to get excited. He always did. He was going to whip round on me with the gun, and make me put my hands up to the collar-pin, and—I warned him not to wave the thing about. So did Bartlett, his valet. You see, it was only loaded with blanks, but there's a hard wadding in a blank cartridge that'll put out somebody's eye if it hits 'em. You'll have noticed what kind of barker it is. That gun was made for a Western bad man who had to shoot sudden and on a split-second: in other words, she's a hair-trigger; and she goes off if you look crooked at her. Vance's arm swung round and hit a lamp-standard when he was reeling off his dramatic speech, and of course his finger was on the trigger. The wadding out of the blank missed me, but it made hay of a cocktail-glass where Bartlett was pouring out drinks. No gun made nowadays could go off like that, but there used to be plenty of accidents with the old style. And there you are."

Masters stared at him.

"It would strike me, sir," the chief inspector argued ponderously, "that none of you can be called too careful. Do you mean he suggested, and you agreed to, the use of a dangerous weapon like that? A weapon that might go off and injure somebody—"

"Give me credit for some sense. No, of course not. Ordinarily it couldn't possibly have hurt anybody. Try to fire it now, and you'll see. It has to be *cocked* first: nobody ever thinks of that, in this day and age. That was why we were yelling at him, because Vance did have the thing cocked. He would. Er—sorry." Gardner corrected himself, and added in a milder tone: "I'll tell you something, Inspector. When I first heard of this business. . . . I mean—you know—the real murder. . . . I thought it might have been another accident. I even thought Vance might have done it himself, because who in the world would kill *Vance?* But then I heard there were two shots, and I knew it couldn't have been an accident or a mistake. Once with a cocked gun, yes. But between the first and the second shot somebody had to pull the hammer back again, and that means it was deliberate."

For some reason, Pollard thought, the mere idea of cocking the gun seemed to give added brutality to the murder. Murder in actuality had come into the room with them now, and they all realized it. He glanced round the group. Since the beginning of the conversation Frances Gale's face had been pink; once she had made a move to get up and go, but H.M. had restrained her. Philip Keating seemed restless but relieved. Benjamin Soar had taken a cigarette from a box at his elbow, had lit it with care, and was engaged in blowing smoke over a down-drawn under lip of such thickness that again it gave him that curious resemblance to Primitive Man.

Masters reflected. "Well, sir, if what you say is true—and I admit you'd be a first-class foolish 'un to lie about something that could be proved by the valet and the waiter—that's all very well. But where does it *get* us?"

"Lord love a duck," said H.M. with sudden energy, "do you think it's only clearin' away rubbish? No, my lad: not by a long way. It's the most illuminatin' and stimulatin' discourse I've heard yet. Let's take one or two little points." He peered at Gardner. "You were quite right in sayin' your group is an almighty ingenious lot. That little trick of the left-handed collar-pin was one of the better ideas. Who thought of it?"

"Vance himself," answered Gardner. "I tell you, a lot of people have underestimated his cleverness. But look here: let me ask *you* a question. Derwent was telling me you were having all sorts of sinister suspicions of me. That was pleasant news. So help me Harry, it never once occurred to me that the reason was this Murder-game scheme on Monday night! And what I still don't understand is how any such mixed-up version ever got about. I didn't suppose either Bartlett or Hawkins would keep quiet about it, but they both know what really happened—"

"It wasn't either of 'em, son." H.M. inclined his head ponderously. "It was Mr. Philip Keating there. He also was present, in a way."

Philip came forward with bouncing earnestness.

"Ron old man," he said, "I owe you an apology, in a way, and I know you'll understand no offence was meant. But what

I say is, fair's fair; the law's the law; and a man's got to tell them what they want to know, or where would the government be?"

Gardner blinked. "You saw us? Never mind the government; where the devil were you?"

"Out in the hall, old man. I didn't see you, and I didn't hear you very well; but I ask you, man to man and no nonsense, how could I know you were up to any such foolishness as that? It never even entered my head. Of course, I suppose I ought to have come in. But after all I thought you three were enough to handle Vance if he got violent—"

"All right; you don't need to look so cut up about it," said Gardner. He studied Philip with an amusement which grew to a roaring chuckle. "There's no harm done. Here! Is that why you were looking so mysterious at Derwent's on Tuesday night? And why you—"

He glanced over towards the girl, who did not return his gaze.

"Let's keep to our beans and potatoes, son," suggested H.M. "Again about Monday night. After you'd rehearsed the star-turn you were to put on for the benefit of the Murder party, what did you do?"

"Well—Vance was in a pretty gay good humor. We got sozzled."

"Disgusting," said Frances.

"Undoubtedly," said Gardner with heavy politeness.

"But you say he was in a gay good humor. Keen on the next night's game?" insisted H.M. "And that's confirmed by Derwent's statement, Masters. I dunno if you recall but Derwent saw Keating on Tuesday morning, and Keating was still devilish keen on it. Burn me, you can bet he was! Now, Masters, observe where we've got to now. The wheel returns; the snake returns; we've been foot-sloggin' round through all kinds of brambles and all kinds of theories, and every time we go straight round in a circle to the same old question. Why did Keating suddenly refuse to attend the Murder party on Tuesday night?"

H.M. hunched his neck into his collar.

"Masters, it's growin' to bigger and bigger dimensions. It's begun to haunt me. There was no reason in the world why he shouldn't have attended that party, and every reason of vanity and enthusiasm why he should have. Yet between morning, when Derwent saw him, and afternoon, when Miss Gale 'phoned him, he sailed off in another direction. I tell you now, you're not goin' to get much forrader by pounding that question of who stole the gun. The scene has shifted. What we want now is a full account of *Keating's* movements, conversations, and interviews (if any) on Tuesday. We ought to learn a lot about it from his valet; the valet's the man I want to see. . . . But, meantime, did any of you besides Miss Gale or Derwent see him on Tuesday?"

There was a pause.

"No," replied Gardner, smoothing his cropped mustache. "I saw him on Wednesday, yesterday, though: only a couple of hours before he was killed. I was downstairs in his flat."

Philip Keating nodded. "That goes for me too, Sir Henry. I rang him up from my office once on Wednesday morning, and again on Wednesday afternoon. But I didn't see hide or hair of the poor chap on Tuesday."

"Any other candidate?" prompted H.M. With some difficulty he twisted round his neck in its formal collar, and looked at Soar.

"Something leads me to believe," said Soar, "that the whole line of this questioning is directed towards me." He squashed out his cigarette in an ashtray; he folded his arms; and he peered round with saturnine good-humor. "No: believe me, I'm not trying to evade the question. I'm only wondering."

"It's like this. In Keating's murder, son, there are three material clews—"

"Just as there was a deliberate material clew in the projected game of Murder?"

"Sure. You got it. The more so since none of the clews, at first glance, seems to make much sense. First, there's a cigarette-case. Second, there's a highly intriguin' and inexplicable hat. Third, there's this. Gimme that valise, Masters."

Masters swung the valise over to him, and H.M. opened it. Out on his lap he spread the Milanese cloth of gold woven into the pattern of peacocks' feathers. More than ever in these surroundings you might realize what a thing of beauty it was. It came with a note of the barbaric into Westminster, of dull gold lights and the profusion of the Gothic.

"As even the newspapers will have told you," rumbled H.M., "the teacups were found on this. I was talkin' to Derwent last night, and he told me a very rummy thing about it. He said that on the day before Keating died—which must 'a' been Tuesday—Keating bought this little exhibit from you under terms of great secrecy and hush-hush. Derwent said you mentioned the fact to him yourself, on Tuesday night. I don't suppose Jem Derwent would manufacture a lie out of thin air: he's much too clever a feller for one thing. But something about the way he said it struck me as peculiar. Have you got anything to tell me about it?"

CHAPTER THIRTEEN

Cloth of Gold

SOAR TOOK another cigarette out of the box at his elbow.

"Yes, I'm afraid I have, though I don't know what it means and I'm not sure I want to know. —By the way, may I ask what struck you as peculiar about anything Derwent said?"

"Now, sir, if you'll excuse my reminding you," Masters broke in, *"we're* here to ask the questions. So if you'll just—"

"It's damnably important, Inspector," Soar told him. He struck a match, and the hairy backs of his hands shielded his face as he lit the cigarette. "However, what particular question do you want me to answer?"

"Did Mr. Keating buy that cloth from you?"

"In one way, yes; in another way, no." He smiled. "Steady, Inspector! Before you crowd me into a corner as you did our friend Gardner, let me explain. I'm trying to tell you the literal truth; and that, I've observed from a close study of criminal cases, is a thing lawyers and policemen never seem to understand. On Tuesday (that's the day you want, isn't it?) someone purporting to be Mr. Vance Keating rang me up at my office, and said he wished to buy this article." Soar touched the rich folds of the cloth. "He wanted it sent immediately, he said, to Mrs. Jeremy Derwent at 33 Vernon Street."

"Notebook, Bob," Masters said briefly to the sergeant. "This is business."

H.M. scowled. "You say 'purporting to be' Keating. So you doubted it was Keating?"

"No, not exactly. That's another yes and no question. I was not surprised. He was an impatient sort; he often did business by telephone—"

"Lummy, yes! He bought a whole house," said Masters,

111

brooding on this, "only a few hours before he was killed. Well, sir?"

"—and he and Mrs. Derwent had both looked at that particular article, and admired it, in my galleries only a week or so before. There you are, gentlemen. Any other considerations were, frankly, none of my damned business." Soar's forehead wrinkled as he raised his eyebrows; there was a slight film over his eyes. "I sent it by personal messenger, my assistant Mr. Wyvern, to 33 Vernon Street. Wyvern later told me that he gave it to the maid at the door. Only one thing bothered me. I was not sure it was Mr. Keating's voice."

"Why not?" asked H.M. softly.

"I don't know. It seemed an *older* voice. And I don't say I doubted it consciously at the time; it stuck in my mind, that's all. By the way, since you like definite times, I received the call at one o'clock. I was just going out to lunch. When I returned from lunch I decided to make sure. So I telephoned to Keating under the pretext of making sure I had delivered what he wanted, and the rest of it. You will guess what I heard. Keating had never made any such phone-call, or asked for any such purchase."

"So? Bit embarrassin', wasn't it?"

Soar made a sound resembling, "Pluh!"—his first sign of animation—and the smoke split in weird eddies round his face.

"Yes, for both of us. I'm afraid that at first he thought I was trying to insult him, or play some game. Naturally I was annoyed. He said that, since the article was delivered, under the circumstances he would prefer to buy it. *I* said that under the circumstances it was not for sale. There was a foolish kind of wrangle, ending in his urging me . . . yes, I know it sounds fantastic; but there it is . . . not to 'lower him' in Mrs. Derwent's eyes, and to let it appear as though he had sent it. I agreed, provided he would accept it at half its actual value."

H.M. blinked. "H'm. When you mentioned the sale of the cloth to Derwent on Tuesday night, did you tell him about that part of it? He said you talked about the sale 'in passing.'"

Soar was amused.

"You have the reputation of being an intelligent man, Sir Henry. I don't think I need even answer that. I no more talk about purchases 'in passing,' especially confidential purchases, than a doctor talks about his patients' kidneys or a hotel-keeper asks to see the marriage-lines of 'Mr. and Mrs. John Smith.' "

"Another realist?"

"No, Derwent is the realist. My private philosophy is a trifle different. —But you don't want to discuss that. I did mention the fact that Mr. Keating had bought the Milanese cloth, yes. I made hints that he might interpret as he liked. You understand why. An expensive, senseless, and possibly dangerous hoax had been played on Keating and myself. Who asked for this cloth to be sent to Mrs. Derwent? And for what purpose? I wanted to find out whether Derwent knew anything about it—don't misunderstand me!—to find out, that is, whether he knew it had been delivered to her at all."

"And did he know about it?"

"No. Or, at least, he said nothing about it to me. I am also willing to bet," said Soar quizzically, "that he said nothing about it to *you*."

It was Masters who intervened here, before H.M. could speak.

"Stop a bit, sir! We don't want to get away from the one good solid piece of evidence we've got. If the cloth was definitely in the possession of Mrs. Derwent before Mr. Keating was murdered—well, you can see what that means. Straight contributory evidence. Eh? Just so. You tell us that your assistant took it to the house and gave it to the maid. And the maid gave it to Mrs. Derwent?"

Soar regarded the tip of his cigarette. "I should certainly think so, Inspector. But I didn't see it; and I can't do your work for you."

"It may be my work," said Masters, "but at the same time it was your tablecloth. Didn't you at least try to find out anything about it from Mrs. Derwent herself? Why didn't you ask her?"

"I did," said Soar imperturbably. "That was why she went upstairs with a splitting headache at half-past nine."

At this point Pollard was conscious of an impression that these two seemed to be speaking in louder tones. Possibly it was because both had heavy voices, but also it was because everyone else in the room sat so quietly.

"Oh, ah? So that's why it was," muttered Masters. "It's —building up the picture, as it were. Yes, sir, but what did she *say* to you about it? It seems to me there's a mix-up and mystery right here where there oughtn't to be one. That's to say, you could have asked her, 'How did you like the nice tablecloth?' You could have said that without being indiscreet, because it came from your shop. And she would have said, 'My, wasn't it good of Mr. Keating to send it to me!'—or something. Like women do."

"That's just the point, Inspector. She didn't say anything; she got a headache. You're quite right: that's why I thought the whole thing looked so queer, and why I tackled Derwent himself about it." Soar frowned. "I understand that you—er—have had some experience of Mrs. Derwent. Can you understand that she said nothing at all?"

This was a facer, and even Masters tacitly admitted its truth, though he was not satisfied. Soar turned to H.M.

"I hope I've answered Derwent's suggestions about the Milanese cloth and about me," he went on. "I don't know whether it does much to answer your particular question as to why Keating didn't attend the Murder party on Tuesday night. Tell me: does this upset about the cloth seem to you a sufficient cause why he should have stayed away?"

"No," said H.M.

"Nor to me. We are speaking now as men of the world; which, I find, is very different from speaking as human beings. You can see now the extent of Keating's infatuation with Mrs. Derwent. If he were so blindly taken with her charms that he would let an unpleasant hoax stand rather than admit he had not ordered a present for her—"

Without a word, without a sound, Frances got composedly to her feet and walked with her free stride towards another door of the room. She seemed even to walk slowly with deliberate intent; but, when she was within a pace or two of the door, she began to run. The door closed after her.

"I beg your pardon," said Soar very quietly. "God help me, I wish I could beg hers properly."

Ronald Gardner spoke without taking his light eyes from Soar. "Very fine, isn't it? We seem to have got things a bit tangled up. That was very pleasant hearing for her."

"Did you stop me?"

"No; I—I forgot. You've got a way of talking and making people listen. . . ."

"Especially myself. Well, go and comfort her. There may be others who would like to do it."

"Thanks," said Gardner curtly, "I will."

He strode out after her. This passage-at-arms had been so brief and unexpected that nobody knew what to say; it showed a new side to Soar, who had spoken between his teeth. H.M., like a very learned owl, made no comment. But Masters went after the obvious lead.

"Sir Henry's told us," said the chief inspector, "that he doesn't care who stole the pistol from Derwent's on Tuesday night. But I care about it. Ah—apropos of what's just been said, sir; and in spite of Mr. Gardner's explanations; do you still think Mr. Gardner was the one who took the gun? He might be, you know."

"I am quite certain he didn't," replied Soar, raising his eyebrows. "What makes you think that?"

Philip Keating walked over towards him and spoke sharply. "Look here, Ben, don't deny you said it. To me. I'm getting a bit tired of being put in the wrong, and having the police think everything I say is a lie. You said to me, as plain as paint, 'Confound that fellow Gardner; he's taken the pistol after all. I wonder if he's trying to insult me?' Or something. I've tried to play fair with everybody—"

"It is conceded," Soar told him, "that your intentions are good. Your only trouble, if you'll pardon my saying so, is that you're the world's most inaccurate reporter. I've noticed it before." The remark about the "insult" seemed to sting him. "I do remember saying something of the kind. What I added to it was, 'No, he couldn't have, because it was in the drawing-room on the mantel at half-past eleven, and he hasn't been in there since.' You see, Inspector, I was standing in the door of Derwent's den when Derwent went with Gardner to the front door."

"Well, I can't be expected to remember everything," growled Philip. "I was going after my hat. Somebody had hidden my hat. At least I'm certain about what people did."

Soar ground out his cigarette. It had grown darker in the room; shadows moved across the wide windows; and the clouds were thickening at last for that storm, delayed day after day, which should end the heat. Pollard thought he heard a vague mutter of thunder, which stirred the glass fittings of the flat.

"Now there I'll contradict you again," Soar said mildly. "The police have probably asked you about it. You're not certain what *I* did, for instance. You can't swear I didn't steal the revolver—just as I can't swear you didn't. And just as none of us can swear it wasn't taken by (say) Mrs. Derwent, who seems to have been generally overlooked for the curious reason that she was under nobody's observation at any time after half-past nine."

"I'll say this for you, sir," observed Masters, in an off-hand tone: "you're a cool one."

"Or take another instance. For the time of the murder of Keating, it happens that I haven't got an alibi. That's unusual. I'm nearly always to be found at number 13 New Bond Street all afternoon. But yesterday I left earlier than usual, at four o'clock. You see, I am moving house. It seems to surprise you, Inspector; but people do change their lodgings sometimes. I left my office, I walked, and no one saw me. That means I'm guilty, or I'm innocent, just as you like to interpret it."

"Mr. Soar," said H.M. abruptly, "what d'you think of the case yourself?"

His use of the proper name appeared to surprise even Masters.

"About my own guilt? That's up to you." Soar grinned. "At the present moment I may be sitting here in a cold sweat of funk while I joke with you, walking on swords and terrified every second that I'll slip, because I killed Vance Keating. Or I may be innocent and serene. Or I may be innocent, but so nervous that I babble like this. It's up to you. And you may never know which."

"No, son. I didn't mean that. I repeat: what do you think of the case?"

"Let me answer that with another question, Sir Henry. Do you believe in the devil?"

"No," said H.M.

"Ah, that's too bad," observed Soar, wrinkling his forehead as though H.M. had spoken of missing a good book or play. "You should have been at Derwent's house on Tuesday night, and I think you might have changed your mind. I don't say you would have, of course. Some people are materialists, like Derwent."

"Uh-huh. Was the devil there?"

"Yes. I don't mean Auld Clootie. I don't mean an operatic bass in red tights. I don't mean the versatile personage in our popular proverbs, who does so much: who quotes Scripture for his own ends: who finds work for idle hands to do: who takes care of his own—in fact, from that description, you might imagine that the devil was standing for Parliament on the Labor platform. No. I mean The Devil. If you don't see the difference, perhaps you feel it.

"You, Inspector, still seem to wonder why I couldn't get any kind of answer at all from Mrs. Derwent when I questioned her about this." He lifted the cloth of gold, which glimmered and rippled. "I'll tell you when and how I asked her. I couldn't get an opportunity to speak with her alone; we were all in the same room. I knew the only opportunity I might get would be during a game of Murder.

"Now follow me. The lights were put out for that short game of Murder we played just before nine-thirty. We began to wander about in the dark. That's when I knew there was something stirring, or moving, that wasn't in the cards we had drawn. Under that roof in the dark were roaming six intelligent, ingenious people, all fascinated by crime; and the devil was with them. It's an impression hard to analyze, but I know it. I've seen it in Pompeii, and I've seen it in the carving of a Florentine cup, and I've seen it in the face of a suburban housewife. I tried to follow Mrs. Derwent. It was bright moonlight; you could see shadows; but I lost her.

"I came on her unexpectedly, when I wandered into Derwent's den. There are two windows, with those Victorian lace curtains. They let in a little moonlight, but not much. Over in a corner by one of the windows there's a padded Victorian sofa. When I saw it I turned cold inside. Mrs. Derwent was lying on that sofa with her head towards the window. Her head was propped up a little; and there was a running-noose round her neck with the knot under her ear; and she was looking at me with her eyes wide open."

You could now hear not a sound in the darkening room except Soar's voice.

"Of course, gentlemen, the physical mechanics of it were plain. Someone had 'murdered' her there in the game; and she was waiting the stipulated number of seconds before she 'screamed.' But I didn't see the physical mechanics of it. It was exactly like a dream in that it had the same half-lights, the same half-tones, the same muffled quality: or prophecy. I said to her, not loudly: 'You have a friend who sent you a fine gift this afternoon. How long have you been accepting presents from him?'

"I don't want to exaggerate. But I've since had an impression that I've never been nearer death than I was at that moment. Wait! Don't misunderstand! The danger was *not* from Mrs. Derwent: she had had nothing to do with it: she was like a beautiful doll or dummy: and the threatening thing, or person, or what you like, was somewhere behind me.

I said a few more words, and she did give the signal that brought the others in. The lights went up; it became an ordinary room again."

The sharp ringing of the flat's doorbell in the hall, at this moment, shook off the somewhat hypnotic effect of Soar's voice. Values altered and shrank. The commonplace was further restored when Philip Keating went to the door, reporting that Alfred Bartlett, manservant, and W. Gladstone Hawkins, waiter, were here and ready to be questioned; furthermore, that a note for H.M. had been sent from Whitehall by Miss Ffolliot.

"We don't mind a ghost story now and then, sir," Masters said to Soar, genially. "Sir Henry and I are used to 'em. But as evidence—no. I must warn you, too, that Mrs. Derwent has a strong alibi for the time of the real murder."

"I think I went out of my way, Inspector, to explain that I did not intend to implicate Mrs. Derwent."

"You like her?"

"Quite well."

"And Mr. Derwent? What about him? He seems a very close-mouthed gentleman; and, just between ourselves, I should like to know what he was doing yesterday afternoon at five o'clock. . . ."

"*I* can tell you what he was doing," offered Soar, and grinned broadly.

"Yes, sir?"

"He was sitting in the offices of the Commissioner of Police."

It was one of the few times when Masters permitted himself, while on official business, to swear. He said only one word; but he said it violently, and Soar's polite amusement did not lessen. The very faint thunder again stirred the glass fittings of the flat; it had now grown so dark that it was barely possible to see. Masters looked at H.M., who was tearing open the envelope of the message Lollypop had sent.

"You're quite right," Masters told him. "Somebody *is* laughing at us. . . . Are you sure of what you say, Mr. Soar?"

"No. Unfortunately I wasn't with him. But I don't think Derwent would lie in such a case. You may have heard that he's been trying to reopen the Dartley case."

"Just so; the Dartley case. I was coming to that. Now, sir—" Masters pointed his finger—"doesn't it strike you as odd that when Mr. Dartley was murdered the teacups had peacocks' feathers painted on them; and when Mr. Keating

118

was killed that cloth had peacocks' feathers on it; and that both things came from your shop?"

"Certainly it strikes me as odd," replied Soar with some asperity; "but I can't explain it, if that's what you mean."

"Did you ever hear of a secret society called the Ten Tea-cups?"

Soar looked up sharply. "The old lead again, Inspector? No, I admit I never encountered it, but I shouldn't be at all surprised if there were such a thing. I've heard fragmentary reports—"

"Any kind of reports will do," said Masters. He glanced in some suspicion at Philip Keating, who nodded doggedly, and then back to Soar. "It's like this. What bothers us is to know what all this flummery *means*. If it does mean anything, that is. The peacock's feathers, and the refraining-from-smoking, and especially these infernal teacups. We've heard about a 'religious' society. But what have teacups got to do with it?"

"Can't you hazard a guess?"

"Not a guess. It's too—hurrum—domestic for me, sir. Where's the harm, or the meaning, of a teacup? You say 'teacup' to me, and I think of a nice fire at home, and a good cup of tea with plenty of sugar and milk, and—ordinary things. Nothing to do with danger, or murder, or the like. Now if it'd been something like that ugly-looking silver box Sir Henry and I once found at Lord Mantling's. . . ."

"Exactly. There," said Soar, pouncing, "there, Mr. Masters, you show the school boy's imagination. I was afraid of that. You can't think of the sinister except in terms of crossed daggers or gory hands. But think again. Do you know anything about the history of tea?"

"History of tea? No. Except . . . stop a bit! . . . that report on the teacups from the South Kensington Museum. I've got it here somewhere. 'They are not, of course, teacups, since tea was not introduced into Europe until the middle of the seventeenth century.'"

"It won't do, Inspector. What your informant means (as any work of reference will tell you) is that tea was not *in general use* in Europe until then. Pepys's famous remark caused some of the confusion. It was brought to Europe from China when China began to trade with Portugal and Italy in 1517: which would make the date of the cups reasonable. Its use did not spread. Don't you realize that what to you is a pleasant, everyday article was once thought of as a secret,

119

dangerous, and exotic drug? Don't you know what a fuss was kicked up about it in England even as late as the early eighteenth century? One medical writer swore it was as bad as opium. Even today, don't you know the powers of bringing hallucinations that used to be attributed to green tea, or Le Fanu's story of the man who used it?"

Masters had gone a somewhat different color.

"Here, I say!" he protested. "You're not going to tell me, sir, that back in the sixteenth century a group of Italians got together and formed a secret society just to drink tea like a lot of maiden ladies at a sewing-circle? I don't believe it."

"Does it shock your romantic soul?" inquired Soar, hitting the nail on the head so exactly that Masters grunted. "Well, be comforted, Inspector. It was a very different kind of tea from any you know. If I'm right in my assumption, it was green tea flavored with opium. Have you read Gardner's travel-book, *The Romany Patteran?* In upper Brazil he found a small Portuguese colony, very ancient and inbred, who had such a practice. I don't know what secrets may have crept out of Lisbon or Milan or Toledo four hundred years ago, to turn up in holes and corners of modern London. I don't know about the Ten Teacups, or what rites they may have practiced. But I do know this. From 1525 to 1529, the first being the date when those Majolican cups were made, the Inquisition was unusually active in southern Europe. On no less than four occasions, batches of ten people—five women and five men—were condemned to be strangled and burnt, with no details of their trials given out. Think it over."

Pollard glanced over at H.M., who had not spoken a word since he had received that letter sent across from his office. H.M. was sitting with his hand shading his eyes, so remote from anything Soar had been saying that even his immobility was disturbing. He took his hand away from his eyes.

"I must 'a' been asleep," H.M. said. "Masters. Bob. Out in the hall with you. I want a word."

Wheezing, he lumbered out into the hall of the flat, and the other two followed him. H.M. shut the door behind them. He held out a note which was marked in his secretary's handwriting, "It came in the first post this morning, but you wouldn't open your mail. I thought you had better have it." Gray light through a window at the end of the hall showed them the typewritten words, and drew from Chief Inspector Masters a sound like a snarl.

THERE WILL BE TEN TEACUPS AT NUMBER 5B, LANCASTER MEWS, W. 1, ON THURSDAY, AUGUST 1, AT 9:30 P.M. PRECISELY. SIR HENRY MERRIVALE IS INVITED AT A DEMONSTRATION, WITH ANY GUESTS HE MAY CHOOSE TO BRING.

Pollard could see no more, for the window darkened; without thunder, without preliminary, with only a sudden impact of rain, the storm tore down.

CHAPTER FOURTEEN

In Which Documents of Importance are Put Before the Reader

TOWARDS SEVEN o'clock that evening, when Pollard climbed aboard a bus to join H.M. and Masters for dinner at H.M.'s favorite tavern, the *Green Man* near St. Bride's Church behind Fleet Street, the town was still a blur of rain. It fell solidly, without fuss and without any slackening, as it had been falling all day. Sergeant Pollard, soaked, pulled himself up the steps to the top deck of the bus, got himself into a corner, and again studied his notebook.

There was a certain piece of evidence he had read twice already. But he meant to read it again as often as should be necessary until he understood H.M.'s comment on it—for H.M. had declared, with some fervency, that it contained several points indicating the solution of the problem. It was not sensational. It was an account of Vance Keating's movements from Tuesday morning until Wednesday afternoon; and, though there were suggestive points in it, Pollard could not find in it anything like a foreshadowing of the solution.

It was headed *Testimony of Alfred Edward Bartlett, valet.* Pollard thought of Bartlett, as H.M. and Masters had questioned him at Lincoln Mansions early that afternoon. Alfred Edward was a lean, grizzled, elderly man with a lean and crooked nose, but with a calm and positive manner. He did not, according to the tradition of valets after murders, look shifty; he looked capable and reliable. The first part of his statement, taken with that of W. G. Hawkins, was merely verification of Gardner's story about the collar-pin device for the Murder party. Bartlett stood easily, his strong white hands folded, and never raised his voice. Pollard picked up the thread of the questioning:

Q: (*by Masters*) —finally, you tell us that when Mr. Keating's arm hit the lamp-standard, the gun went off and the wadding from the blank cartridge broke the glass on the tray you were carrying?

A: Yes. It hit the glass not an inch above my hand. That was why I dropped the tray on the table.

Q: How far was Mr. Keating away from you then?

A: About as far as I am from you now. (Six feet? Seven feet?)

Q: From where you were standing, could you see the door to the hall?

A: Yes, I could have seen it, but I was not looking at it.

Q: So you did not see Mr. Philip Keating there?

A: No.

Q: What did Mr. Vance Keating and Mr. Gardner do after this?

A: They had dinner. Then they started drinking and talking.

Q: Did they drink a lot?

A: Yes, a fairish amount.

Q: Were you in the room at this time?

A: Yes, they made me stay up and drink with them. I used to be a barman and I can mix any drink in the world.

Q: Did Mr. Keating say anything about the Ten Teacups, or about an appointment for Wednesday?

A: No, I am sure he did not or I would have noticed it.

Q: Did he say anything about any other people in their group: I mean, anything that would help us to find out who killed him?

A: Not anything particular that I remember. He talked about them, but nothing particular.

Q: Did he seem to be on good terms with all of them?

A: Yes, very good terms. Oh, once he wanted to ring up Mrs. Derwent on the telephone and talk to her, but it was half-past one in the morning and we stopped him.

Q: Did he talk much about Mrs. Derwent?

A: Nothing more than usual.

Q: Come, now, none of that! What did he say about Mrs. Derwent?

A: He said he was going to make that bitch come across if it was the last thing he ever did in the world.

Q: What did Mr. Gardner say to that?

A: Mr. Gardner said it was all right now, but he would have to stop playing about after he was married. Mr. Keating said, "That's right, that's right," and they shook hands five or six times, and had another drink on it.

Q: But mightn't he have said something you didn't overhear?

A: I do not think so, because I was with them until Mr. Gardner left. Mr. Gardner insisted on walking downstairs instead of going by the lift. They are those curved stairs that none of the drunken gentlemen can resist walking down. Mr. Keating said he would go along. I went along too, because I did not know whether they could manage it and I was afraid they might start singing in the halls.

Q: Now, about the next morning, Tuesday morning. I want to hear about every visitor, phone-call, or letter he had. Was there any mail that morning?

A: No.

Q: What time did Mr. Keating get up?

A: About ten o'clock. That is, he woke up about ten o'clock, but he did not get up until nearly one. He stayed in bed with a wet towel on his head, groaning. Mr. Derwent came to the flat to see him.

Q: What time did Mr. Derwent get here?

A: I think it was a little past eleven in the morning.

Q: Was it usual for Mr. Derwent to come to the flat?

A: No, it was the first time he had ever been.

Q: What did they talk about?

A: I don't know. Mr. Derwent went into the bedroom to see him, and the door was closed.

Q: Did you overhear anything?

A: Not a word.

Q: But did it seem a friendly sort of interview?

A: Well, yes, as far as I could judge. Mr. Derwent certainly seemed all right when he left.

Q: What about Mr. Keating?

A: Yes, he seemed cheerful enough.

Q: Did Mr. Derwent say anything that you over-heard as he was going?

A: Yes, he looked over his shoulder and said some-thing to Mr. Keating in French. I think it was French. I do not understand French. Mr. Keating said some-thing back in the same language.

Q: Did Mr. Keating have any other callers?

A: No, not all day. About half-past two, I think it was, Mr. Soar rang up about a gold shawl or something.

Here, Pollard noticed, the witness completely verified Soar's story, so far as it could be verified by one listening to only one side of the conversation. Bartlett agreed that his employer had never ordered any such article from Soar, and had certainly not put through any call to Soar at one o'clock. It was a strong point in the art-dealer's favor.

Q: Did Mr. Keating make any comment to you about this?

A: No.

Q: But how did he seem? Angry? Upset?

A: Yes, rather angry.

Q: What happened then?

A: He had a Turkish bath at the flat. There is a steam-cabinet fixed up in the bathroom. Then was when I first heard he was not going to the Murder party at Mr. Derwent's that night. I asked him whether he would dress formally or informally. He said never mind which, because he was not going.

Q: (by H.M.) Didn't that surprise you?

A: Very much.

Q: Why did you think he had changed his mind all of a sudden?

A: I supposed it was because of the difficulty with Mr. Soar about the shawl.

Q: Did that sound reasonable to you? If somebody played a hoax on him by ordering the shawl in his name, and having Mr. Soar send it to Mrs. Derwent in his name, wouldn't he be more likely to go to Mrs. Der-went and find out what it was all about?

A: I do not know. That was none of my business. If you do your job well, you do not think about anything your employer does and then you do not get into trouble.

Q: (*by Masters again*) Were there any other messages that day?

A: Miss Gale rang up late in the afternoon, about five. I do not know what they talked about. I was mixing an after-Turkish-bath cocktail in the kitchen, and Mr. Keating answered the phone.

Q: How did he spend the evening?

A: At home. He sent me out to buy half a dozen detective novels, and he spent the evening reading and listening to the wireless.

Q: Was he usually as home-loving as that?

A: No, but he did it sometimes.

Q: Finally, about Wednesday—the day he was killed. . . .

A: I was coming to that. Wednesday morning he received a letter that seemed to excite him a good deal.

Q: Did you see the letter?

A: Naturally not, but there were two keys in it. One looked like a front-door key and the other just an ordinary door-key.

Q: You think they were the keys to 4 Berwick Terrace?

A: I suppose so now. That is none of my business. You asked me.

Q: What did he do?

A: He fidgeted about all morning, and at noon he said he had got to go out. Just as he was going out—

Q: Wait. Look at this hat, gray Homburg, size 7¾, with the name "Philip Keating" inside. When he left the flat on Wednesday, was he wearing this hat?

A: No, he was not. It is not his hat.

Q: What hat was he wearing, then?

A: None at all. He seldom wore a hat in the hot weather.

Here, Pollard remembered, a wrangle had taken place. They had been questioning Bartlett in the living-room of Philip's flat, with all other witnesses excluded. But Philip himself was brought in to hear this part of it. Inquiries all over the building brought the hall-porter of the flats into the discussion: the hall-porter declaring that, when Vance Keating had come downstairs in the lift about noon on Wednesday, he had been wearing a gray hat. Nevertheless, Bartlett was not to be shaken in his positive declaration as to Keating's having left the flat bareheaded.

Q: Could he have picked up the hat somewhere between the time he left his own flat and the time he went downstairs in the lift?

A: He might have done, but I don't know anything about that. All I say is that he did not have a hat when he left me. Anybody who says he did is not telling the truth.

Q: Could he have picked it up here at Mr. Philip Keating's?

Philip Keating: No, he could not. I tell you again, I never saw that God damned hat in my life.

Q: Were you in your flat at noon on Wednesday?

Philip Keating: No, I was at my office like any decent working man.

When Philip was got rid of, with as little fuss as possible, the examination of Bartlett was concluded:

Q: Now, we have evidence that Mr. Keating went to Berwick Terrace early on Wednesday afternoon; that he left there at ten minutes past two; that he took a cab and returned to his flat for a very brief visit about three o'clock. —Why did he come back to his flat?

A: I don't know. He was like that.

Q: What do you mean, he was like that?

A: I mean he would always dash in and dash out.

Q: What did he do when he came back here?

A: He went into the bedroom, and closed the door, and came out again in a couple of seconds. I do not know what he did there.

Q: Was he wearing the famous hat then?

A: Yes, he was. It was not what you could call becoming, and Mr. Gardner said, "Where did you get the funny-looking tile?"

Q: Mr. Gardner? He was there?

A: Yes, he came in some time before to find out why Mr. Keating had not been at the Murder party, and he waited.

Q: What did Mr. Keating say about the hat?

A: It was something foolish. I am not certain about it.

126

Q: Yes, but what was it?

A: He said the hat had magical powers. He said he had to go out again; but he told Mr. Gardner to wait there until he came back, and he would have some great news. Then out he went again.

Q: Did Mr. Gardner wait?

A: He waited until about twenty minutes to five, and then he got mad and left.

Q: Did anything else happen while Mr. Keating was at the flat?

A: No, he was there only a few minutes. Oh, Mr. Philip Keating rang up, but Mr. Keating said he did not have time to talk to him. They had a slight argument, and swore at each other a bit: but that was nothing unusual.

Q: Why did they swear at each other?

A: I think Mr. Philip Keating was trying to borrow some money. He had already rung up once before, in the morning.

Q: Can you explain how an ordinary fifteen-and-six-penny hat from Prance & Sons could have magical powers?

A: I do not think it has magical powers. I am only telling you what Mr. Keating said, and that is different.

Considerably different, Pollard thought as he closed up the notes in some disgust and stared out at the eternal twilight of the rain. The bus itself, lumbering down the slope into Fleet Street, seemed to be hooting at him. There was still the problem of Keating's sudden refusal to attend the Murder party. There was still the problem of Nobody's Hat. Not even a helpful quarrel had been recorded. The one lead towards an alibi—among the few suggestive points as Pollard saw it—proved little except doubt. Pollard had established, by corroboration of the hall-porter, that Ronald Gardner really had left the flat on Wednesday afternoon at about twenty minutes to five. It would therefore require a lot of speed for him to have got out to Berwick Terrace in time to kill Keating at five. But, granted phenomenal luck with successive Underground trains, it was just possible; and none of the suspects could definitely be eliminated.

Nor was the sergeant alone in his state of mind. Arriving at the *Green Man*, where H.M. and Masters were installed in a snug room upstairs, he found Masters raving.

"So there'll be ten teacups, will there, at number 5b Lancaster Mews?" said the chief inspector. "And they'll be there tonight, will they? Tonight? Does this maniac think he can get away with it twice on successive days?"

H.M., who had been studying a menu, put it down, and peered up at him over his glasses. H.M. looked somber; he spoke in a worried growl.

"Don't go so fast: that's all I ask. I say, Masters, have you made sure this new teacup letter is strictly on the level?"

The chief inspector mopped his forehead. "So help me, sir, I don't know what to make of you! You don't seem like yourself. You don't seem to want to ask any questions, or take any interest— Yes, it seems to be on the level as far as these murders are on the level. I found that out, while you took your siesta this afternoon. And I've got a bit of a feeling that something pretty terrific is going to happen tonight: I haven't had the feeling quite so bad since the War."

The dingy-paneled little dining-room, with its gas-lights and eighteenth-century pewter, was very warm. Even the rain, dripping thick and sluggish outside the windows, looked warm.

"Yes. I know," said H.M. "What about the house?"

"5b Lancaster Mews is in a poky little but rather swank street—all in a huddle, as it were—at the back of Park Lane. You know the sort of thing: what used to be the stables and coach-houses of the big mansions turned into private residences. The house has been empty for some time. It belongs to Lord Heyling. Lord Heyling is out of town, and we couldn't get hold of anybody belonging to him. Doesn't matter, though. I've got a search warrant; we can break in any time we like."

"Empty!" said H.M. violently. "You're not goin' to tell me that the usual load of furniture arrived there today?"

"It did. And nobody knows the name of the hauling company. Just so, sir; if you tell me it's getting a bit creepy, I'll agree with you. But why should it surprise you?"

There was a silence, while the waiter brought soup. H.M. opened and shut his big hand on the table. He said:

"Because there's no point to it, that's why! There's no point to it at all, unless my whole glimmer of reason about this case turns black and I have to start all over again. Which, you'll say, is extremely probable. Wait, now; don't hustle me, dammit! What have you done to prevent another dance of the teacups?"

"The house is watched—"

"Uh-huh. I seem to remember you did that before."

Masters glared. "Oh, ah; but we've learned a thing or two about the customer we're dealing with. And will you just tell me what other precautions you can take against a murderer who seems to be invisible? Very well. Every bolt-hole is stopped. I'm getting half-hourly reports from our men there. Nobody has been near the house all day. As soon as anyone so much as sticks his nose inside the door, we're ready to close in at any time we like. But that's not all. We're not working blind now. We know our circle of suspects. Every person under suspicion in this case has been shadowed since that letter came this morning. They won't be able to draw a breath, any of 'em, that we don't know about. . . ."

"That's better, son. That's somethin' like it."

"Our own crowd is on the job. As soon as I hear of anybody inside—" he looked at Pollard—"you and I are moving in—"

"Well . . . now," said H.M., scratching the side of his jaw. "I expect I'll be taggin' along myself."

"There may be funny business, and there may be more than one of 'em. I wish we could be armed; but of course the Home Office won't allow that. When trouble breaks loose, the English copper has got to use his hands and trust in God. Ur!" said Masters, more relieved now that he knew his ground. "I don't expect that real trouble will break loose before half-past nine, just as it says in the letter. This—this teacup maniac seems to be very neat and precise about doing his work to schedule. But we're ready for him at any time. That's what I can't understand. This chap must know we're ready. How the blazes does he think he can get away with it again?"

It was noteworthy that none of them ate much soup. They had other interests.

"It still looks fishy!" roared H.M., paddling with his spoon. "Look here: did you compare that letter this morning with the other teacup letters, to see if they were written on the same typewriter?"

"Doesn't mean a thing, I'm afraid, sir. I think I've told you before: of all the documents of any kind in this business, no two of 'em were written on the same typewriter."

"Meanin' that there may be an Organization?"

"Just as you like, sir. While you were sleeping this afternoon—or sitting and thinking if you prefer it—I've got together a few more bits of information. Which reminds me."

He turned to Pollard. "Let's hear what you've got to say, Bob. I may tell you, sir, that I sent the sergeant out to Kensington to interview Mrs. Derwent. I thought he might be a bit better at polite give-and-take than an old old-style copper like me."

H.M. looked round curiously, and Pollard shook his head. "No good in that," Pollard said. "I didn't even see her."

"Didn't even see her?" snapped Masters.

"No, sir. She's got two doctors and a nurse in the house. I asked the doctors whether they were going to certify her. They said she was prostrated with complete nervous shock, and could see nobody. They were within their rights, and they knew it. I saw the maid, though—the one who received the gold cloth from Soar's assistant on Tuesday afternoon. The maid is willing to swear she gave the parcel to Mrs. Derwent. Mrs. Derwent was then in an upstairs sitting-room. *And there was somebody with her.*"

"Who?"

"That's just it. The maid doesn't know. She didn't know there was anybody in the house at all until she heard Mrs. Derwent talking behind a closed door. The maid hadn't seen anybody come into the house or anybody leave it. Mrs. Derwent opened the sitting-room door, took the parcel, and shut the door again. And that's all," said Pollard, remembering the dreary house in the gardens. "Mrs. Derwent sent me a message, though. She said she was sorry to be too ill to see me, and she thought I ought to have some refreshment after my long trip for nothing; so how would I like a nice hot cup of tea?"

H.M. laid down his spoon.

"Smart cracks again, hey?" he demanded.

"You ought to have expected that," Masters said gloomily. "It's exactly the answer she would have sent. Now *I'll* tell you something. First, you can discard all our fancy ideas about people hiding in divans or guns hidden in gas-pipes. Inspector Cotteril has almost torn that attic room to pieces at Berwick Terrace. As for that brown divan—the one Miss Gale said had a hollow place inside it—the hollow place is just about flat. It wouldn't hold anything bigger than a picture postcard. Lummy, I wonder why a sensible girl like Miss Gale bothered us with that at all!" He brooded. "As for the gas-pipe, it's an ordinary gas-pipe. Nothing else. No flummeries in the room. No secret passages. No gun-mechanism. No mechanical device. . . .

"That's the first point. The second point is this: we needn't suspect Mr. Jeremy Derwent any longer. He's definitely out of it. He's got a cast-iron alibi."

"Then Soar was right," mumbled H.M., "when he said that at five o'clock on the afternoon of Keating's murder Jem Derwent was sittin' in the office of the Commissioner of Police?"

Masters smiled without amusement. "He was even right to a shade. He didn't say 'office.' He said 'offices.' Mr. Derwent wasn't actually with the Commissioner, but he was in an outer office trying to see him; and there's no doubt about that. It's one of the few instances I know of where Scotland Yard itself can swear to a suspect's innocence. As a suspect he is *o-u-t*, out; and at least it clears the air."

He sat back as the waiter brought them a second course that they were never to eat, and the waiter bent over Masters.

"Message for you downstairs," he said.

They all knew what it was. H.M. took out his watch, which ticked loudly as its hands pointed to a quarter past eight. Masters was not long away from the table; when he returned he was calm and almost genial.

"Get ready, sir," he said. "The car's waiting. A man has just gone into 5b Lancaster Mews."

CHAPTER FIFTEEN

The Dark Window

IT WAS not possible to see far ahead. A narrow, cobblestoned lane ran to the north. To the right of the lane were high walls like warehouse walls. To the left stood cramped houses hanging over it, all as dark as though they remained stables and coach-houses. About halfway down the lane on the right, a narrower alley pierced it at right-angles and stretched away to a dead wall. The squat, two-storied house at the corner of the lane and the alley—with a door fronting on each—was number 5b Lancaster Mews.

Some dozen yards away from this corner there was a street-lamp, which the wash of rain blurred to a mere spark of gas. Its glass box streamed; its spark was distorted by the downpour; it made faint images waver and change. If you got close enough to 5b, you could make out that the front door (with an iron knocker) gave on the lane, the side door on the alley. Not a hundred yards away was the life of Park Lane: this was one of those semi-fashionable mazes which seem more dingy than a slum. A dozen eyes watched the house, but no movement could have been heard under the multitudinous noises of the rain. In some places it fell with a flat smack, in others with a drizzle, in others with a steady splashing; but always sluggish, and like nothing so much as warm tea.

Masters kept to the left-hand wall of the lane, with Pollard behind him, and H.M. following. Pollard could barely see the shape of the chief inspector's back ahead of him; he almost bumped into Masters when the latter stopped. There was a bare alteration in the darkness, but a new voice whispered.

"All present and correct, sir," the voice said. "There are three of 'em inside now."

"Three?"

"Yes. Looks like a meeting, all right. The first one came when I got in touch with you, fifteen minutes ago—"

"Did you get a good look at him?"

"Not at his face. Not much of anything. He had on a big mackintosh and a soft hat; his head was down, naturally. He opened the front door with a key, and ducked in. I don't know whether he put a light on inside. You can't tell from here. The second man—"

"S-sst!" urged Masters softly, and Pollard thought that he held up his hand. The monotonous drip-and-splash was louder than their voices. "I thought I heard something. No, it's all right; go on."

"—the second man got here only a minute or so after the first one. Another mackintosh. He tried the front door, and poked round the windows, and then he went to the side door in that alley. I don't know whether he opened it with a key; I think so; but he opened it. The third man arrived only a little before you did: wore some sort of box-pleated cape and a soft hat. *He* was let in by someone who opened the front door—still without a glim showing in the whole house. They're up to no good, sir, I can tell you that."

"How many ways in or out?"

"Only those two doors. All the windows are covered. I've got a skeleton key that'll fit the side door. Here, you'd better take it."

"Right. Stand by until. . . . *Goddelmighty, what's the old fool up to?*"

Masters, spinning round in the dark, had almost spoken the words in an audible voice. Somebody brushed past Pollard in the dark. H.M. lumbered out slowly, a dim bulk against the spark of the street-lamp, and was walking across towards the front door of number 5b. Over the crown of his ancient top-hat (the present from Queen Victoria) he had laid a large handkerchief to protect it from the weather; and the draped effect was somewhat weird in silhouette. He trudged steadily, the handkerchief swinging. He stopped before the door of the house. He examined it. Then H.M. lifted the iron knocker, and it banged thunderously in Lancaster Mews.

Touching Pollard's arm for him to follow, Masters hurried across to the house. There was no reply to the knocking: except its own echoes, and the rain. Nothing stirred in the house. The three of them stood in a row facing the door, and Masters spoke in a blurred ventriloquial mutter.

"Are you clear off your chump?" inquired the chief inspector. "Do you want 'em to get ready for us? What's the game?"

"I had an idea," H.M. explained in the same tone.

"Just so. Was your idea right?"

"No, it was wrong," said H.M. He added: "Don't move, and don't look up. There's a window just above the door; and there's somebody's hand with a gun in it; and I rather think it's trained straight at the middle of your forehead."

None of the three moved a muscle. Pollard heard the rain beating on him, and saw trickles of it past his eyes, while they stood looking at the door. After a silence Masters joggled his arm, slipping a piece of cold metal into his hand.

"Skeleton key to the side door," said Masters. "Walk back there, get Sugden and Wright, and go into the alley. Send Banks to me. Don't hurry. When you hear me whistle, rush the side door. Banks and I will break in this one, and take him from this side. You, sir, move back against the wall when you hear the signal. . . ."

"Why waste good men?" said H.M. "Follow the old man, son."

He turned round, settling his shoulders, and waddled away from the door with a sour expression. There was nothing to do but follow him; two seconds of unhurried walking, and the three of them were in the pitch-dark alley with no bullet fired. As Pollard turned away from the door, he cocked one eye up at the window. Behind the pane he could see

133

now nothing but a grimy white-gloved hand which suddenly appeared and flattened itself out against the pane like a starfish.

Swollen gutters ran in the alley, where they took conference. "Do we," Masters muttered, "do we go in, or don't we?"

"We go in," said H.M., "but by a door where we got a reasonable chance. Have I tipped the beans all over the floor? I dunno. I didn't think there was goin' to be dirty work. Now I know there is. Try this door, son."

Pollard groped after it, a thinner door with peeling paint that might once have been gray. His finger was searching for the keyhole when he heard a faint click, and the knob moved in his hand. He knew what had happened even before he put the skeleton key into the lock.

"They've opened the door for us from the inside, sir," he said. "Have you got a flashlight?"

Masters snapped on a torch, and, as Pollard pushed the door open with his foot, Masters flourished the beam of the torch inside like a broom. Straight ahead ran a spacious passage with a low roof. It was not altogether dark: some faint illumination came from behind a door at the far end, standing a few inches open. They could see that the passage was carpeted with thick coconut matting, of a dull yellowish color. In the wall on either side there was a large niche, such as used to be found along the staircases of old-fashioned houses. In each niche stood a porcelain jar or vase with a curious top: Pollard thought of Masters's description of one set of teacups, "orange and yellow and blue, shiny-like, and it seemed to move."

Masters went swiftly down the passage, but he stopped halfway along it, and directed his light down. There were no water-stains or footmarks in the place, except one or two near the door. But halfway along, two feet or more from the right-hand wall, there was a small darkish spot on the matting. The chief inspector touched it, and held up his finger to show that it was blood. He found another and smaller spot near the door at the end of the passage.

"All right," Masters said under his breath, and pushed the door open.

The room beyond was large, and also low of ceiling. A table lamp burned between two embrasured windows at the rear, without greatly disturbing the darkness. The walls were of light brown eighteenth-century wood, cracked in places, with a number of bookshelves, and over the mantel-piece hung a portrait of a more modern old man in eyeglasses. But first of all you noticed the big chairs and divans shrouded in their close-fitting white dust-covers—for the room looked raw and disarranged, like the dust-covers.

Then they smelled the smoke of a cigar.

"Good evening, gentlemen," said Mr. Jeremy Derwent, getting up from a chair whose back had been turned towards the door. "I have been expecting you. Please come in."

For the space of possibly five seconds they stared at him, listening to the water drip off their raincoats on the floor. The elderly solicitor looked as lean and brushed as he had looked last night; his wiry white side-hair was brushed close to his bald skull; and under frosty eyebrows a pair of very sharp eyes regarded them amusedly. Again he wore a dinner-jacket. In one hand he held a cigar, and in the other a book with his finger between the pages. He was very much at home in the raw, unused room.

"Who—?" blurted Masters.

"Evenin', Jem," said H.M. in his most wooden tone. "I don't think you two have met. This is Chief Inspector Masters, and that's our notorious friend Derwent."

Derwent acknowledged this with his usual slightly pedantic style of speech.

"Ah, I am glad you have brought the police," he went on. "I told you last night, Henry, how much I regretted that we could not sit down and discuss crime comfortably over a cigar and a glass of port. And I thought the oversight had better be rectified. By the way, I have been glancing over—" he held up the book—"De Quincey's, *On Murder, Considered as one of the Fine Arts*. It is magnificent writing, of course; but I fear it contains few hints for the practical modern craftsman."

Masters wiped a wet sleeve across a wet face.

"I *will* have some sense out of this," said Masters. "Don't you think, Mr. Derwent, that you've got a devil of a lot of nerve?"

"Yes, I am afraid I have," admitted the other, considering this.

"Do you know that this house is surrounded?"

"Yes. I noticed that."

In his calmness, as Pollard had noticed last night, there was again something a trifle sinister. Masters dragged out the latest teacup note from under his waterproof.

"Well, then—did you write this?"

"Let me see it, please. Yes, this is the one I wrote. But why not take off your coats and sit down, gentlemen? It is a nasty night, and—"

"Easy, Masters," growled H.M., putting his hand on the chief inspector's sleeve. "I warn you, Jem: you better speak up and do a lot of explainin' before the rest of us get apoplexy. We've been takin' these teacup letters at their word, because this feller always keeps his word. Is there going to be a meeting of the Ten Teacups tonight? And above all are you the President or Grand Llama or whatnot of the teacups?"

Derwent put down the book in the chair.

"First of all, I can solemnly assure you that I am not in any way connected with any society of teacups. Next, there will be no meeting of a society here or anywhere else, tonight or any other time, and for a very good reason. There is no such thing."

"No such thing?" said Masters.

"I mean that it does not exist. . . . Gentlemen, forgive my little hoax. I wrote that letter, which is a sham and a delusion. But I want to show you that I had reason for writing it. It was the only way I could get this house watched, without a great deal of preliminary fuss and argument. It was the only way I could get you here quickly, equipped with a search-warrant, without a great deal of fuss and argument. Quickness was necessary, and also an effect on a certain person's nerves. I have been trying to make Scotland Yard move for many weeks: I have learned that only a sharp jab with a pin will make justice stir at all. Justice may not be blind, like a goddess; but it has flat feet, like a policeman."

"If you've brought us here on a wild-goose chase," snapped Masters, "then I warn you—"

"Oh, no," said Derwent rather sharply, and raised his cigar. "I may not be able to show you any teacups, gentlemen. But I can show you the evidence in the murder of William Dartley."

From the direction of the interior of the house they heard footsteps. A door, giving on the interior of the house, opened; and Benjamin Soar came in.

In this case there had been several encounters which produced startling results. But Pollard would never have imagined that the stocky, the swarthy, the quiet Mr. Soar could have been given such a turn. For a second there peeped out of his expression something that you might have called atavistic: certainly dangerous, and from no shaven civilization. It was gone very quickly. Soar touched the bridge of his nose, as though to assure himself that his eyeglasses were firm. He was wearing a heavy black dressing-gown.

"Hello!" he said, rather huskily. "How did you people get here? What are you doing here?"

"That, sir, is what we should like to know ourselves," replied Masters with a certain grimness. "We thought we should find ten teacups and maybe a corpse—"

"Did you let them in, Derwent?" inquired Soar.

"I did."

"—and now we're told that it was a sort of hoax," said Masters. "But I'll tell you this: we have had, and do have, very good reason to believe it's the real thing. This house, for instance. It doesn't belong to anybody, and a vanload of furniture was delivered here just as it was done when Mr. Dartley and Mr. Keating were mur—"

"What do you mean, it doesn't belong to anybody?" demanded Soar. "Damn you, sir, this is *my* house; bought and paid for. And of course a vanload of furniture was delivered here. Didn't I tell you myself this morning that I was moving house, and that's why I didn't have an alibi at the time of Keating's murder?"

There was a silence, except for the rain.

"Yes, he did, Masters," said H.M., scratching his nose. "A murder-case is the last mess in the world where anybody should say I-told-you-so; but there was somethin' awful fishy about that ten-teacup letter from the start. I say, Jem: I suppose you calculated the effect of that empty-house-and-furniture on us? . . . It would seem, Masters, it would *seem*—" he turned round with a dull, curious look—"that we have merely walked into a man's private house—"

"Which, we are told by the law, is his castle," said Soar. "I don't object to your presence here. But I can't say I welcome it, and I've had a long day. Unless you have any pressing business I think we might say good night."

"Why, sir," Masters told him with deceptive offhandedness, "I think we have some pressing business. If this is just a cozy private house, as you claim, then why was somebody standing at the upstairs window, not very long ago, in the dark, with a revolver in his hand?"

"You're drunk," said Soar, articulating the words distinctly through stiff jaws. "You're raving mad. Sir Henry Merrivale,

137

do you countenance this? Derwent, will you kindly tell this lunatic that there has been nobody in this house except us two?"

Derwent, seeming to switch his thoughts back to this, looked puzzled.

"Yes, that is true—whatever else may or may not be true," Derwent declared. "Soar and I are alone here, so far as I know."

"I have been upstairs, changing into my dressing-gown," Soar went on with the same intensity, "and I can tell you *I* wasn't standing at the window in the dark, with a gun in my hand. Who else could it have been? There aren't any servants here yet. In fact, the house isn't finished. Except for this room and my bedroom at the back, the furniture is all piled into the center of the floor. And there are light-bulbs for only two rooms, which is why it is so dark; but if you think—"

Masters held up his hand.

"Would it interest you to know, sir, that this house has been watched all evening?" he asked, and saw the sweat come out on Soar's forehead. "We happen to know that there are three persons in the house now. One of you got here at a quarter past eight, and entered by the front door—"

"That was me," said Soar. It is conceivable that, when Benjamin Soar neglected his grammar, he had received a very nasty jolt.

"The second man got here a minute or two later, and came in by the side door—"

Masters paused interrogatively, but both Derwent and Soar only looked at him.

"—with a key. The third man arrived at about half-past eight, and was let in at the front door. He wore a box-pleated cape."

"You humble servant, Inspector," said Derwent. "I affect such a cape. You will find it in the hall. And I believe Mr. Soar did let me in at the front door at half-past eight. But I know of nobody who came in by the side door." He looked round politely. "Er—perhaps Mr. Soar does?"

"No, I don't. It's rubbish. It's damned rot. If there was supposed to be anyone like that, where is he now?"

"That," Masters said, "is what I propose to find out. Because there was blood in that passage leading to the side door."

"No, you don't, son," said H.M. sharply. His big hand

138

descended on Masters's arm as the chief inspector drew out a police whistle. "Not just yet. Not for a minute or two. We know there's an extra feller in the house; we also know he can't slip away. If he's dead, he won't get out of here. If he's alive, he can't get out of here. Once you start the search and get the hounds bayin', you'll muddle up the real reason why we came here at all tonight. And I very, very much want to know that reason. . . . Mr. Soar, you got other worries."

"Blood!" Soar was saying, in such an ordinary tone that Masters's eyes narrowed. "Blood! I certainly can't explain that. And you're quite at liberty to search if you. . . . I beg your pardon. What were you saying?"

"Read this," said H.M. He took the teacup-letter and thrust it into Soar's hands.

Soar read it without comment, but at the end he looked steadily at Derwent. It was understanding; it was as though these two read each other's minds. In some ways they were curiously alike, even to their dexterity in playing with words; but Soar was the emotional and Derwent the logical; or was it by any chance the other way round? In any case it became plain that Soar was keying himself up for a great effort.

"Sit down, gentlemen," he suggested, and sat down himself on the arm of a chair across the room. The dim light shone on his glasses. "Derwent," he said, "this letter is a fake. You wrote it."

"Yes. I wrote it."

"Why?"

"That's what I want to know!" interposed Masters with some violence. He had allowed H.M. to push him into a chair, but he half rose again. "You've done a lot of talking, Mr. Derwent. But you still haven't given any good, sound, solid reason why you should have played an asinine trick that may get you into trouble, and that's got the whole C.I.D. out—"

"If you will let me explain," said Derwent, with a slight gesture of a cigar that had gone out. He leaned back in his own chair. "I think I can show you that it was the only way to obtain the proof I needed."

"Proof?" Soar prompted.

"Proof of who killed William Morris Dartley at Pendragon Gardens on the night of Monday, April 30th, 1934."

"And you think I killed him?"

"No, strangely enough, I do not," replied Derwent.

"Who did, then?"

Derwent's eyes wandered up to the portrait in oils that hung over the mantelpiece. It was that of a very old man who bore a great resemblance to Soar himself, even to the eyeglasses; but it seemed of even more savage and imaginative cast.

"I think your father killed him," Derwent said, "and I am prepared to prove it."

CHAPTER SIXTEEN

The Blue Jug

DERWENT LAID down his cigar on the edge of the table. He put his fingertips together, tapping them gently, and looked up at the dimly lighted portrait in the dim brown room.

"You don't mean," Masters said, "you don't mean the old gentleman who died six months or a year ago? But he couldn't have killed Vance Keating. He's dead. He—"

"You misunderstand me," Derwent corrected sharply. "I did not say he killed Keating; I said only that he killed Dartley. There, I think, is where your whole case has gone wrong. I told you you were paying too much attention to Keating, and too little to Dartley."

H.M. uttered something like a groan.

"So you've tumbled to that, have you?" he asked, and Derwent turned to him.

"You mean you agree with me?" inquired Derwent, not too pleased.

"I want to hear your ideas, son. All of 'em."

"Very well." The other shut his eyes. "Let me again summarize briefly, for the sake of clearness, the facts in Dartley's murder.

"William Morris Dartley was shot twice with a .32 automatic pistol in the one furnished room of 18 Pendragon Gardens. He lay on his face between the table and the door, wearing his topcoat. His hat and gloves were on a chair. There were fingerprints of his in the room, and fingerprints of the moving-men who had handled the furniture; but no others. A wood fire had burnt out in the grate, and in this fire were found remnants of a large cardboard box, together with fragments of a piece of wrapping paper. This was not the box which had contained the teacups on the table; the container for the teacups was an ordinary dark wooden box some two feet long by one foot high—and this had been stolen, together with the paper in which *it* had been wrapped.

"Finally, on the table the ten teacups were ranged in a circle. They were without a fingerprint of any kind; not only without a fingerprint, but they had not even a glove-smudge or the mark of having been wiped.

"I began my investigation," ran on Derwent's smooth, pleasant voice, "with the facts concerning the sale of the teacups—notably the extreme, almost incredible *secrecy* of the sale. We are informed that Dartley himself bought these cups, on the very afternoon of the day he was murdered; that he bought them from old Mr. Benjamin Soar; and that he paid twenty-five hundred pounds in cash. Yet the fact that the cups had been sold at all came as a surprise to everyone until Mr. Soar senior announced it after Dartley's death. We know (a point I stressed to my friend Merrivale last night) that on the afternoon of April 30 Dartley did not go to Soar's shop, and Soar did not visit him—although he paid cash. No receipt for such money is found in Dartley's accounts— although he paid cash. Mr. Soar's assistants, including his own son, knew nothing of this sale. Dartley's sister, and his servants, never actually saw the teacups in Dartley's possession. It began to look as though Dartley had never bought the cups at all. What is the only piece of real evidence we have as to this? The only piece of evidence is that—at half-past nine on the night of the 30—Dartley left his house on South Audley Street, carrying 'a biggish box or parcel, wrapped up in paper, such as *might* have contained the teacups.'

"But did it? You have assumed that Dartley got the cups in the afternoon, and took them home with him: you must assume this, since you say he took them away in a parcel when he left his own home at half-past nine. You have assumed that he himself took them to Pendragon Gardens. —Now what is the first thing an avid collector does when he acquires a fine new item? He examines it. He touches it. He even fondles it. Dartley would certainly have handled the teacups at home. If he took them to Pendragon Gardens that night, he would certainly have handled them: for his fingerprints are all over the room. His fingerprints are everywhere *except* on the cups. On those cups there is no print at all, not even a smudge or a mark to show they have been wiped.

"Dartley, then, did not buy the cups and did not take them to Pendragon Gardens. The person who took them there must have been the murderer. But how are we to explain the fact that, whoever took them there, we find no mark on them at all? Somebody must have touched them, if only to range them on the table. This can be explained in only one way. We are informed that the cups had been packed in a big wooden box, each in its wrapping of excelsior and tissue paper; and they appear without a mark because someone has put each on the table and slid off its wrapping without touching the cup at all. This is clearly the man who later tells so obvious a lie about the sale of the cups to Dartley: the only man who had the cups in his possession at all: Mr. Soar himself.

"Shall I go on?" inquired Derwent.

He picked up his cigar again, and snapped on a lighter.

"On the other hand, we know beyond any doubt that Dartley did carry something to Pendragon Gardens that night, the biggish box wrapped up in paper, which was seen by both his butler and the taxi-driver.—You will have noted that the fragments of a big cardboard box, and also wrapping-paper, were found in the fireplace. What was Dartley carrying in that cardboard box? It is a curious fact that the only thing missing from his collection, and inexplicably missing, was a certain large puzzle-jug in which he took a curious kind of pride."

Masters got up from his chair, extending his hand slowly to snap his fingers.

"Lord, sir, I believe— You mean that there was an appointment arranged by the murderer; and to that appointment Dartley brought the puzzle-jug, while the murderer brought the teacups? You mean Dartley was killed just so the murderer could steal that puzzle-jug?"

"Exactly."

"But the thing wasn't valuable, was it?" Masters demanded. "The jug, I mean. Everybody said it wasn't. What did the murderer want with it? Ah, and wait! If old Mr. Soar did this (as you claim he did, mind), why did he go and leave the teacups behind all spread out on the table? Eh? They were worth twenty-five hundred quid. What's more, they pointed straight to him: so he had to invent a lot of lies afterwards to account for 'em. It even looks as though poor old Dartley can't even have seen the cups at all: you say the murderer removed 'em from the wrappings, but nobody touched 'em. If that's so, it must have been done after Dartley was shot. Why did the murderer leave those cups behind?"

Derwent's forehead wrinkled. "About your last question, Inspector, your native shrewdness should tell you the answer. As for the first . . . why not take a look at the puzzle-jug itself?"

"Take a look at the puzzle-jug?'"

Derwent got up on his feet and looked at young Soar. Briefly, the cold light in which Derwent moved changed to something like a human quality.

"Young man," he said, "I'm sorry. But before you begin to curse the old devil, remember that your father used *my* house to stage his murder." He pointed to the portrait over the fireplace. "Behind that picture there is a wall-safe. It has a letter-combination which is opened by the word *Leeds*. You will find the puzzle-jug in there, behind the puzzle-lock. You have your search-warrant, gentlemen. Now take your damned evidence, and let me go home."

Benjamin Soar junior still sat motionless on the arm of the big shrouded chair.

"I don't know whether you're an old devil," he said, "but I do know you're a very patient one. Derwent, you persuaded me to take this house."

"Yes."

"Because you'd looked at it yourself, and you knew the combination of that safe—" Soar got up from the arm of the chair. Padding in his slippers, he went quietly to the mantel-piece, took down the picture, and opened a powerful wall-safe behind. Out of it he took the jug, a monstrosity over a foot high, with long spreading spouts like arms, and a great ear of a handle. It seemed less like a jug than a fantastic teapot, for it had a close-fitting lid. Although it appeared to be of blue china or porcelain, it seemed extremely heavy; and, when Soar banged it down on the table, it gave out a steely kind of sound.

"You've been trying for over two years to prove either my father or I had this. And, even when you knew where it was, you couldn't get the police here except by a fake letter about ten teacups. You deserve a reward," said Soar. "Now take your damned evidence, and let me go to jail."

Masters came up to the table.

"You admit, sir, that your father—?"

143

"Yes, my father killed Bill Dartley," Soar returned with savage bitterness. "It's a pity you can't arrest him, isn't it? I suppose you can salve your conscience by arresting me." He stopped. "Sorry, Inspector; I know it's your job. I suppose it isn't any good my telling you I never knew my father had killed him, or anything about this jug, until an hour before my father died?"

"Just a moment, sir; hold on!" urged Masters. "But what's the point of this jug? Why did he want it? And, though it's all in favor of my business that you didn't, I still wonder why you didn't get rid of it or destroy it?"

"How." Soar said, digging his hands into the pockets of his dressing-gown, "would you go about 'destroying' a steel deed-box, Inspector, short of dropping it into a blast furnace? That thing is steel, under a porcelain shell. Try to remove that lid. You can't; it has a combination of its own. Do you know what the thing is, actually? It's a private safe, a little safe. That's why Dartley was so proud of it. That's where Dartley kept some of his papers. Do you know what Dartley was?"

"Oh, ah. I'm beginning to remember. The firm of Soar & Son," Masters told him, "was at one time suspected of selling bogus antiques. And Dartley, I recall, was at one time a bit tied up with blackmailing business deals. And I noted in the report that the things he chose to buy from your father he managed to get at a low price, a very low price."

Soar's dark eyebrows drew together. "My father—made mistakes. That I admit. There were times when we were in very low water. Dartley had retired, and consequently he couldn't use his favorite blackmail tactics in business: so he merely used them in his hobby. He bought up all the evidence. Then he got my father to sign a statement admitting it. When I think of how that mild little swine went to work afterwards, I could—" He brought his fist down on the table so hard that even the steel jug was shaken. Then he turned composedly. "It wasn't even straight-forward blackmail. Dartley wasn't even honest or cynical enough for that. He didn't say, 'Soar, I like that eighteenth-dynasty canopic jar you have there; hand it over.' No; he said, 'My dear fellow, I like that eighteenth-dynasty canopic jar; the price you quote is sixty pounds, but I feel sure that to an old friend you will let it go for thirty.' He didn't even think of it as blackmail: he called it good business. Well, I don't do business like that. Neither, God help him, did my father. Wyvern and I never suspected; we thought the old man had gone soft-headed.

But in the course of a few years Dartley's good business nearly ruined the firm, for he was a steady customer."

"Your moral tone," remarked Derwent dryly, "is commendably high. So your father took a heroic resolution—and shot him?"

"What would you have done?"

"I don't know," said the other with some abruptness. "That is the difference between us."

"Possibly. Will you continue with your Holmesian analysis, or do you think it would spoil your effect if I merely confessed?"

"Excuse me. You seem to think that all this comes from personal vindictiveness. Soar, that is not true. Remember, if you can, that there are other people in the world besides yourself; other people under suspicion. I tried, in the only way I could, to clear myself—"

"Rubbish," retorted Soar, making a flicking motion of his thumb and forefinger. "If you knew my father killed Dartley, you also knew quite well he didn't kill Keating. And it's only Keating the police are interested in. You've dragged a dead man out of his grave for nothing."

Derwent shook his head, with a slow and rather fishy smile which did not go well with him.

"No, I think not. I have proved the one point in which the police are most interested: whether there is or is not a secret society called the Ten Teacups. I have tried to show, and I think I have shown to their satisfaction, that such a society does not exist. This is a point, I notice, over which you have constantly tried to mislead them."

"You haven't proved it yet," the other told him grimly. "But I'm going to prove it now. Look here, Inspector, let's get this over with.

"My father wanted to get back that 'confession' he had given to Dartley. He was willing to give Dartley a price for it, but if Dartley didn't hand it over he meant to kill him. There: that's short and sweet. What Dartley most wanted in the world was that set of Majolica teacups; as you know, it was unique. My father offered to trade him the teacups for the confession.

"But he didn't trust Dartley an inch. Neither should I have trusted him. He went ahead with his preparations for murder. You may be interested to know, Inspector, that the police's original theory of the crime—at least, so far as it was suggested in the papers—was the correct one. Dartley was to be 'lured' into an empty house, which he thought was the murderer's own house; and then, when the body was found, there would be nothing to point towards the real murderer. Your ex-house, Derwent, was chosen only because of its 'haunted' reputation, a circumstance which seized on my father's imagination. He showed the kind of imagination with which I have been cursed by heredity. He ordered the furniture anonymously and—"

Masters interposed. "That's all very well. That's what we thought all along. But if your father did all this funny business, why in the name of sense did he write to the police? That's senseless."

"Haven't you guessed it yet, Inspector?" inquired Soar. "He didn't. It was *Dartley* who wrote that note to the police. You recall its phrasing, 'There will be ten teacups at number 18 Pendragon Gardens,' and the rest of it, concluding with the businesslike, 'The police are warned to keep an eye out.' You can rather bet Dartley wrote it! Haven't you heard that the first teacup letter was written on a different typewriter from those sent as instructions to the Domestic Furnishing Company and the Cartwright Hauling Company? Dartley didn't trust my father any more than my father trusted him. He couldn't tip off the whole show to the police; but he thought he could protect himself. He protected himself in another way too. He didn't shove my father's 'confession' into an envelope and take it along in his pocket. Not he. My father was old, but he was a large and powerful man: Dartley was a featherweight little stick. So Dartley took along his puzzle-jug; his real puzzle-jug, his private safe with the confession inside it; the safe that couldn't be smashed on the floor and couldn't be opened by anyone who didn't know the secret of taking off the lid.

"Yes. And he died because he wrote to the police, and because he took that jug along."

Though Soar's voice shook, he was speaking in a steady tone; and Pollard could sense what an effort that calmness cost him.

"You don't get any grisly details from me, Inspector. Except to explain how it happened. It happened when Dartley took that puzzle-jug out of the cardboard box and flourished it; it happened when Dartley announced how he had written to the police. My father tells me that something went wrong in his own head then. Just like that. Dartley was standing over by the fire. My father got his hands on him, and his

146

hand over Dartley's mouth before Dartley could squeal. He got out the pistol, but Dartley was wriggling and the first shot went through the back of his neck. Dartley crawled towards the table, and was finished by a shot through the back of the head.

"So you're looking horrified, are you? I don't blame you. I'm not extenuating. I'm not defending. I'm only telling you, as I've seen the thing in nightmares ever since I've heard of it. If you think it's brutal, what do you suppose *I* think of it?

"Thank you: I'll wind this up as quickly as I can. What you want to know is how my father came to leave the teacups behind, all ranged on the table, when they were still in their box and Dartley hadn't even seen them that night. Well, the reason is just as ordinary and just as horrible as any other point. I imagine Derwent has guessed it, by his look: a little deduction from the facts, and you'll have it.

"The cups were left—but their wooden box, two feet long by a foot high, was missing. When my father had set on Dartley, Dartley was standing by the fire. The cardboard box and the wrapping-paper for the puzzle-jug were kicked into the fire accidentally when Dartley tried to get away. My father couldn't save them; for his hands were busy in another way. After the pig-sticking was all over, how the devil do you think he was going to carry that jug away without its being noticed by everybody for half a mile? Look at the jug! It's over a foot high in itself; it's got spouts like cathedral spires sticking up at all angles to add another ten inches; it's bright blue—one glimpse of it, remembered by anybody afterwards, would finish whoever carried it. He couldn't conceal it under his coat. He couldn't even wrap it up in a piece of paper; try it and see. Yet the whole jug had to be carried away, because he didn't know the secret of taking off the lid and the paper was still inside.

"If you can think of any uglier position than the possibility of being seen walking through London streets with a monstrosity nearly two feet high. . . . There was only one thing he could do. He could pack that jug in the teacup-box: an ordinary commonplace wooden box, which a dozen people could see without thinking anything odd. But he had to leave the teacups behind. He obviously couldn't take both. Both alternatives were dangerous; but I think he chose the better one. For his imagination supplied a little flourish, a little brain-teaser, a little suggestion which has turned you dizzy ever since. You know what he did. He slid the wrappings off

147

the cups, put them in a mysterious circle on the table like a symbol, and left them. He had turned damning evidence into a clew pointing away from himself. He covered up by opening up. He created the Myth of the Ten Teacups."

Soar's heavy breathing had grown a trifle slower. He took a turn up and down in front of the fireplace, his black dressing-gown flapping like a monk's robe; then he faced them with sardonic weariness.

"Derwent's right, gentlemen. There was never any such society as the Ten Teacups, so far as I know. The English love of mystery, imagined one. Forgive me for the amount of hints and gas and camouflage I had to inflict on you today. What I told you about the history of tea was quite true. And when I told you that those Majolica cups really were the first teacups ever found in Europe, that was also true. The rest was bunkum. But I had to save my face and the old man's face— or try to save it. Now do whatever you like; I've had my say."

For once Chief Inspector Masters, in a sort of hypnosis, used an expression of H.M.'s; he used it as though it were drawn up from a subconscious well.

"Lordloveaduck," said Masters. Then he turned round to the big swathed chair where H.M., silent for so long a time, had been sitting with his eyes shut. "I'm just beginning to remember a few questions you asked me at the beginning of this business. . . . Here! Blast it! The old beggar's asleep!"

"I wasn't asleep, damn you," said H.M., opening one eye. "I was cogitatin'. That's the way I cogitate."

"—a few questions you asked me," Masters insisted. "Are you going to tell me you knew all this, Sir Henry?"

"Well . . . now. Knowing's a large word. I sort of thought it might be the case, yes. The evidence was all spread out in front of us."

"Then why couldn't you have told me? That never occurred to you, I suppose?"

"To tell you? Oh, sure. But I didn't think it was altogether wise, son. Can't you guess why? I was very curious to see how many people in this affair would come chargin' up to us and swear there *was* a society of teacups. You were workin' along the right line, too much so for my taste, because you steadily and wholeheartedly refused to believe in any such society. Consequently, if you'd had proof of it, you'd have greeted any person who told you about the society with a resoundin' raspberry. And he'd have shut up. He'd have seen we knew better. There's one thing you must never tell a criminal, son: you must never tell him you know better. . . . Are you thinking about Vance Keating now?"

"Yes. I am thinking of Keating."

H.M. scratched the side of his jaw.

"Then you'll see, Masters," he said apologetically, "what we've come to at last. The Dartley case is settled. The mythical society of the Ten Teacups is exploded as a hoax and a delusion—though, burn me, I hate to see it go; it was good fun while it lasted. We're back to this: some very ingenious murderer merely *used* the Dartley case to throw dust, to kill Vance Keating in such a way that the police should go whoopin' away after a terrible secret society, and neglect motives closer to home. We were intended to see the murder of Keating as only a link in a sort of foreign chain. That was why the murderer set his stage as he did—and deliberately reproduced as many features of Dartley's murder as he could. He couldn't find any more teacups with peacock designs on 'em, because they were unique; so he did the next best thing by snafflin' a Milanese cloth with a design resembling the first. Do you begin to see somethin' else? That was also why he scattered so many clews—scattered 'em lavishly—scattered 'em like a paperchase. He did a little something to cast suspicion on just about everybody in the case: so we might think a number of people were all concerned together in the sinister Clan of the Teacups. The bogy was decked out in everybody's clothes. It very nearly succeeded in foolin' us, Masters. But I believe there's only one person who killed Vance Keating: one person that I'm more interested in than I've ever been in a throat-cutter before: and he's the person we want.

"Or should I say *she?*" added H.M. "Because Keating himself believed there was a Society of Teacups: that's how the murderer got him: that's how he was lured into that house and shot."

CHAPTER SEVENTEEN

Suspects' Gathering

THE LOW lamplight, coming from across the room between the two windows, made an even greater monstrosity of the many-armed blue jug on the table in the middle. They gathered round that jug, while H.M. still sprawled in his chair.

"You don't think it was a woman?" asked Masters.

"I wonder what our friends are thinkin'?" H.M. returned.

Derwent peered round at him obscurely, the wrinkles going up the side of his thin neck. "Throughout this case, when any person refers to a woman," he said, "I find he merely means my wife. That, I submit, is nonsense."

"What about you, son?"

"Me?" said Soar. He picked up the heavy jug and banged it down again. "In my present mood, I'm thinking of only one thing. I say, to the devil with Keating and Keating's case. What you say may be all very true; but what I want to know is where *I* stand. With regard to this."

"You stand in a pretty bad position," replied Masters grimly. "You stand in the position of accessory after the fact to the murder of Mr. Dartley—by your own confession before witnesses. That'll do for a starter."

"Accessory after the fact. God save the law," Soar said with some heartiness. "I'll ask you again, Mr. Masters: will you believe that I never knew anything at all about this until an hour before my father died? And what did you expect me to do then? Expect me to rush out to Scotland Yard and say, 'Here, see what a good citizen I am. Here are all the facts; now hang a dead man and ruin me?' Whatever the law thinks about my citizenship, I presume it doesn't think I'm raving mad?"

Masters was bitter.

"You can use words, sir. All of you can, as slick as slick. But in the first place we've got no proof your father only told you this when he was dying—"

"Yes, I can give you that," interrupted Soar, a gleam of hope in his sallow face. "He wrote out a statement. It's in that jug, if you'll let me show you the trick of opening it. But whether or not it satisfies you, I don't suppose it will satisfy Derwent."

Ever since Soar's acknowledgment of the facts in the Dartley case, a certain reaction (possibly relief) had shaken Derwent. He tried to fight it: it was little more than a jerk or shiver: but Pollard suddenly realized that this stringy amused man was over seventy. They were all a little surprised to hear him speak with a quaver in his voice.

He said: "Must everybody think that I, of all people, do nothing but act on malice? I do not want you arrested, Soar. I don't want anybody arrested. What I was trying to do, as I patiently tried to show, was clear myself of suspicion in the murder of Dartley. So long as they accept that, I am not concerned with what they think otherwise. As for poor Keating's death, I am sorry for it but I am not afraid about it. It—ah—happens that I. . . ."

"Have an alibi," supplied Soar. For the first time he spoke in a friendlier tone, though there was despondency in it. "Yes, both you and Mrs. Derwent have alibis. Which means that I'm left holding the baby in both cases. Even if they don't think I'm accessory after the fact in Dartley's murder, they may think I'm the actual villain of the piece in Keating's." He appeared to come to a decision; there was in his face a light like fanaticism or inspiration. "There may be a way to convince you," he told Masters. "If I were you, Inspector, I should lose no more time. I should search this house."

"I mean to do just that," agreed Masters; "but why should you be so anxious for it all of a sudden?"

Soar pointed at him. "Because you're either bluffing, or you can clear me. You say, I repeat that you *say*, that there is someone in this house besides Derwent and myself. You say this person came in by the side door at a quarter past eight—"

"We know it."

"Then I should handle the nest with gloves," said Soar. "Because you've got the murderer of Keating."

"Nonsense," said Derwent. "There is nobody here except us. Why should there be?"

"Because you brought him, unfortunately. You played a neat little trick, Derwent, to get the police here. Look at it! 'There will be ten teacups at number 5b, Lancaster Mews on Thursday, August 1, at 9:30 P.M. precisely.' Since the murderer didn't write it, don't you think he would be interested in it and why it was written? Don't you think he might have dropped in to inquire? . . . What do you say, Sir Henry?"

"It's a possibility," acknowledged H.M. "You just thought of that: didn't you, son?"

"Why do you say that?"

"Well . . . now. I doubt whether you'd have stood there so freely and blithely, with the door to the hall open, tellin' us things that knock the murderer's ten-teacup scheme higher than blazes, if you thought he might be standin' out in that hall listening, with a gun in his hand. I told you, Masters, we had to hear about this. We had to hear about Dartley, or we shouldn't 'a' known where we stood. But I also tell you that for the past ten minutes I've been sittin' here with gooseflesh up my back like a nutmeg grater."

Soar smiled bleakly. "No, it doesn't worry me. Besides, you forget this murderer can appear and disappear when he likes. Maybe he's gone. Or perhaps he hasn't chosen to show himself just yet; it can't be quite nine-thirty. But if he really wants to turn a hoax round on us, it's a pity he doesn't choose to appear now."

Softly and steadily through the main hall of the house, the front-door knocker began to rap.

Masters afterwards declared that there was no man in the room, possibly including H.M. himself, who did not have his heart in his mouth. The rapping of the knocker rose above a swish of rain on the windows; it left off, but began again immediately.

"That's not our people," said the chief inspector. "They're not to move until I blow the whistle or give a light signal. Here." He turned to Pollard. "Go to the front door, and take this torch. Let in—whoever it is. Bring whoever it is back here; but don't let anybody out. When you've done that, go to the front door again; give two flashes of the torch, and then three. That'll bring Wright and Banks. Hop to it."

The unused hall was very dark; but a fanlight over the door let in a faint glow from the mews outside. Pollard passed the newel-post of a staircase on his right. To his left he heard a mellow ticking, which had a velvety sound in the rawness of the house; briefly, he flashed his light on the dial of a grandfather clock, to see that it was five minutes past nine. Then he opened the front door.

The red tail-light of a taxi was just bumping away in the mews. In the doorway, silhouetted against a gas-spark and silver skeins of rain, stood a Rubensque woman in a white velvet wrap which came high up round her neck. Above it the heavy-piled golden hair gleamed low on the neck.

"Is this Mr. Benjamin Soar's house?" asked the large blonde melodiously.

"Yes, madam."

"I am Mrs. Jeremy Derwent. Is my husband here?"

"Yes, madam. Will you come inside, please?"

She studied him in the gloom with her head a little on one side. Although he could not make out her features, even a flicker of heavy eyelids, he sensed humor.

"But what a butler!" she said. "Surely you are the young police-officer who made such terribly determined efforts to see me this afternoon? Under the circumstances, I really don't think I need come in. If—"

"Your taxi has gone," said Pollard, as she turned away. "You will get wet. I think you had better come in." He reached out and closed his fingers round her arm, which was a smooth soft arm under the wrap. "I am *not* making love to you, Mrs. Derwent, and I warn you that if you let out a yip this time it'll be heard only by our men out in the street."

She laughed, and he stood back to let her go past him into the hall. Following, he indicated the path with his light; and she did not turn round. What her appearance meant he did not know, but he realized that here at last was something he had hoped and cursed for—a meeting between Janet Derwent and Sir Henry Merrivale.

"Mrs. Derwent, sir," he said at the door of the library, and saw that he had produced a sensation.

He saw their faces craned, although he had been told to return to the front door and he was afraid he might not hear anything else. Pollard swore under his breath, wondering what might be the revealing first words at that interview. The ticking of the grandfather clock was loud in the front hall. Poking his neck out into the wet, Pollard flashed the torch down twice, and then three times. After a few seconds' silence, two figures materialized out of the drizzle, moved across the mews, and closed in on the front door. Sergeant Banks he knew fairly well; Plainclothesman Wright was known as a good man.

Banks closed the door and drew Pollard aside. He spoke so low that his words were not as loud as the ticking of the clock.

Banks said: "What the hell's going on around here? I've just been round the beats, and—"

"Wait; listen!" said Pollard, as Banks shook his hat and sent a shower of water over him. "Has anybody tried to get out of here since we got in?"

"No. As I tell you, I've just been round the beats. And that's the point. I never heard of so many coppers assembled in one place since the battle of Sidney Street. (Brrh! Can we smoke in here?) Did you know His Nibs has been having everybody in this business tailed since afternoon? Yes; well, most of 'em have wound up here, or hereabouts. We only just found that out. That lawyer, Derwent, is inside. Soar is inside. And now some woman—Mrs. Derwent, I'm pretty sure."

"Look here, since they've all been tailed. . . . Yes, Derwent's

153

here; and Soar's here; but who was the third man who let himself in by the side door at a quarter past eight?"

"I don't know," said Banks. "Nobody seems to know. But do you know a fellow named Gardner?"

"Is *he* in the house?"

"No, he's not in the house. Do you know what he's doing? He's sitting up on top of a wall with Constable Mitchell. This Gardner is wise, and he's been wise all day to the fact that Mitchell was tailing him. He led Mitchell one beggar of a dance. Clear across town to the Tower of London; all through every exhibit in the Tower; back again by way of Cheapside to St. Paul's; clear up a hundred million stairs into the dome of St. Paul's; three times round the Whispering Gallery— Mitchell thought he heard smart remarks floating out of the air in the Whispering Gallery—back again by bus to Westminster Abbey. . . . Well, he kept up that kind of thing until he came here tonight. Then he waited for Mitchell to catch up to him, and said, 'Look here, my lad, I've given you an instructive day with an opportunity to improve your mind; but we both want companionship now, so let's sit down and see what happens.' They've been sitting up on top of a warehouse wall under a tree, smoking cigarettes and talking about guns. I ask you again, what's going *on?*"

"God knows. What about Philip Keating?"

"I can't tell you. No sign of him anywhere near here, though, as far as I can find out."

"Then who's the third man in the house? You're certain he went in and didn't come out, are you?"

"Positive. I don't know who he is; that's not my job. My job—"

"Yes; I was forgetting. Come back to the Chief Inspector."

In the library, the yellow shade of the lamp was now tilted slightly, but it did not give much more light. Janet Derwent sat in the chair previously occupied by her husband, who stood behind her. In a similar illumination, she was just as Pollard remembered her from last night, except that she now wore white instead of black. The white velvet wrap was thrown back, revealing a very low-cut silver gown which flashed as she moved her Rubensesque proportions. Her elbow was on the arm of the chair, her forearm raised so that the wrap fell away from the wrist to show a diamond bracelet. Nobody spoke as Pollard reported; but there was an atmosphere of successful retort. Through the crack of the door behind him Pollard just managed to hear P. C. Wright's hoarse whisper:

"Half-a-crown Sir Henry does her down."

"Small pickings," muttered Banks. "Three and six on the blonde."

"Five bob."

"Done. Let's see your mon—"

Masters, without commenting on the news about Gardner, gave them their orders outside. "There's somebody hiding in this house. I don't know whether he's alive or dead; but I want him. Don't miss an inch of the house; turn it upside down; but get him. If he's alive he's armed, so button up your faces and watch out for him. No, Bob, you stay here: I want you to take down this lady's answers."

He closed the door with unnecessary violence, and turned back.

"Now, then, ma'am! Do you still refuse to tell us why you came here tonight?"

"But my dear Mr. Masters." She spoke with low, melodious, almost pleading gentleness. "You're putting me so horribly in the wrong, aren't you? You know I don't *refuse* to do anything the police tell me to do. You ought to know that, after all we've been through together—"

Masters's voice grew harsh.

"Stow it, lady. Stow it right here and now. That cat won't jump any longer. You've walked in on us, when we didn't ask you—" as he spoke, her knuckles went up slowly to her full lips—"and, now that you're here, you're ruddy well going to answer some questions before you get out."

"Jeremy, darling?"

"Yes?" said Derwent.

"Has he the right to talk to me like that?"

"No, my dear."

"Are you going to let him talk to me like that, Jeremy?"

"Yes, my dear," said Derwent.

"Well, I suppose I must put up with being bullied," said Mrs. Derwent, looking round quickly, "if there's nobody to defend me. But I really think it's too bad, when all I tried to do in coming here was what a wife should, and take care of my husband—"

"You came here tonight to take care of Mr. Derwent?"

"But of course! Why else?" She slid her hand up gently and took Derwent's hand, which was on the back of the chair. "Of course I wouldn't have mentioned such a thing, until you

155

dragged it out of me; but we have the strictest doctor's orders; and poor Jeremy isn't as young as he might be, and sometimes he's a little—"

"Janet," said Derwent. The slight quaver and loosening he had shown a while ago were now gone; he was his dry, urbane self. "What do you mean, exactly? Do you mean touched in the head? Feebleminded? Mad?"

"No, of course not! Nothing of the kind. Only—" She looked slowly up round at him, exposing the full line of her throat; and, to the stupefaction of the others, she added the following revolting question: "Diddums need to take care of ums nice old husband?"

Yet this was to be noticed. Such was the enormous physical vitality of the woman, dominating that room, that it paled the ironic self-possession of her husband. It made him look ineffectual. She was deliberately playing off that vitality against him, and succeeding. Before Masters had time to think, she turned round again.

"So if he does write you notes saying that he's the head of some shocking organization like this Ten Teacups," said Mrs. Derwent, "where they say women do the most dreadful things —well, you will try not to believe him, won't you? Or, if you must believe him, I am sure you will give him a fair trial and see that his age is taken into consideration? Promise me, Mr. Masters."

Masters blinked. Up on the floor over their heads, faint footsteps had begun to stir back and forth, up and down, as Banks and Wright searched. They advanced, they retreated, they died away altogether, and came back again: by this time those footfalls were beginning to have an odd effect on Pollard, for they should have tracked down *something*. Evidently they were having an effect on Soar. Soar had sat down in his favorite chair away from the light, where he shook a little, and twice glanced sharply at the ceiling when the steps passed. H.M. remained wooden.

"We haven't quite got your husband in the dock yet, Mrs. Derwent," the chief inspector pointed out. "Where did you learn about this note your husband wrote?"

"But I read it, of course."

She leaned back in the chair as though relaxing. Her breast had been heaving a little, with a certain subdued excitement she had shown since she entered here. But now she became quiet, speculative—what was the word?—almost boneless: lying back as Pollard had pictured her lying back last night in the limousine, and studying Masters.

"He showed it to you, ma'am?"

"How absurd!" She smiled. "When I returned last night from that journey which you and I so much enjoyed, I saw that Jeremy had given Arabella, our maid, a letter to take out to the post-box so that it should be delivered early in the morning. I saw that it was addressed to Sir Henry Merrivale"—she never once looked towards H.M.—"and, since the flap was imperfectly gummed down, I did so wish to make sure that the dear boy did not inadvertently do himself some mischief. . . . Are you so terribly shocked? My dear Humphrey, if you tried to arrest all the women who read their husbands' correspondence, there would not be enough jails in England to hold them. Doesn't *your* wife read your correspondence, Humphrey?"

"Never you mind my wife, ma'am." Masters looked at her with sudden suspicion. "You thought *who* might 'inadvertently do himself some mischief'?"

"My husband," she replied, reaching up again to hold Derwent's hand.

"What made you think he might?"

"You did, Humphrey, during our *tête-à-tête*."

"Oh? I mentioned Mr. Derwent?"

"No, but you talked a tremendous lot about the Ten Teacups."

"Just so, ma'am; I was coming to that. You've said yourself, a minute ago, that you knew certain things about a certain secret society, of whose existence you know, called the Ten Teacups. What else can you tell me about it?"

There was a silence, while every person watched the trap.

"Oh, come, Humphrey!" urged Mrs. Derwent, fixing her eyes on him and speaking with gentle, melodious scoffing. "You know perfectly well there isn't any such thing."

"How do you know that?"

"I don't; but you seem so terribly eager to get me to say there is such a thing, that I feel certain there can't be. Don't tease me, Humphrey, please."

"And may I ask," demanded Masters uncontrollably, "how the blazes you happen to know my first name?"

"I rang up your wife, and told her what a nice man you are. She told me things about you. If you ever try to put me into one of those dreadful boxes at any inquest, and try to tell them I said anything at all to you, I shall have a nice character-witness against you."

"They don't have character-witnesses at inquests, Mrs. Derwent."

"Oh?" cooed the other. "Aren't you glad?"

"And you know nothing about the Ten Teacups?"

"Nothing except what you've told me."

Masters turned. "Although," he said suddenly, "the gold cloth that was draped across the table in the room where Mr. Vance Keating was murdered was delivered to you, and was last known to be in your hands?"

She regarded him from under heavy eyelids. Pollard was thinking: Why doesn't H.M. get into this? For H.M. had remained graven, the corners of his mouth drawn down, his top-hat across his knees. The effect was more than a little ominous, as the woman may have realized, since she was challenging him with every word. Upstairs the footsteps prowled.

"Well, Mrs. Derwent?"

"Stuff! Does that prove I know anything about any teacups?"

"Answer the question, please."

"What question, Humphrey dear?"

"Do you deny receiving the gold cloth?"

"But of course not!"

"Who sent it to you?"

"Poor dear Vance had it sent to me, only the day before he—he passed away—"

"We happen to know, you see, that that isn't true."

Her beautiful face expressed astonishment and concern. "But didn't he? Then you mustn't speak to me. Mr. Soar has been telling the most dreadful falsehoods, or rather his assistant has; or perhaps it was Arabella the maid. They said it was poor Vance, and how should I know any different?"

"Yes. We know you received it. But what did you do with it afterwards?"

"Why, it was so tremendously valuable. . . . You know, of course, that no decent woman who valued her good name could ever dream of taking such an expensive present from any man except her husband. Naturally I could not accept it. So I gave it to my husband, to lock in his safe until he could return it to Vance." She leaned back and threw her head round so that she could see Derwent; at the same time her hand tightened on his. "I suppose he did put it away, for I haven't seen it since. *Didn't you, darling?*"

158

Masters looked from one to the other of them.

"Very neat," the chief inspector said with a sudden chuckle. "But I think you'll find it a bit difficult to get Mr. Derwent to confirm that. Now, now——"

"Didn't you, darling?"

"Yes," said Derwent.

There was a sharp knock at the door, and Sergeant Banks poked his head in.

"Excuse me, sir," he growled to Masters, "but would you come out here for a second? It's something pretty serious."

The chief inspector was so intent on this fresh evasion, glaring from Derwent to the decorous placidity of Mrs. Derwent, that he was on the verge of ordering Banks away; but Banks's expression satisfied him. He went out into the hall; Pollard followed, and shut the door.

In one hand Banks had a big electric lamp, and in the other a crumpled newspaper held like a bowl in his palm. He flashed the light on its contents. The first was a .32 caliber automatic pistol. The second was a pair of white kid evening gloves, man's gloves, smudged in a certain way. The third was a knife or dagger, eight inches long, with a heavy, grooved, double-edged blade, with a silver crosspiece and an ebony handle. Someone had evidently tried to wipe it and clean it in the newspaper, but there were traces of blood up as far as the cross-piece.

"This thing has been used within the last hour," said Masters heavily. "Where did you find it?"

"Found the lot wrapped up in this paper, shoved away on the shelf of a cupboard in an upstairs front bedroom," answered Banks. "The trouble is——"

"Well?"

"It's been used right enough, sir," said Banks. "The trouble is—Wright and I have combed every square inch of this place; upstairs and down and everywhere; and, except for the people you know, there's nobody else in the house at all."

CHAPTER EIGHTEEN

Conjuror's Chair

MASTERS WAS on the point of crushing the paper together.

"Don't give me any of that, my lad," he snapped.

"There's *got* to be somebody else in the house, alive or

dead. There were three men known to be here when we got here!—and only two of 'em are accounted for. Have they let anybody out?"

"No, sir, they have not. All I can tell you is that there's nobody here now. Come and search for yourself. It's a little house, and only a couple of the rooms are furnished. There's no cellar and only a little box-room of an attic, not a ghost of a place where anybody could hide."

"It looks as though the vanishing murderer had vanished again," said Pollard.

"More like a vanishing corpse, by the blood on that knife," suggested Banks doggedly. He turned to Masters. "I've just talked to the patrols, sir. Would you like to speak to Sugden? You talked to him when you first got here."

The chief inspector tramped with him to the door, and Banks flashed his light.

"What's the good of secrecy now?" snarled Masters. "We'd better give 'em the whistle. Bring everybody here. I want this house turned inside out. If the man we want has managed to slip through your hands, of every ruddy hulking fathead I've had watching this house, and made a monkey out of me after everything I swore to the Assistant Commissioner; so help me Harry, I'll break every—"

"Easy, sir," said Pollard. "Here's Sugden."

Masters took a turn down the hall, his head lowered to cool it, and managed to keep down his rage. He gave brief directions for an invasion of the house. Then he returned to the library, carrying the articles still wrapped in the newspaper. Banks overtook him with more information.

"They've traced another of the gang, sir," he reported. "Philip Keating."

"Philip Keating," said Masters, lingering over the name. "So he's here too, is he?"

"No, he's not here. But he's in a pub over near the Marble Arch, about five or ten minutes' walk from here, downing double whiskies."

"Look here," said Pollard. "Can we be certain there isn't some kind of an organization after all, in spite of what's been told us? If there isn't any such thing, what are they all doing here?"

Masters considered even before he glowered. "Now, now. *I* can tell you what they're all doing here, my lad. It's Mrs. Janet Derwent's passion for using the telephone. She saw that fake letter her husband wrote last night. So she up and phoned everybody today—"

"Do you think she's in it?"

"I don't know, and that's the truth. Sometimes I'm sure she is, and sometimes I think she wouldn't dare have such a blasted cheek unless she was innocent. No, that's not what I want to know. Right now there's a murderer or a corpse somewhere in this house; and, whichever it is, I want to know *who* it is. If Philip Keating has been tailed all evening, and didn't come into this house, who was the chap who came in at a quarter past eight? It wasn't Gardner; he's been covered and he's up on the wall now. It wasn't Soar: we know when he came in. It wasn't Derwent: ditto. But that's the lot. So who was it?"

Again Masters chewed at the problem.

"We've come to a blank wall with that woman again. You saw what happened. She's got some kind of hold over her old man; that's really-'appened-certain-sure. When she came out with the news that she'd turned the gold cloth over to him, she made him back her up. I don't know what kind of hold. Maybe the old chap really is cracked in the head after all. Sometimes he sounds like it. Maybe any of 'em is cracked. See this .32 automatic? Remember Dartley was shot with a .32 automatic. I'd lay you a tanner this gun belongs to Soar; and I bet a whole lot more that the gloves belong to him, because they're his size. Choose your solution, my lad. Who was standing at an upstairs window, with a white glove and a gun pointing at the middle of my head, when we first got here?"

He stumped down the hall, and opened the library door.

You could feel that not a word had been spoken since Masters left the room. Its occupants stood or sat like dummies in a waxworks; and over them, alone in the middle of the divan, was the huge Chinese waxwork of H.M. There was a kind of symbolism in the grotesque, many-armed puzzle-jug on the table. Masters saw that the atmosphere was good, and he did not speak. Without a word he put on the table the knife, the gloves, and the automatic pistol.

"That's very good," observed H.M. suddenly. "Now that we're all locked in for the night, as the ghost said in the story, maybe you'd like to know what really happened."

Every person looked at the three new articles on the table. Pollard had a feeling that nobody spoke because nobody dared to speak. Janet Derwent turned slowly round to H.M.

"It would be awfully kind of you," she assured him. "I've

161

really been most disappointed in you." A slight flush had come into her heavy, beautiful face; sometimes her light-blue eyes could take on a sort of bovine expression, which was deceptive. "Perhaps (one never can tell, can one?) perhaps one of the reasons why I came here tonight was to meet you."

"Thanke'e," said H.M. vaguely.

"Well, *aren't* you going to say anything, or ask anything?"

"Oh, all right." H.M. fished out a grimy bit of notepaper from an inside pocket. "Let's see. June 28, present year. Does that mean anything to you?"

"June 28? No."

"Uh-huh. In that case, we'll pass on to developments after that. What about July 15?"

"Really, this is quite incomprehensible. Why should you think the date June 28 meant anything to me?"

Over H.M.'s face stole his rare and terrifying smile. "No," he said. "No. That's a trick you got, my gal. You get asked a question. You give a short answer and a dig in the ribs. That stings the other feller so much that he elaborates all over the place; so you know what's in his mind and by that time you can kick the question round like a football."

Her eyes were dancing. "How clever of you, Sir Henry! We know you're not to be caught like that."

"That's what I mean," said H.M. "I gave you a handle about a sixteenth of an inch long, and you're twistin' it already. I forget what I was sayin'? Oh, yes. Well, if neither the 28 of June interests you, or subsequent developments on the 15 of July—"

"You want me to admit," cooed Mrs. Derwent, "that June 28 was the date on which poor Vance made a will leaving me all his property. I'm sure I didn't want his money. And now you're trying to suggest, without actually saying so, that on this 15 of July Vance made a new and different will. Now, I am in a position to know he did nothing of the kind. I can only suggest what I told Humphrey: don't tease me, please. —That's what you were trying to scare me with, wasn't it?"

"Ho ho," said H.M., "who's elaboratin' now? No, it wasn't what I was tryin' to suggest. I never even thought it. You're quite right: Vance Keating didn't alter the will he made on June 28, leavin' all his money to you; and it's a perfectly good will."

"Then—really, I don't see what you're driving at."

"I only wanted to know about July 15," H.M. said, with an air of patience.

Masters interposed. "But what about July 15?" Masters demanded. "Or June 28 either? Where did you get all these dates?"

Janet turned towards him, as quick as a politician to scent a shifting wind towards a possible ally who had previously been an enemy. A slight change had come over her in the past few minutes. She was still mistress of the over-blown rose; but at the moment you might not have thought so much of a Rubens woman, or of Mademoiselle de Maupin, as of Boadicea. It is certain that a vast relief went through her when H.M. admitted the validity of Keating's will.

"The dates?" rumbled H.M., scratching the side of his chin. "I got 'em by followin' my nose, at the time this afternoon when you said I was sleeping. One thing that's always struck me as interestin' in this business, Masters, is the behavior of our friend Frances Gale. . . ."

"Dear little Frances," said Mrs. Derwent coyly, and glanced at Soar, who was sitting motionless. "Mr. Soar only met her on Tuesday night, but I think he was terribly struck with her. . . ."

"Yes," said Soar. "I was."

"A part of her behavior might 'a' been rational enough," pursued H.M., "considering that, after all, she'd just lost her fiancé in rather a nasty way. But it didn't altogether explain certain jumps and hops and nervous tricks. When she came to call on me at my office this morning, she said something that was an eye-opener. See if you can recall the first words she said when she came whirlin' over the threshold. She said that she'd run out of her own house, run away, to get away from her father's arguing *with a whole crowd of solicitors.* A whole crowd of solicitors, Masters? That's a very literal-speaking young lady. It's conceivable that her father, with his gal remotely mixed up in a murder case, might consult a solicitor to find out where she stood. But what is old Bokey Gale, who's not a rich man, doin' in the midst of a whole buzzing crowd? And what are they arguin' about? And why does she sneak out rather than face 'em? At least it was suggestive. I know old Bokey Gale pretty well; so I thought I'd better ring him up and ask. . . . Masters, do you know what Vance Keating did on the afternoon of July 15?"

"Well?"

"He got married," said H.M. "He married Frances Gale."

Over the face of Mr. Jeremy Derwent, lately shaken, began to twitch and shake a very fine smile. It was not the mere

163

sardonic loop he had shown before. It was a relief, it was a breaking of the shell, and it broadened until Derwent was convulsed with dry laughter. His wife flashed one look at him over her shoulder, and then got her voice.

"But how too, too terribly charming of them!" Mrs. Derwent cried prettily. "A runaway elopement after Vance's most poetic style? To Gretna Green, was it? I only hope it is legal, because the dear child is under twenty-one. And in any case, Sir Henry, you acknowledge yourself that it does not in the least affect my position, since Vance did not alter his will."

"No," said H.M. "He didn't need to."

"Didn't need to?"

"Why don't you ask your husband why he's laughing?" said H.M. "Mrs. Jem, I got to break the news. Keating never altered his will: your tame solicitor who drew it would have informed you if he had. It's a perfectly good will, except that it's no good. Accordin' to the law, when any testator marries, any previous will he may have drawn automatically becomes invalid. And that's too bad. If you're mixed up in this business, if you've touched dirt at all or helped to commit one of the scummiest crimes in my experience, you've had all your pains for nothing. You'll never touch a penny."

"Jeremy," Mrs. Derwent said quietly, after a pause. "Is this true, what he says—about the law?"

"Quite true, my dear."

"It might also interest you to know," continued H.M., never moving and never taking his eyes from her face, "just how Keating played this delicate little joke on you. For that's what it was: a joke. The whole ponderous will was a joke. That's why the ingenious Mr. Keating married Frances Gale in secret. She didn't love him overly. She marred him in a burst of spite, because she'd shown Ronald Gardner how she felt and Gardner didn't love her: Gardner has never made eyes at her and, to do him justice, he never will if she's as rich as Great Catherine. She's barely twenty, d'ye see. She cares nothin' for money, if only because she's not old enough ever to 'a' felt the need for it.

"Now listen to me, Mrs. Derwent: that will and that secret marriage were goin' to be used against you. Keating had come to have one ambition in life. You know what it was. He was goin' to make you his mistress—just once—if it was the last thing he ever did. You'd led him an awful dance around the gooseberry-bush, Mrs. Jem; and, burn me, but didn't Keating feel it! He knew you were anglin' for marriage. But, once he'd done what he set out to do, he was goin' to announce that he was already married, thank you; that for months you had been living in a hashish-paradise of promises that didn't exist and a will that wasn't the paper to start a fire; and so good-by, cheero, and be damned to you. . . .

"Better shove your hand over her mouth, Masters," H.M. added bleakly. "I think she's goin' to yell."

She did not scream, though she opened her mouth to do so. Janet Derwent was sitting upright in the chair; and it struck Pollard that she had never looked so beautiful, because she was upheld now by a certain dignity. You might call it the dignity of humiliation. In less than five minutes she had taken such a fall as she might never before have known; and you suddenly found that it was possible to sympathize with her.

"I say, Merrívale," Derwent interposed. "This has gone far enough."

"Oh, I know," said H.M. despondently. "I get into some almighty messes, don't I, with my sittin' and thinkin'? Cases get to be too human all of a sudden, don't they? Real, living people gather up round you: you're not analyzin' X and Y: and you feel as you'd feel at a party if you spat in the soup or slapped the hostess's face. Do you think I enjoy this?"

"May I compliment you on that much elementary decency," said Mrs. Derwent, in no affected tone now. She rose. "If you will allow me to go—"

"No," said H.M.

His voice was heavy and quiet. And there occurred a slight, almost imperceptible tipping of the scales, when all things had been balanced. For a quality of expression, quick and crafty and unpleasant, flashed across Janet Derwent's face; and they all saw it. She turned round to her husband.

"Jeremy," she said, "Jeremy darling, take me out of here. Oh, for God's sake take me out of here! I'll do anything you ask, anything; only protect me, and back me up whatever they say about me; and take me out of here now, before—"

"Just one moment, Jem," interrupted H.M. "There's another side to it. You know now, don't you, when Keating planned to explode his little surprise-cracker about the will and the secret marriage? He was goin' to explode it yesterday afternoon, when he *thought* he was going to the shrine of the Ten Tea-cups: when he *thought* he was going to meet your wife there. And that's why she'll have to explain her connection with it, whether she's innocent or not. What sort of mumbo-jumbo ritual, or assignation, or promise of an assignation Keating

165

thought he would find at Berwick Terrace—well, I dunno. It doesn't matter a hoot, because we know there's no such thing as the Ten Teacups. We know the entire stage-settin' was a trap and a hoax, built up on the circumstances of Dartley's murder, to entice Keating in and get the eyes of the police full of sand. We know what Keating did find: a broken spine and the back blown out of his head. But that's not all, son. Because, d'ye see, the Enemy is here again tonight. At least, he's been here."

"The enemy?" repeated Derwent.

The door to the hall opened, and Sergeant Banks, followed by Sugden and Wright, came in. The hall behind them was illuminated now.

"Sir," the sergeant reported to Masters, "we've just finished proving—what I told you it'd be. Every room in the house is lighted; we sent round to a hotel and got a box of electric globes. We've sounded the walls, we've seen to everything in the house, and there's still nobody here. I suppose you've had a good look in this room yourself, have you?"

"Yes, I've had a good look in this room," Masters replied grimly. "But fire away! Everything you like. Comb it through."

"Quiet, everybody," said H.M. "Now watch 'em."

In silence, with not even a curious glance at its occupants, the three began their search—though there was nowhere to search. There was no cupboard in the room; and their tappings on the wall disclosed no secret panel. They took up a part of the carpet; they shifted the tables; they even probed under the divan (three inches off the floor) and pulled the dust-covers off the big leather chairs that were not occupied. Nobody spoke while it was being done.

"Satisfied, sir?" inquired Banks.

H.M. lumbered up from the divan. He walked across and stood in front of Soar, who had not moved; only Soar's eyes moved.

"Son," said H.M. gently, "you'd better own up. What you've done tonight is one of the hardest tests for sheer pluck I can think of; and I've been wonderin' whether any of the rest of us would have had the guts to go through with it. I don't know why you're doin' it at all. But you'd better get up now."

"Get up?" Soar asked huskily. "What's wrong? Why should I get up?"

"Because there's a dead man sitting in that chair under you," said H.M. "And you've had the nerve to cover him

166

ever since they began to search the house, so they'd never think of looking there."

With one hand he yanked Soar to his feet. With the other he pulled the white dust-cover from the chair. It was not a great leather chair like the others: it was of wood and wicker, with a high back and a top like a canopy. A man, whom they could not identify because a piece of board had been propped up across his breast and face, sat bolt upright in the chair. Another piece of board lay across his lap; so that, with the chair draped, it would take the outline of any other. The man's arms were tied to the chair-arms with twine, and other pieces of twine ran round his chest through the wicker back. Only his white hands and knuckles showed, and legs ending in two polished shoes that had been pushed back flat at angles in a parody of life.

Masters flung away the boards and slashed at the twine with a pocket-knife. The body pitched sideways and out, its grizzled hair rumpled; and they could see that it was Alfred Edward Bartlett, valet; and by the blood and the ragged tear they could see that Bartlett had been stabbed to death through the back.

CHAPTER NINETEEN

H.M.'s Way

"No," Masters said heavily. "Nobody leaves this room."

Janet Derwent's screams were real screams now; not of lung-power, but of thin and piercing intensity. They shook the raw nerves of everyone present, and were ended only by her bolting for the door, where Banks caught her. There seemed an overpowering silence after them.

The dead man, with his crooked nose and his grizzled hair, lay on his left side near the chair. There was about his brown mackintosh no trace of mud or wetness, except the blood which had made sodden the back of his coat. They looked from him to the heavy double-edged blade on the table, where it lay between the pistol and the stained gloves.

With unsteady steps Benjamin Soar walked as far away as he could from his late place, and sat down again. He was breathing like a man who has been long under water; but, after resting quietly for a moment, he peered up with a sweated and whimsical smile.

"Well, I'm glad that's over," he said to Masters in a startling ordinary tone. "You've given me a bad time all evening. First I thought you were out to nab me for the murder of Keating. Then you almost did nab me for the murder of Dartley. And all the time—that lifeless piece of sawdust was under the cover of the chair. Unless there's something wrong with my income-tax, I don't see what more I could have done."

It is only when a man begins making feeble jokes that you realize the reaction has set in. Masters regarded him with grim satisfaction.

"You've done quite enough for one evening," Masters told him. "This has just about torn it, my lad." He became formal. "I must tell you I've not got a warrant, but I'll risk that. Benjamin Soar: I arrest you for the murder of A. E. Bartlett. It is my duty to tell you that anything you say will be taken down in writing and may be used as evidence."

"So that's the proper formula, is it?" asked Soar, looking at him curiously. His mind seemed to be fixed with heavy dullness on one small point, and to play with it and slap at it like a cat with a ball of wool. " 'Taken down in writing, and—' I'd heard we usually got the wording wrong, and that 'in evidence against you' was never used. So that's right."

"Do you understand what I'm saying to you?" Masters questioned sharply. The chief inspector seemed uneasy. "Mr. Soar! Do you hear me?"

"Eh? Oh, yes. Quite."

Janet Derwent, near the door with Banks's hand on her arm, drew a slight breath; and her looks took on an immovable placidity as she fastened the white velvet wrap round her neck.

"So you have caught him," she observed without rancor, but with a melodious far-away air like a heroine in a play. "There is only one thing I cannot forgive. I cannot forgive your sending that gold cloth to me, Benjy, sending it to me yourself, to throw nasty suspicion—"

Soar put up his head and became rational again.

"Look here, Mrs. Derwent. I am the only one here who hasn't pitched into you tonight. I don't advise you to begin pitching into me." He addressed Masters. "Inspector, I didn't do it."

"You are not obliged," said Masters, "to make any state—"

"Oh, have something to chew on," offered Soar. "You won't believe me: I can't reasonably expect that you should: but,

168

just for the information of future ages, I—did—not—kill him. Why should I kill him, may I ask? Bartlett, of all people!"

"Just so. Why should anybody kill him? And if you didn't kill him, who did?"

"I don't know. I hid the body—yes, yes, I admit that; make what you can of it. Which appears to mean that I've been accessory after the fact on two occasions, once for Dartley and once for that poor devil over there. However, since I'm under arrest for murder. . . ."

"You're not under arrest for murder, son," interposed H.M.

Masters whirled round. "Here, stop a bit! What's this? Why isn't he under arrest? If—"

"Because I say he ain't," roared H.M., with such a sudden blast that Banks let go of Mrs. Derwent's arm. "Another little reason is that he's not guilty. God damn my scarlet socks and britches, Masters, but you've been complainin' all day how I've acted like Old Man River, and how I've stayed asleep in spite of all your piteous pleas. All right. I'm awake now, and I'm takin' charge. Siddown. You, Mrs. Jem, oblige me by goin' back to where you were sittin' before." He faced them from in front of the fireplace. "No, Masters: don't move that body. It'll serve its purpose where it is."

"In that case," said Masters, "I shall have to have a reason or two. Sugden!"

"Sir?"

"You still stick to your report that, before we got here tonight, only three men came into this house?"

Sugden had been asked the question so many times that he was tending to sizzle. "Yes, sir. It wasn't only me that saw 'em; ask any of the others. They—"

"No back-talk, my lad. We've identified these as Mr. Soar, Mr. Derwent, and the unknown who came in by the side door at eight-fifteen. That unknown was Bartlett, who was stabbed here. . . . Do you deny that, Sir Henry?"

"No. Oh, no. That was Bartlett, all right."

"Just so. And by what you'd call the process of elimination," Masters declared, "the murderer must have been only one of two people. Mr. Soar—or Mr. Derwent. Eh? If you don't choose Mr. Soar, you choose the other."

"Jeremy darling," cried Mrs. Derwent piteously, "you *didn't!*"

Derwent, who had been standing regarding them with a mysterious pleasantness, with his hands clasped behind his back, inclined his head.

"To be quite frank about it, my dear, I didn't," he said. "Nevertheless, I see the force of the inspector's proposition, and I do not object to it. Was that your idea, Merrivale?"

"Not necessarily. No, Jem, not necessarily."

"You don't mean the invisible murderer?" demanded Masters.

"Yes," said H.M., nodding his head gravely, "I mean the invisible murderer." He looked at Soar. "Let's hear what happened here tonight, son. We understand you got here at close on a quarter past eight yourself, and Bartlett walked in only a minute or so later. I rather suspect you'd been in a blue and corpse-like funk all day, hadn't you, ever since you got a phone message from Mrs. Derwent sayin' that she'd heard—she'd *heard*—the Ten Teacups were to meet at your place tonight? What did you think of it?"

Soar considered. He was still so jumpy that he could not keep his eyes off the body on the floor, but H.M. made no move to have it covered.

"I thought Derwent had gone out of his head at last."

"That seems to be the general impression," Derwent observed, taking out his cigar-case with great deliberation. "But why?"

"Because you've a perseverant ghost. Because for a long time you've been at your haunting. Because you've been trying to convict my father or me of Dartley's murder for two years. When you couldn't do it, I thought the obsession might have gone far enough for you really to commit murder—in my house—so that I should hang for it."

"Your Celtic imagination," said Derwent, lighting a cigar and looking at him sideways out of the smoke.

Pollard thought: Something's going to happen here. Look out! Danger! Or is this my own far-from-Celtic imagination?

"You're right," Soar continued, to H.M., "about my being in what you call a blue and corpse-like funk. I wouldn't have come back to the house at all. I'd have gone to the police: I'd have gone among friends and established an alibi: there were a dozen things I might have done to strike back—if only I hadn't remembered that cursed puzzle-jug locked up in my safe. So I had to come back. I can tell you it wasn't a pleasant house to come home to in the rain, especially as I thought I saw a policeman's helmet over near that street-lamp outside.

"I came in by the front door and hung up my hat and coat in the hall. It wasn't a few seconds more than that when I heard a noise like a bump, coming from the direction of this

170

room. I came back here, but nothing seemed to be wrong. Then I opened the door to that passage leading out to the side door. And I saw *him*." Soar nodded towards Bartlett. "He was lying on his face in the passage, with his head towards me. He had a mackintosh on, and a bowler hat fallen off, and the handle of that knife was sticking up between his shoulder blades."

"Dead?" asked Masters.

"Not quite. You see, he was—crawling. He was crawling towards me."

"Just so. Like Dartley."

"A very subtle thrust, Inspector. Thanks: like my nightmares of Dartley, yes. There was no light in the passage, except what came from this room, so I dragged him in here. I suppose he had just got out of a cab; his mack and shoes were hardly wet, and there was very little blood. But it was no good. He died before I could do anything."

Masters went over and opened the door to the passage. Carpeted in yellowish-brown matting, with the blue vases in niches against the walls, it stretched away straight to the side door. There was no other door.

"Assuming this is true—which I don't say it is, mind!" insisted Masters, pouncing. "What did you think had happened to the murderer?"

"You flatter me," Soar said dryly. "I did not think. Afterwards I supposed he must have followed that poor devil through the side door, stabbed him in the back, and slipped out the side door again."

"Was the side door locked then?"

"No. I remember, because I locked it afterwards. That was how Bartlett must have got in. He certainly didn't have a key."

Masters addressed his subordinates.

"Now, then, let's hear from our watchdogs. What d'you all say about this? Could anybody have followed Bartlett through the side door, stabbed him, and gone out again? You were watching." He listened with a certain satisfaction while he received sizzling testimony that no other person had been anywhere near that side door, either to go in or to go out. "That seems pretty clear; eh, Mr. Soar? Just so. Consequently, if we believe your story, the murderer must have come *into* the house, by the way of that passage and through this room? That is to say, however he approached Bartlett, he must have left the body and come back through this room, since he didn't go out the side door?"

"Oh, God, I suppose so."

"And you must have seen him, then. Yet you say you didn't."

Soar opened one eye. "If it comes to that, Inspector, your whole confounded force has been searching this house without seeing him, either. Yet they swear he is still inside. I have done some abnormally foolish things, I admit; but still that doesn't give you the right to have it both ways. If you can believe them, you can believe me."

"Can I, by George? We'll see about that. Mr. Soar, I arr—"

"That's the second time you've done it," said H.M. "Lord love a duck, Masters, will you be quiet a second? So Bartlett died on your hands, did he, son? What happened then?"

"Somebody knocked at the front door," answered the other.

There was a pause.

"You will kindly think of my position," suggested Soar. "I had reason to think that somebody was deliberately maneuvering me into a snare which should end with a well-soaped rope and a ten-foot drop. Here was proof of it. Here was a dead man lying on the floor, with a newspaper spread out under him to take any splashes of blood; lying there like an unwrapped parcel; and the door-knocker rapping away without a stop. I ran upstairs and looked out of the window over the front door. It was Derwent; I knew him by his pleated cape. At that moment I could have believed he was the devil. I also knew it was no good refusing to answer the door; for I thought he would only bring the police in if I didn't. . . .

"Well, you know what I did: the old Purloined Letter trick: body out in plain sight, but unnoticed by anybody because at a pinch I could sit on it as a chair. And I did it in not much more than two minutes, with twine and short bookcase-shelves as boards: one of the advantages of moving house is that string and loose bookcase shelves are all over the place. I had to take the knife out of him, though, because he wouldn't sit back in the wicker chair. Then I draped a white chair-cover over the whole affair, letting the long edges slop so that you couldn't see his feet. I wrapped the knife in a newspaper, and hung up his bowler hat in the hall, and I answered the door. But I forgot the evening-gloves I had put on to do it, so that I shouldn't get blood on my hands; and I had to shove my hands into my pockets when I met you. I was hardly, however, in a mood to shake hands."

172

"You thought," Derwent said harshly, "that *I* had—" he pointed to the body.

Soar was polite. "Will you tell me what I was bound to think," he returned, "when immediately after you arrived there was a thunderous whacking at the front door? I had to go upstairs again and look out, even at risk of leaving you alone here."

Masters nodded. "That's better! Then it was you standing up at that window, with your gloves on, and a gun in your hand?"

"Rather than make you think I intended to put a bullet through you," the other said, his heavy chest swelling, "I will admit I was of half a mind to put a bullet through myself. Why moralize? There it is. I tell you I stood in the dark up there and I had a hundred feelings at once. But you went away—or I thought you did. I took off my gloves and put on a dressing-gown. Then I came downstairs; and found you here. Why I didn't give the show away then and there, I don't know. And then Derwent flung that business of my father in my face. I saw a line of soaped ropes and a line of hangmen, like a drunken man. It was only when things kept on moving and *still* nobody spotted the body that I began to think you would never find it; and I challenged you, I threw it in your face. If I could keep still enough, and keep myself from wabbling in that dummy's lap, I thought you might be satisfied and go away. I'm like that. My God, I need brandy!" added Soar. "But I don't think there's any in the house."

Masters turned to H.M. "Do you believe this, sir?"

H.M. nodded. He lumbered over and stood in front of Janet Derwent, who had sat down again.

"I'm goin' to ask you whether *you* believe it," said H.M. "But you didn't expect that, did you?" He jerked his thumb grimly towards Bartlett. "Mrs. Jem, I can't play about any longer. I'm givin' you your last chance. Will you speak up and tell us what you know about this business, or have I got to turn nasty? I don't honest-Injun dislike you, but I could wish you'd 'a' been a little less virtuous, and an awful mess might 'a' been avoided. Now I warn you: on Tuesday night, at the Murder party, our friend Soar had a vision of you with a rope around your neck. If you keep on in the present way, it'll be less a vision than a prophecy."

"You don't mean that. You are bluffing me. You—you don't even know why Bartlett was killed. . . ."

"Oh, yes, I do," replied H.M. almost gently. "He was

173

killed because he knew too much. He knew why Vance Keating wore a hat."

You would have said it was a commonplace enough reply, not to say a meaningless reply; but Janet Derwent lost her nerve. She lost it as abruptly as though a chemical process had got out of control: as though that great white marbly beauty were disintegrating or growing flabby. As she looked back up at him, H.M.'s expression became more grim.

"I'm sorry to see you know as well," H.M. growled. "I sorta hoped you didn't. Now play your ace of trumps: say I don't know how the invisible murderer worked the trick of invisibility, and consequently I can't make an arrest."

"You don't and you can't."

"The first shot," said H.M., "was much more muffled than the second. Does that mean anything to you?"

She put her hands up to her temples. "I never did it! I never killed him! I knew nothing about it. I—"

"But you're a sensible woman, Mrs. Jem," pursued H.M., "and you'll have realized it's the end of you now. Once, a couple of years ago (I think it was in that White Priory case) I made a generalization. I said there were only three *motives* for a murderer to create a locked-room situation. I said there was first, the suicide-fake; second, the ghost-fake; third, a series of accidents which the murderer couldn't help. Well, I was wrong. When I was gradually tumblin' to the way in which this little sleight-o'-hand trick was worked, I saw a fourth motive, the neatest and most intelligent of all. A super-cunning criminal has at last realized the legal value of impossibility; and he's realized that, if he can really create an impossible situation, he can never be convicted for murder no matter if all the other evidence is strong enough to hang a bench of bishops. He is not tryin' to evade the detecting power of the law so much as to evade the punishing power. He's realized that, set beside impossibility, all other methods of coverin' his tracks are clumsy and uncertain.

"Look here! An ordinary criminal sets out to commit a murder and cover his tracks—how? Usually with an alibi. He tampers with clocks. He gets on and off bicycles or trains; he fools about with time-tables or steeplejack stunts; he winds himself up in shroud of red tape, doin' the most dangerous thing of all because every point must depend on somebody else, every point brings complication after complication, every point puts him into fresh danger of bein' caught in a lie.

174

"But, suppose, on the other hand, he can kill his victim in such a way that the police can't tell *how* it was done?—a locked room, a body alone in snow, whatever you like? The police may be certain he did it. He may be found with blood on his hands and blood-money in his pocket. If they dare to bring him to court, judge and jury may be certain he did it. Yet if the Crown can't show how he did it, he must be acquitted. A court of law ain't a court of probability; it's a court of certainty. He's pinnin' his faith to the whole crux of criminal law—the reasonable doubt.

"This person's not, in the sense we know it, a super-criminal. I doubt if the intentions are basically criminal at all. The murderer of Vance Keating is only a mighty intelligent and mighty imaginative person who's realized a new way to dodge justice, by riskin' an awful long chance. But once any dunder-headed investigator tumbles to the trick, the murderer's done for. Of course, he's done for whatever trick he uses, once they know how he faked his alibi or concealed his weapon; but he's finished, tied, and triple-damned when the impossible situation is shown not to be impossible at all. Mrs. Jem, I'm givin' you your last chance to turn King's Evidence. Who killed Keating and Bartlett? Will you tell me, or shall I tell you?"

"I—"

"All right," said H.M. in a different voice. "If you won't, you won't. Now, Masters, I'll just put the facts smack out in front of you, and you can deci—"

"I beg your pardon," the woman interrupted in a calm, cold voice. "I am not, as you say, a fool. You cannot bully or trap me into saying anything I do not wish to say; and you cannot make me hysterical; but I know my duty, and any mistaken altruism that may have led me to shield the murderer is gone now. You might as well know that Keating was killed by—"

The door to the hall opened, and a figure in a long raincoat walked in so quickly, so quietly: so much without fuss or effort: that the man was halfway across the room before they were aware of his presence. Pollard saw water drip from a sodden cap and from a black raincoat; there was a whirl of water from the newcomer, like a dog shaking itself, as he reached across the table and picked up the double-edged knife.

Whether he meant to use it on the woman, or on himself, none of them knew. It is possible that he did not know himself. Even as his hand shot across the table to take it, Pollard lifted the steel puzzle-jug and brought it down on his right wrist. Then Masters had the newcomer from one side, and Pollard from the other; but force was not necessary.

The murderer of Vance Keating, breathing hard, looked about with hot, puzzled, miserable eyes: he looked at the woman, who regarded him levelly: and then he gave H.M. a bitter nod.

"All right. You win," said Ronald Gardner.

CHAPTER TWENTY

In Which It Is Shown That We Do Not Always
Think of Everything

ON Sunday evening, in long clear light when there was a touch of coolness in the air, four men drove up to number 4 Berwick Terrace in H.M.'s Lanchester. They were H.M. himself, Masters, Pollard, and Benjamin Soar. They had the air of men going to a conference. They went up to the top of the house, to the little attic room where the furniture remained. The cloth and the teacups had been replaced on the table.

Masters sat down at this table, spreading out his papers. Pollard stood against the wall with his notebook. While Soar prowled restlessly, H.M. leaned back against the wall behind the divan, settled himself with no small amount of cursing, and puffed solace from a particularly vile cigar.

"If you people will just stop movin' about—!" H.M. roared querulously.

"Gents, there's one fortunate thing about this case; and it's time we got a fortunate one. It's unrolled itself, so to speak. We got a problem, and not long afterwards we got the answer to that problem; we got another problem, and the answer, and so on through a whole series of happenings. So now, you'd say, there remains only to tell you how and why Gardner worked his various vanishin' tricks; and we can close the book.

"But there's much, much more than that, even when you can see the mechanism work; it's a question of adjusting the nice proportion of guilt; and no slide-rule will ever work as far as that. You know the solid facts. Ronald Gardner killed Keating and Bartlett; he killed 'em alone and unaided, as far as the mechanics of murder went; and his roarin' fire of inspiration was Mrs. Janet Derwent. He didn't do it for money;

he did it for Mrs. Derwent. But there's the trouble: just how much did that clever lady know? How far was she entangled in it? How far did she set him on? And how much, when that ingenious pair come up for trial, are you goin' to be able to prove against her?"

"Never mind the motive, sir," interposed Masters, shaking his head. "Let's hear about the mechanics."

"Never mind the mechanics," said Soar. "Let's hear about the motive."

"And since all the rubbish is cleared out of the way except them two things," said H.M., annoyed at the interruption, "I'm goin' to take you step by step through the formin' of the picture, with points from your own observation or from Bob's notebook, and show you how it appeared to me.

"I can begin by admitting that, up to the time I heard a certain statement from Bartlett, the old man was completely fooled. Burn me, I didn't even realize how many pieces of the truth I had, when an irrelevancy came blazin' in; and I groaned. Now, what was the situation as we first had it?

"We had Berwick Terrace—a narrow street just twenty yards, or sixty feet, broad. It has four houses on each side of the street; built together, each exactly alike, looking like one house except for the area rails. The windows and doors of the house across the street, where Hollis of L Division was watching, face the windows and doors of this one. Uh-huh. *If* it could be shown that the two shots that killed Keating had been fired from some distance away (say only sixty feet away, from the attic window of the house opposite correspondin' with this), we shouldn't have had any such stiff problem—as Masters himself said."

"You're not going to tell us they were?" demanded Masters.

"Oh, no; just you wait a minute. We're only sittin' and thinkin' about the evidence. As I say, in such a case it'd have been remarkably easy: particularly considerin' the size of the window in this room." He pointed. "You've been told the dimensions of that window—four feet by five and a half, which is a whale of a big 'un, notably in its width.[1]

"But we were certain from the medical evidence that this couldn't have happened. The wound in Keating's back, for instance, was actually smokin' and showin' sparks on the cloth when Bob Pollard charged in there. It's true the first shot sounded a bit muffled and far away;[2] but the second

[1] Page 91.
[2] Page 30.

blasted so loud and close that there was no doubt about its bein' fired in there; and the powder-burns on the back of Keating's head showed that both bullets must have been fired close against him.

"So I was gropin' blind, even next day when a very rummy fact popped up. You brought it up, Masters, with your sinister talk about guns in gas-pipes. You mentioned that there was—of all things—a powder-burn on the carpet close up against where Keating had been lying.[3] Powder-burn on the carpet! How did it get there? How could it have got there, if in both cases the gun had been held against Keating? I didn't know. I only kept sittin' and thinkin' without result. . . .

"Swift on the heels of that messenger, we got from Gardner himself (who had to tell the truth about things that could be proved) a few truths about the old Remington .45 belonging to Tom Shannon. That gun was a hair-trigger. In Gardner's own incautious words, she was an old-style model, before the common use of safety devices, and she 'went off if you looked crooked at her.'[4] It occurred to me then that you could get a bad powder-burn *on the carpet* if you dropped a cocked gun on the floor, and she exploded as she hit the floor sideways; but that wasn't helpful, because there were two shots, and because the gun had to be cocked deliberately, and because the carpet was so thick that it wouldn't give a sufficient jar.

"I had got so far in my blindness when—well, gents, that tore it. There was somethin' that unsealed my eyes and caused the groan I mentioned before. I questioned Bartlett about the activities of Keating and Gardner on Monday night; and Bartlett, for no apparent reason under heaven, *told a deliberate, flat, spankin' lie.*

"I couldn't quite understand: because, mind you, I wasn't at all suspicious of Gardner or even of Bartlett. The tale about the plannin' of the hoax for the Murder party on Tuesday night; the tale of how Keating got excited and fired a blank cartridge while he and Gardner were rehearsing it; all that sounded quite reasonable. More to clarify the details than from any suspicion, Bartlett was asked about the firin' of that blank cartridge. Now just read me what he said."

Under H.M.'s sardonic eye, Pollard opened his notebook.

"Q: (by Masters)—finally, you tell us that when Mr.

[3] Page 91.
[4] Page 107.

Keating's arm hit the lamp-standard, the gun went off and the wadding from the blank cartridge broke the glass on the tray you were carrying?

"A: Yes. It hit the glass not an inch above my hand. That was why I dropped the tray.

"Q: How far was Mr. Keating away from you then?

"A: About as far as I am from you now. (Six feet? Seven feet?)"

Masters frowned. "Yes, but . . . what's wrong with it?" the chief inspector asked. "There *is* a wadding in blank cartridges. And it is fired with pretty terrific force; enough force to smash a glass on a tray."

H.M.'s face had an evil mirth.

"Oh, sure, son. Sure; and that's not all it has. That's the trouble. Masters, were you ever human enough to enjoy amateur theatricals? I dunno; but I'll tell you this: the most dangerous thing in the world to give a group of amateurs on a small stage (and sometimes professionals on a big stage) is a gun loaded with blanks. If they get excited, they play the devil with it. A professional actor who's got to fire one on a stage learns one painful truth: that pistol has to be pointed either at the floor, or in a direction where there's nobody in front. Why? Because there's not only a wadding in the cartridge: there's a heavy charge of coarse-grained powder. One of the nastiest things I ever saw in a peace-lovin' English community occurred when a nephew of mine (the one with the feet) got his crowd of amateurs playin' a gangster melodrama at Christmas. Wow! The villain got excited and pointed the gun at the heroine. She got scared, and turned her back, and this fathead pulled the trigger. She was wearin' a low-cut evenin' dress. Mind you, she was ten feet and more away from him: yet the powder-grains so slashed and tore her back that the poor gal spent a week in bed.

"Now Bartlett, by his own confession, says he was standin' only six or seven feet from Keating when Keating fired. In fact, he says the wadding took the glass out of his hand. Masters, he lied. If that wadding had come anywhere near his hand, close enough to hit a glass, his hand would have been in bandages now. But you noticed the smooth, large, white surface of those completely untouched hands.[5] . . .

"That was a staggerer. Love a duck, *why* should he lie? Where's the point? And right away my mind started turnin'

[5] Page 122.

over the strange confusion that seems to date from that innocent Murder rehearsal on Monday night. Now, just what did we know about it? Certain facts can't be disputed, because they are confirmed by too many witnesses. We knew that there really was an honest-to-God rehearsal of a trick for a Murder game on Tuesday (from Bartlett, *confirmed* by Hawkins the waiter; from Gardner, *confirmed* by the mistaken testimony of Philip Keating. We knew that there really wasn't any quarrel between Vance Keating and Gardner (from the independent testimony of the waiter, *confirmed* by Vance Keating himself when speakin' to Derwent and Frances Gale next day). We know that a shot was fired, as confirmed by everybody.

"But that's all we know. How many people actually *saw* what happened, and *saw* the shot fired? Philip Keating didn't, as he admitted. (By the way, that was the first question which Gardner—rather rummily, I thought—asked Philip: did you see anything?) The waiter didn't, because he appeared in the door to the dining-room only after the shot. They could all hear. But the only ones in a position to see were Vance Keating (now dead), Bartlett (who lied about being hit by the blank shot), and Gardner (who prepared and arranged this lie). Still, somebody fired a shot, and right away we see . . . well, we see that from this time onwards begins to date Vance Keating's weird behavior.

"What did he do? Did he leave his flat next day? No; he never poked his nose out. The only person he saw (aside from Bartlett) was Derwent. It's a curious thing, my lads—but when Derwent saw him, Keating had a wet towel round his head. It's a curious thing—but, as the day wore on, Keating decided not to go out at all on the Murder party to which he'd been lookin' forward so much. It's a curious thing—but next day, when at last he did go out on a summons from the Ten Teacups, he only went out wearin' a hat several sizes too large for him, which came down over his ears and concealed the back of his head."

H.M. broke off with the same evil glee, and looked at his companions.

"You mean—" said Masters.

"The hat, my son," declared H.M., nodding violently. "The hat is the startin' point and the finishin' point of this case. It should have given me my first lead. It should have been the ordinary commonsense point which gave a shove to our wits: why does Vance Keating, a fastidious feller of much vanity and conceit, choose to walk about in a hat ridiculously too large for him? It ain't sense. Granted that he's in the habit of borrowing things. But he's deliberately taken the one thing in the world that nobody borrows—a hat that doesn't fit. Now, suppose two young fellers share digs together: they'll borrow. If they're anything like friends, they'll use each other's razorblades and each other's toothpaste; they'll take a shirt here and there, and they'll pinch each other's neckties to a point of grand larceny; but can you conceive of anyone strolling out in a hat that flattens out the ears?

"This wasn't even a hat belonging to Philip; it was nobody's hat; it was one specially procured, with Philip's name inside it to explain the incongruity if anyone should question Vance. Why does he want that hat? To conceal the back of his head. But why not take one of Philip's? Because Philip wears only bowlers, and this had to be a soft hat. . . .

"Well, gents, with all this pilin' up, I began to see a vision of a Christmas party at my place, where a girl's back was badly slashed and burned by a blank cartridge. I also saw a vision of what might have happened at Vance Keating's flat on Monday night. Just suppose (until we get more evidence) suppose *Gardner* fired that blank shot about which both Gardner and Bartlett lied? They're handlin' the gun between them. Gardner lifts the hair-trigger pistol . . . either accidentally, or jokingly, or with a deadly intention Keating doesn't understand . . . and presents it. And Keating flinches. He flinches: just consider that. We've heard he was secretly afraid of firearms, though he, the swashbuckling adventurer, would have died rather than admit it. He flinches like a school-girl before his friend and his valet. He turns away, with a kind of yell; and Gardner's finger, either accidentally or deliberately, jars the trigger. Hence the valet's shout, heard by everybody, 'For God's sake, sir, look out!' and the valet's dropping the tray of glasses when the pistol explodes . . . not ten, or seven, or six feet away, but within a short distance of the back of Keating's head. Powder-burns? It would burn that head like blazes.

"Y'know—Gardner presented to us a jovial, and intelligent, and imaginative face. Yes. But I'm wonderin' what his face looked like when he pressed that trigger.

"What'll happen then? Well, I was sittin' and thinkin', and I thought to myself: Here! There's one notion that'll be scorched in Keating's mind like his scorched head: the fact that he funked the sight of a pistol shoved at his head, and

181

everybody saw it. So when Gardner says hurriedly—you remember, he said something so low that Philip couldn't hear it out in the hall—'Good Lord, sorry, accident: here, it's your flat; take this gun or I shall get into trouble,' then Vance takes the gun.

"That was what Philip saw when he peeped briefly round the edge of the door. It was all he saw; because, as he said, Vance was facing him and the room was very dimly lighted. But you'll note that Vance looked *scared*. It was all the waiter saw, because he was shooed out.

"Now Vance Keating, when he came to think it over, was in a position that made him wild: a comic position, a ludicrous position, the sort of position he hated. For the next night an elaborate Murder party had been arranged, at which he had been goin' to act as detective. It isn't merely that here he stands with his hair singed and burnt and powder-freckled, with an amusin' lump made by the wadding, to show to his *fiancée* and his prospective mistress: though that's bad enough for a feller of his vanity. But now, if he shows up at that Murder party, and tells a story of how he heroically got popped in the back of the head with a blank cartridge, it will be plain to the dullest wits that he was cookin' up some flummery with Gardner so that he could be the hero of the Murder party; and he'll look twice as big a fool.

"He hoped they might be able to smooth out the burns and the mess so that he could appear on Tuesday night. When he saw Derwent on Tuesday with a wet towel round his head, he still hoped so. But he couldn't; the burn was worse than they'd thought. He raved; but there was nothin' to be done. And that, gents, is why Vance Keating didn't attend the Murder party on Tuesday night.

"There was only one thing that would draw him out, one summons he would obey: a summons from the Ten Teacups. He would have gone to that, to get his revenge on Mrs. Derwent, if he had to go on crutches. And the murderer was now ready to send a Teacup summons . . . for here was Vance with a ragged black burn in the back of his skull. And in the attic room of the opposite house stood the murderer, with Tom Shannon's gun and soft nose expanding bullets that'd make rather a mess of that skull. Let Vance stand with his back to a window four feet by five and a half. Let the murderer drill him through the back of the head with one of those expanding bullets. And no doctor would afterwards have reason to suspect, since both burns and bullet

182

came from the same pistol, that his head was not burned at the same time the bullet tore open his head."

H.M. paused with sour irony, peering around the group. Masters swore softly, and strode to the window.

"So that, sir," Pollard suggested, "was why I—standing outside the door here—heard the first shot as muffled and far away, and the second blazing straight out behind the door?"

"Stop a bit," urged Masters. "If that's true, what about the second shot, the one that broke his spine? It's absolutely certain the second shot was fired in here; the back of the coat was still burning from it when Bob came in. And the pistol was found in here!"

H.M. nodded.

"Sure. But don't you see it yet, Masters? Yes, the first shot was fired from across the street: the hilarious part of it bein' that it was actually fired from the attic floor of the house in which Hollis and you, Masters, stood watchin' this very window. Of course, it didn't sound any louder to you, because four of these solid thick-built floors were between you and a bullet fired into the open air. You were watchin' the window of this room. Your whole hearts and eyes and souls and ears were fixed and glued here. If somethin' happened, you expected it to happen here. When you heard a shot in this general direction, you all naturally assumed it came from here. There was a brief silence, and then a second explosion that actually and beyond any doubt did come from in here.[6] . . .

"I got a pretty sharp picture about that first shot, son. I can see Keating standin' with his back to the window. I can see the murderer raisin' the pistol. And then—what? Remember, Keating screamed just a fraction of a second before he was shot, so how did he see what was goin' to happen to him? Well, you may recollect that he was turnin' over a cigarette-case in his fingers, wonderin' whether he dared smoke in the shrine of the teacups. You may also recollect that it was a polished silver case as bright as a mirror. On one occasion, y'know, Keating handed that case to Frances Gale to use as a mirror. He lifts it—and reflected in the mir-

[6] Here may be mentioned a point which did not develop until the trial: that Gardner had entered the empty house across the street by the back door, the same way as Hollis had entered, while Hollis & Masters were at the front. For Keating to be standing with his back to the open window was a part of the rigid "instructions" he had received from the Teacups.

ror, reflected over his shoulder, is a certain window across the street. He sees the murderer's gun, the last thing he ever does see in his life. He pitched across the table, smashing two teacups on a slightly different side of the clock-dial. He pulls the tablecloth a bit, rolls off, and lands on his left-hand side. . . .

"Then there's the second explosion. You notice, Masters, I don't say shot: I say explosion. In doin' so I call your attention to four very revealin' facts:

"1. When Bob Pollard broke into the room, he found Keating lyin' at full length on his left-hand side, with his back towards the window.

"2. The .45 revolver lay on the floor close to Keating at his left-hand side.

"3. The wound in the back, accordin' to the medical evidence, is a bit astonishin'. Instead of going in fairly straight, the bullet's entered between the third and fourth lumbar vertebrae, low down, and taken a very steep oblique upward slant through the body.

"4. Near the body, on the left-hand side, there is that rummy powder-burn on the carpet we were considerin' a while ago.

"How did that burn get there? I was askin' myself that. Now, if somebody had dropped the pistol on the carpet beside Keating, with its muzzle pointin' towards his body; and if in that position the revolver had exploded—well, you'd have had a wound, a position of the gun, a burn on the carpet, exactly correspondin'. But the carpet was too soft to jar the trigger. You'd have had an explosion like that only, d'ye see, if the revolver had been—hey?"

"Thrown," said Soar.

Soar took a step forward, and his face assumed an expression of cynicism.

"Yes, I see it now," he agreed. "The murderer wasn't definitely trying to hit Keating in a certain place with a second shot. He was trying to do two things, Sir Henry. First, he wanted to throw the weapon across into the room, so that it should be found there and show Keating was actually shot in here. Second, there was Keating's body stretched out like a target with its back to him just beyond a window five and a half feet wide. The murderer knew that if he threw the gun, cocked, through the window, he could at least make it land somewhere close to the place where Keating lay. With luck, he could put another bullet into Keating.

But in any event the pistol would explode, to produce another shot, any sort of shot, that would show both bullets were fired in this room."

"Here, I say!" protested Masters. "How could that be? Wouldn't Hollis and I have seen the gun when he threw it?"

"No, my lad, you wouldn't," said H.M. with ghoulish relish. "You'd have seen if anybody climbed in or out that window. But you wouldn't have seen a dark-metal gun,[7] on a dark-metal day,[8] thrown forty feet up over your heads by a first-class cricketer[9] who was bowlin' much the same length as an ordinary cricket pitch. . . . You wouldn't have seen it, Masters, because you hadn't bothered to clean the window."

"To do what?"

H.M. glanced at Pollard. "Looky here, son. When you got to Berwick Terrace on Wednesday afternoon, you were hailed by Sergeant Hollis, who was watchin' number 4 from the house across the street. Hey? Right. Well, when Hollis spoke to you from where he was watchin' could you see him? No? And why? Because the window was too thick with dust.[10] Masters, what chance had you to see that dark flyin' speck forty feet up, then, if a man smack outside the window couldn't see a man smack inside? I'm sorry. It's painfully, heartbreakin'ly simple when you know the secret. You even saw the gun was light enough to throw easily.[11] And it was all a compact little plan evolved by the murderer. . . ."

There was an odd silence, after which Soar spoke thoughtfully.

"The murderer," said Soar. "Ronald Gardner."

"It don't surprise you much, does it?" asked H.M. in the same tone, so quietly that Soar gave him a sharp glance.

"You are the seer of secrets," Soar told him with a certain dryness. "No, it does not surprise me. I perceive that your sittin' and thinkin' proceeds along very sensible lines. Mine, I regret to say, doesn't. I say it does not surprise me; and I should have been certain if I hadn't been somewhat thrown off by my doubts about Derwent. I've believed for some time that Gardner was Mrs. Derwent's lover. There was a kind of—of affinity between them; will you understand that it isn't merely Celtic imagination when I say that? You were

[7] Page 32.
[8] Page 31.
[9] Page 98.
[10] Page 23.
[11] Page 32.

185

looking for the Man in the Case, I think. They have the same sort of slow, heavy good looks. They have the same love of the bizarre and the florid; you know Mrs. Derwent, and you may have read Gardner's exotic travel-book. I tried to give you some hint of this."

"Oh-oh? That wasn't the reason, was it, for your sharp brush with Gardner over the subject of Frances Gale? I thought you flared out a bit oddly, son.'"

"No; that was unpremeditated, though," Soar spoke still more thoughtfully, "my real ideas were stirring under it, I suppose. No, I meant the hints I tried to convey about a dangerous associate hanging close to her. And more particularly an odd bit of information I found useful in hoaxing you about the Ten Teacups. You may recall the elaborate secret society I conjured up; and I said that the practice of drinking tea laced with opium out of old-fashioned cups, and done as a secret rite, was to be found mentioned by Gardner in his book. So it is—mentioned as a fact. But I, who had very good reason to know the whole business was rank fraud, knew that Gardner lied."

Masters whistled. "Look here, sir! You don't mean he deliberately shoved a lie into a book that was supposed to be true, so that later, when it seemed to come true in London, there'd be confirmation?"

"Why not? South America is the one remaining unknown continent. If he said he found in upper Brazil a small group of Portuguese addicted to weird rites and practices, who was to deny him? And that's not all. You see, Sir Henry?"

H.M. nodded disconsolately. "Oh, yes. It would intrigue Keating's interest. And when Gardner, the authority, asked him in a whisper whether he wouldn't like to be initiated into the society of the Ten Teacups, of which Mrs. Derwent was a member . . . cruel neat and elegant, gents."

"That shows a long degree of premeditation," Masters said. "You think they were concerned in the murder with equal deepness, then, Gardner and Mrs. Derwent? I mean, she knew all about it even if it was Gardner alone who managed the mechanics?"

"I'm quite certain of it, son," returned H.M., chewing his cigar, "and if you'll just stop interruptin' me I'll show you why. Why, to begin with, do you think she had that rounded, smackin' alibi of the aunts and the hired limousine?— *prepared for two weeks in advance, as Derwent told us.*

That's premeditation, for a fiver. Next, it was pretty plain that no *hoax* concerning the teacups could have been put across Keating without her knowledge. Think a moment! If there'd really been a society of cups, and she really had been a member, it was possible Keating might have been inveigled into a trap without her knowledge. But, since the society was a myth, she had to know. Why was Keating so certain she would meet him at 4 Berwick Terrace? Why was he certain she was a member? Suppose all this had been done without her knowledge, and Keating had let slip a hint or a word to her? Wouldn't Keating have found out?—unless she confirmed his belief? I'm inclined to think so. Finally, she pinched that pistol off the mantelpiece at her own house, while she was supposed to be upstairs with a headache.

"You want to know why she had a headache? Because you gave it to her, Soar, intentionally or unintentionally. You came across her in the dark, just after the gold shawl had been sent to her, and you whispered: 'You have a friend who sent you a fine gift this afternoon. How long have you been accepting presents from him?' I can kind of see you were in danger at that moment, son. She thought you'd tumbled to her relations with Gardner: a thing her husband hadn't tumbled to and even Keating hadn't tumbled to. It'd have wrecked the game immediately."

"Oh, ah. The gold shawl," said Masters, scowling. "Then Gardner phoned and had it sent? And what was the point of the shawl?"

"I can explain that best," continued H.M., "by indicatin' the way in which this ingenious pair went to work on their scheme. And here we get back to the eternal problem, the eternal cussedness, of measurin' out guilt in a pair of scales; of puttin' a pinch this side, a pinch that side and tryin' to determine which of two people is the more guilty. You've got the same puzzle wherever a woman and a man murder another man for the sake of their joint interests or their own appetites. On one side you got Janet Derwent: chilly, vicious, screamin' for attention and luxury and cushions. On the other side you got Ronald Gardner: clever, impulsive, even generous—and yet without any cartilage of moral sense to hold him together. Janet Derwent murdered calmly for money; Gardner didn't care a curse about the money, and he murdered hotly for Janet Derwent. *Yet* at the pinch it was Gardner who was a dozen times more ruthless than his

187

deliberate mistress. I'll give you two instances that'll sort of round out the case.

"Now note how, at every part of the case, these two supported and interlaced each other's testimony. The woman was allowed to have a firm alibi for the time of Keating's murder; but, at the same time, it was to be shown that the man did not and could not have pinched that revolver out of Derwent's house on Tuesday night. Which was just as good as an alibi. But on one point their apparent good sense seemed to go skew-wiff. I mean, my fatheads, that obvious sendin' of the gold cloth to Mrs. Derwent. It's true Gardner had to have some fancy stage-settin', if only to impress Keating. He would scrape up a hundred quid for some furniture in the shrine of the teacups. (By the way, you'll have noticed that it was all *light* furniture which one man could handle, and seemed to indicate only one man had set the scene.) But he wanted something elaborate. That's all very well. *You'll* retort, 'Even if he did want a fancy bit o' work for the table cover, why send it so obviously to Mrs. Derwent?' To tighten her into the plot, gents. To show she was in as deep as he was: a gentle, ugly hint not to try any games: as Gardner was realist enough to know she might.

"Last of all, there's the murder of Bartlett—as workmanlike, calm, and savage a piece of brutality as any in the case."

Soar lifted his shoulders uncomfortably.

"As *I* have good reason to know," he observed. "But that's what I wanted to ask you about. I can see how, once you have deduced the way in which the impossible-murder trick was worked here, it pointed straight to Gardner and to nobody else. But didn't it pull Bartlett into the plot as well? After all, Bartlett had lied and thrown in his testimony with Gardner's—"

"Yes. And he was murdered before he could retract it." H.M. reflected. "That was the whole scheme: that was why he had to be killed. Naturally, the first thing the old man thought of was that Bartlett and Gardner were in the crooked together. But that was just the trouble; that was the part which wouldn't make sense. Bartlett lied about the firin' of the blank cartridge, yes. He lied about the hat, which he bought himself at Vance Keating's order. But, if he were mixed up in the really fishy business, he did *not* lie about the one crucial point on which he'd have been certain to tell a whopper. *I mean that he and Gardner didn't give each other an alibi."*

"Eh?" demanded Masters.

"They didn't, you know. Bartlett said Gardner had left Lincoln Mansions on Wednesday afternoon, the afternoon of the murder, at twenty minutes to five: just time enough, with a lot of luck, for Gardner to get out to Berwick Terrace. That was no alibi. And Bartlett had no alibi. If they'd been concerned in it together, you can lay your shirt on the belief that they'd have said they were in each other's company all day. Why not? Gardner could have slipped downstairs in the service lift or by the back stairs; and who'd ever have known he wasn't in the flat with Bartlett? It would have been *aes triplex*, which no amount of batterin' would be able to break in court. At the same time, Bartlett himself would have taken care to have some sort of alibi in case they tried to drag him in afterwards, even if he only talked to a chambermaid or the liftman. But he didn't; he stayed alone in that flat.

"No, son. Bartlett was lyin' because he'd already lied accordin' to Keating's order, while Keating was alive, about that burnt head. In the first place he had to stick to his story, which he'd already told all over the place and which might sound very fishy to future employers (to say nothin' of the police) if he altered it now. In the second place, he saw no reason under the sun why he shouldn't stick to his story, because he didn't connect it with the murder. What did he know about the murder, at the time we first saw him? Only the guarded report allowed to the press bulletin, which made no reference to any impossible situation, and said only that Keating had been shot twice by someone who must have been in the room with him. Now, it's certain that within a very short time—twenty-four hours at the most, and probably less—he'd have learned what was what; and then he'd have told the truth fast enough. But in the meantime why should he be suspicious? Because, d'ye see, he had no reason to be suspicious of Gardner. The relations between Keating and Gardner had always been jovial: on that very night of the blank-cartridge-firin' they wound up in a friendly guzzlin' party at which Keating forgave Gardner for the 'accident.' And there you were, for a few watch-ticks. But in the brief time before Bartlett learned how puzzled the police were by a burnt head, his mouth had to be stopped.

"It was a ticklish position for Gardner, right enough; and

for Mrs. Derwent too. Gardner must have been fired with inspiration when Jem Derwent played straight into their hands by writin' that letter to the police with the announcement that there would be Ten Teacups at Soar's house on Thursday night. Wow!—what an opportunity to tumble another victim of the Teacups across somebody's threshold! And who but the predestined Bartlett? Our friend Gardner acted with the same quickness, the same complete triple-brass audacity and skill, as when on the occasion of Keating's murder he'd whipped out to Kensington, got in through the back door of an empty house while the police were standin' in the front room, and got upstairs to the attic to fire his gun. How he persuaded Bartlett into followin' Soar home on Thursday night we're not goin' to know until the trial. I got an idea it was with some idea of makin' Bartlett an amateur detective to track down the guilty, because Bartlett liked Keating and he liked Gardner. . . . "

"And so we come to the final vanishing trick?" inquired Soar.

"Ho ho ho," said H.M. "You mean how Gardner managed to kill Bartlett and disappear? Yes, if you can call it a vanishin' trick. Gardner was bein' tailed all that day; what's more, he knew he was bein' tailed. He had a fine time: he led his follower a devil of a dance, to get him mad and careless and tired. Finally, after dark, he went to number 5b Lancaster Mews, where he'd arranged to see Bartlett for mutual detective-work. Mind, he was well in advance of his tailer, and it was dark. In his pocket he'd got what he was preparin' to use if a good opportunity came: the knife. And he did get an opportunity. He nipped up on the wall you saw opposite the side door, just as Bartlett—after tryin' the windows —had found the side door open and was preparin' to explore. You remember, Masters, when we went in the side door a bit later, we saw no marks of any wetness or light footmarks except just inside the door? Yes. The reason bein' that he must have just gone over the threshold when he collapsed.

"Bartlett, d'ye see, had just got the side door open when Gardner threw the knife. He threw it from up on the wall. It's seldom dark enough but what you can see a man's outline; but the police watchers couldn't see the knife because—d'ye remember?—it was too dark for 'em to make sure whether or not Bartlett had a key. Bartlett went inside, and he closed the door, and he fell. Gardner merely nipped down off the wall, met the tail as the tail caught up to him,

190

and suggested that they sit down and take it easy. Oh, a cool one, Gardner. An amiable, cool, practical one. He was so dexterous that I hadda force Mrs. Derwent into betrayin' him so there would be enough evidence to yank him to trial."

H.M.'s cigar had gone out. He contemplated it; he looked round the forlorn room with the powder-burn still on the carpet, while the stirring of evening noises crept up the steep hill of Kensington.

"Which is about all, gents," concluded H.M. in a dull tone. "You've seen the blocks fit into place and the ends of the cussedness converge. You've seen the little part that each person had to play to make up one pattern. There only remain little human problems: what'll happen to Jem Derwent, whose head really ain't as strong as it used to be— and that woman has been holdin' it over him unmercifully? What'll happen to Frances Gale—"

"I hope I can tell you that, in a year or so," said Soar.

"—and what'll happen at the trial? I think it'll be a real up-and-at-'em sizzler of a trial, with enough dramatic effect to stock another record. And what'll be the result of that? My own guess is that Gardner will take all the blame, and he'll hang; the woman will probably get off with a lecture from the bench. Again our Rheingold maiden will float among us and comb her long hair. Is it right, or is it wrong, or what's the answer?"

Masters's face was set stubbornly.

"Just so. I gather, anyway," the chief inspector said, "that Gardner is going to plead like that." He brooded. "There's just one thing, though. We were led such a dance over that confounded secret society that I'm bound to admit I'm sorry it doesn't exist. Lummy, it *ought* to exist! But if it doesn't, where's the thread of point or motive that connects all the trappings—as you said there was? The sixpenny teacups on the expensive shawl? The peacocks' feathers. . . ."

H.M. grunted.

"Ain't you seen it, son?" he inquired. "Don't you follow Mrs. Jem's dreamy brain in workin' out that point? Keating was the sixpenny teacup that was to be smashed: as he was smashed: on the cloth of luxury and pampered women. And there's another analogy that I'm too materialistic to draw, though I wonder our friend Soar hasn't drawn it. The peacocks' eye was the symbol on the robes of a certain army, in a certain battle that was fought long ago, when Lucifer

191

went down from the sky with his peacock host. But I got a materialistic mind, as I say; and I also got a suspicion the early theologians mixed up their Latin and their Hebrew. Because, d'ye see, *lucifer* in Latin means 'light-bearer'—another of the names of Venus."

THE END